The Black Farm

THE
BLACK
FARM

ELIAS WITHEROW

THOUGHT
CATALOG
Books

Copyright © 2017 by The Thought & Expression Co.

All rights reserved. Cover photography by © photo_arena

Published by Thought Catalog Books, a division of The Thought & Expression Co.,
Williamsburg, Brooklyn. Founded in 2010, Thought Catalog is a website and
imprint dedicated to your ideas and stories. We publish fiction and non-fiction
from emerging and established writers across all genres. For general information
and submissions: manuscripts@thoughtcatalog.com.

First edition, 2017

ISBN: 978-1945796500

Printed and bound in the United States.

10 9 8 7 6 5 4 3 2 1

This one is for all six of my brothers and baby sister.
I love you all and miss you every day.

Thanks also to my good pals Matt and Dave for providing constant feedback as I crafted this story. You guys kept me sane in more ways than one.

And I'd like to offer a massive thanks to you, the reader.
I'll keep writing for as long as you let me.

One last thing:

<u>*This story is not for the faint of heart*</u>

1

I exhaled slowly, my eyes trained up at the night sky. Stars twinkled down at me like curious crystals and I felt my chest heave. They looked so beautiful. They looked hopeful. They looked like happiness, dragging me towards them, millions of light years away.

A warm wind rustled through my hair and I closed my eyes, breathing in the soft serenity. Crickets chirped around me, filling the darkness with unseen life.

"I can't do this anymore," I whispered to the sky, opening my bloodshot eyes to stare at a cool sliver of moon. "God help me, I just can't."

I was standing in the front yard of my small house. The countryside rolled with untainted darkness and I took it all in for the last time. I could hear my girlfriend crying from inside. Her sorrow drifted out through the open door behind me and settled around my shoulders like a heavy cape.

"God," I whispered, feeling my eyes well up, "If you're out there…tell me I shouldn't do this. Please…" My voice cracked and I dragged the back of my hand across my face. The weight of my life pressed down on me and I felt like I would be crushed beneath it.

"Life wasn't supposed to be like this," I sobbed. I listened to the quiet and gritted my teeth.

"How did things get so bad?" I prayed. "If you can hear me...please...help me..." I didn't even believe in the existence of God, but if he was out there...I needed him.

The empty hills before me offered no answer and I listened to the grass rustle in the wind.

I thought I liked isolation. I thought I liked being away from everyone. Maybe things wouldn't have gotten so bleak if I had been around more people.

But it was too late to think about that.

Too late to think about all the bad luck and poor choices I had made over the course of my thirty years on this earth.

I heard Jess continue to sob from inside and it killed me. I had done this to her. I had moved us out here. She hated the country, but I had insisted on getting the house. She loved me; I was her life, her everything. Of course, she followed me here. We were supposed to start a family. We were supposed to grow old together.

I put my hands over my face and fought back the sorrow threatening to overwhelm me. It was the baby that had put us into this situation. Our unborn son.

"But we couldn't even have that," I hissed to no one, my voice a muted croak.

Jess had been devastated by the miscarriage, an onslaught of crushing misery that swept her away in its violent arms. She hadn't spoken for a month and even when she finally did, it was clear that something had shattered inside of her that would never heal.

I dealt with the loss in my own way. Drinking, pondering, just trying to make sense of it all. When things got too heavy,

I would slip out into the night and walk through the sprawling fields surrounding our house. I would stare up at the sky, tears running down my face, and weep for what my life was becoming.

That was a year ago. They say time heals all, but not for us. I kept waiting for things to get easier, kept waiting for life to show its beautiful color again. But it hadn't. Each day took us one step closer to where we found ourselves now.

Three months after the miscarriage my father had died in a drunk driving accident. Two months later I lost my job. Three months later I got an eviction notice. Our lives were crumbling before our very eyes and events seemed to be spiraling out of control to an extent where I thought I was going mad.

Jess was a ghost of her older self during all of this. Her job at the local jewelry store wasn't nearly enough to keep us afloat. Our state of living declined at a rapid pace and I couldn't find work anywhere.

And then a month ago, Jess's younger sister had been diagnosed with terminal cancer at the age of twenty-four. Any progress Jess had made since the miscarriage vanished. Her skin grew pale and sickly, she barely ate, and she spent most of her time just sitting in the living room staring at the TV.

I scrubbed my face and let out a long, tired breath. It was all just too much, each tragedy like the drop of a hammer on our miserable lives. My mind couldn't function anymore, my head in a constant state of strained anxiety. My days were filled with worry, my nights with sleepless despair. I had sunk down to the bottom and now the mud was sucking me deeper.

I was exhausted. The thought of facing another day terrified me. I couldn't keep this up. Everything just compounded in my chest and boiled up into my screaming mind like a poison. The loss of our son, the death of my father, the cancer, the upcoming eviction, Jess's decline…

"No more," I whispered into the wind. I realized I was crying. I brushed my cheek and turned to go inside.

I closed the front door behind me and went into the living room. Jess was on the couch, a ball of pale flesh curled into herself. Her hair was dirty and her eyes dilated as they rose to meet mine. On the coffee table before her were an array of pills scattered across the wood top.

Easily enough to kill us both.

Wordlessly, I went and sat beside her, pulling her cold body into mine. She rested her cheek against my shoulder and I felt dampness begin to spread across my arm. I stroked her hair and kissed the top of her head.

"Are you sure this is what you want?" I asked, breaking the silence.

Without looking at me, she answered in a soft voice, "Yes. Nick, I just can't do this anymore. Any of it. It's too much. I am in pain…" She shifted and looked up at me, her eyes watering, "I'm in pain all the time."

My lip trembled, my heart breaking to see her like this.

"Me, too," I said gently.

"I'm sorry," Jess sobbed, still looking at me, "I'm so sorry about our son."

I gripped her shoulders, feeling my own tears streak down my face. "Hey, you don't have anything to be sorry for. It wasn't your fault. We did everything we were supposed to. I love you."

She collapsed in my chest, shaking. "I love you, too."

We sat like that for some time, both of us staring at the death before us. My eyes ran over the pills again. I shifted Jess in my arms and I felt her sigh.

"You don't have to do this with me," she said without looking at me. "I want you to be happy. I want your life to get better."

I rubbed her arm. "You're my life. And you're my death. I can't survive without you. I want to..." I paused. "I want to just drift off to sleep, right here, with you in my arms and never wake up. Doesn't that sound nice?"

Jess nodded, sliding down to rest her head on my lap. "It does."

"What do you think our families are going to say?"

"Who cares..."

I didn't respond to that, letting the words die in the air. She was right. Who cares? No one understood the day-to-day hell we were living. The worry, the stress, the constant state of panic. It was just too much with no hope in sight. Hope...I had given up on that notion a long time ago.

The muted night bugs echoed outside and I let their dark song fill my head. It seemed like a peaceful melody to die to.

"Are you ready?" Jess asked suddenly.

The question filled my chest with warmth and the sudden confrontation of choice loomed before me. I licked my dry lips and exhaled. There wasn't anything to be afraid of. The monsters were all on this side of life. What awaited us was blissful nothing, an unaware existence of absolute emptiness. No more worries...no more stress...everything would float away like sticks in a river. I could close my eyes and slowly submerge myself under death's eternal current.

"I'm ready," I said, heart racing despite myself.

Jess leaned forward and scooped up a handful of pills. She dumped them into my palm and then gathered her own. She didn't move, her head still resting on my lap.

"Baby?" Jess said, turning her eyes to me. I smiled down at

her a sad, loving smile. She was so beautiful even in this ruined state. Her blue eyes, her blond hair, the smattering of freckles across her nose. She was everything to me.

"Yes, love?" I whispered, a weight in my chest and grief in my eyes.

"If there is an afterlife…will you come find me?"

I leaned down and kissed her cold lips. "Of course I will. Existence is meaningless unless you're with me, no matter where that is."

She crumpled a little at that, her blue eyes brimming with fresh tears, "I'm so sorry, Nick. I'm sorry this is where our lives have led us. I love you so much."

"I love you, Jess."

Jess grabbed the glass of water from the coffee table and looked up at me, "Is it ok if I go first?"

I sniffled, realizing I was openly crying now. "Of course."

My heart ripped in two as I watched the woman I loved fill her mouth with pills. She tipped the glass to her lips and began to ingest them. She paused and then poured the remaining pills into her mouth. When she was done, she held the glass up to me.

My heart hammered in my chest as I took the glass from her. My hand holding the collection of pills was sweaty and shook slightly. I let out a long breath, clearing my mind of everything.

I raised my hand and shoved the pills down my throat.

Shaking, I drank deeply from the glass.

It was over. The decision had been made and the task was finished. I suddenly felt peace wash over me, an acceptance of what we had done. It was the relief that comes with making a hard choice and realizing you did the right thing.

"Hold me," Jess said, taking the empty glass from me and placing it on the floor.

I wrapped her in my arms and pulled her close. I stroked her hair gently and rested my head against the back of the couch. I closed my eyes, listening to the midnight bugs beyond the walls. I smiled, swimming in the dark behind my eyelids, and losing myself in the gentle chorus.

Who knew death could be so gentle?

We were silent for a while, the gravity of our actions weighing on us. I focused on the crickets outside and the minutes stretched out before us as we waited.

"We never gave him a name."

I looked down at Jess and saw tears budding in her eyes. I ran my hands over her arms, trying to comfort her in our final moments.

"It hurt too much to think about," I whispered, "but now that we're here…at the end…I think we should give him one."

Jess smiled sadly, staring off into the distance, "Michael. He was always Michael to me. I think he would have had your smile. I know he would have." She turned to look up at me. "Slightly crooked and totally adorable."

I was starting to feel sleepy, a deep pull in my head and body. "Michael is a great name."

Jess's eyes were starting to droop, "Yeah…"

"He would have had your beautiful blue eyes," I said quietly. "And your sense of humor."

A tear quietly rolled down her cheek, "My poor sweet boy. Maybe it was for the best. There's nothing good left in the world for him. It's all evil and sadness."

I said nothing, a sharp pain developing in my stomach as my head swam and sank. I didn't know how to respond. She was right. Nothing but bad out there. Nothing but disappointment and misery. I didn't want to watch my child get ripped apart by life. I didn't want to watch him drown in sadness like his parents.

"It doesn't matter anymore," I said, squeezing my eyes shut as a jolt of searing fire ripped through my gut and then vanished. I noticed Jess was clenching her middle as well.

I almost welcomed the uncomfortable sensation. It was a reminder of why I was leaving this earth. My thoughts began to swim together and images rose and vanished like patches of morning fog. Memories bled through the swarm of shifting color, still-shots of when I first met Jess. Our first date. Our first kiss. The brief couple of months we were happy before life started destroying us, one tragedy at a time. I gritted my teeth, feeling my eyes slide shut.

Jess was motionless on my lap and I heard her breath begin to slow. I rested my hand on her chest and felt her weakly grasp it. Another bout of pain rocketed through my stomach, but I found I didn't have the energy to cry out.

Hot darkness pressed down into my skull and I was dimly aware that I felt like I was going to throw up. The crickets outside were muted and seemed very far away, like I was driving down a long tunnel away from them. Warmth dripped down my chin, but I paid it no attention. Nothing seemed to matter anymore. Nothing.

Just the warmth…and the darkness…

I shuddered suddenly…and then died.

2

Darkness. So much...darkness. I was falling through it...no...that wasn't quite right. I was sliding in it, its strange chill pressing in around my body like a wet coffin. I shivered as its cool walls coated me, pulling me deeper through the threshold of death. I was vaguely aware of something dripping onto my head, something colder than the darkness.

I coughed in the black and tried to focus my thoughts. That's when the first bolt of unease shot up my spine like lightning.

I wasn't supposed to have thoughts. I wasn't supposed to be aware of anything. I was dead; I should feel...nothing. Why could I think? Why could I feel?

I coughed again as the darkness slid across my skin like frozen paste. It coated me, slid around me, engulfed me. I shivered and my mind began to realign. I let out a breath and concentrated, begging my senses to come to life.

My mouth tasted like stale bile and I groggily scraped my tongue along my teeth. I tried to spit but found my lips weren't functioning quite yet. Something wet was dripping on my head...no...not *just* my head, but everywhere. It felt like...rain?

I slid through the darkness again and I hacked, realizing my throat was in pain. It felt like sharp claws were throttling me, choking me. What the hell was happening?

Eyes. I needed to open my eyes.

I searched my mind, desperately trying to remember how I did that but found I couldn't. It was like all motor functions had been scrambled and I couldn't find the controls to work my body.

Sound. I could hear something in the distance, but it was muted, muffled. After a moment I realized I felt pressure in my ears, something clogging them and compressing my head. Panic began to dance across my fractured consciousness as the darkness slid around me once again. Agony briefly seared my throat and I gagged.

You have got to get your shit together, I thought, forcing myself to calm, *what is happening to me!? Eyes...you have got to open your eyes, Nick. Just do it. Do it!*

Ever so slowly, I found my eyelids in the chaos and pulled them open. It was like cranking open two rusty garage doors.

The darkness edged itself out of my vision and was instead filled with dull gray. At first it was just a blur, but after blinking a few times, shapes began to take form. As the gray sharpened, my other senses began to come back to me.

Cold...pain...thirst...

And then I realized what was happening.

Something massive was dragging me through mud by a chain coiled around my throat. The cold darkness I felt was the soaked earth sliding across my skin as I was pulled. Heavy rain fell from an overcast sky that was blanketed by impossibly dark clouds.

I suddenly retched as the chain tightened around my throat and I was pulled further through the mud. Through bloodshot eyes I craned my head and saw that a huge shirtless man held the chain in his hands, his back turned to me. He was fat, his bloated stomach bulging over the waist of a dirty pair of ragged pants. His back was a series of cuts and scars and his soaking black hair hung down past his shoulders and stuck to his skin like greasy leeches.

Where the fuck am I?! My mind screamed as I took all of this in with horrifying clarity.

Weakly, I reached out and grasped the chain, begging for some relief. My chaffed skin howled as the iron scraped around my neck, drawing blood. My fingers found the wet leash and I gripped it, trying in vain to halt our progress.

The massive man felt the slight resistance and turned, his eyes meeting mine. I felt a sickly horror rise in my chest as I gazed upon him. The bottom half of his face was blown out, his nose and jaw a mess of mangled gore. His mouth hung loosely from a tattered cheek and what few teeth he had jutted from exposed, open gums. His tongue was a stretch of angry red that dangled from his chinless face.

He grunted when he saw I was awake and turned to face me. I cried out as he advanced, pulling something from his back pocket. I sputtered in the rain as he towered over me, his stench gagging me. I dug my fingers into the mud and attempted to pull myself away from his reach, but he caught me easily by the throat and slammed my head into the ground.

Stars exploded across my vision and that familiar darkness danced in the corners of my eyes. I rolled over on my back and gasped, coughing against the cold rain. I blinked and tried to clear my mind, stretching it out in hopes to gain insight on this horrific new reality.

As the fat man leaned down toward me, I noticed something wrong with the sky.

Red gashes spotted the heavy storm clouds, like deep cuts in human flesh. These strange orifices gave way to long hanging strips of vermilion ooze that hung from the gashes like strands of drool. They swayed gently in the wind, like frozen strings of blood clutching an open wound. They were long and thick and my mind reeled beneath them.

I didn't have long to process what I was seeing as my captor grabbed a fistful of my hair and wrapped something dirty and wet around my eyes, blinding me.

"S-stop it, please," I croaked, hands clawing at him, "Why are you doing this? Where am I?"

Darkness wrapped around my face once again as the man ignored my cries.

"What do you want from me?" I sobbed, feeling him begin to tie my hands.

He suddenly answered, his voice sounding like broken thunder, "Naw suppose-a-be awake."

I struggled against his powerful grasp as he bound my hands, futile cries pouring from my lips.

Now, blind and restrained, I could do nothing as the man took his place at the end of the chain and began to drag me through the mud once more.

Fear engulfed me in a sudden wave of cold ice. I realized I was completely helpless and had no idea where I was. Worse, this monster of a man was taking me somewhere as his prisoner and my imagination shook with unknown terror.

I began to scream. My throat creaked as I let panic fill me, overwhelm me. I thrashed about, cold mud slapping my face and filling my mouth. It poured into my ears and stuffed itself up my nostrils. The chain around my throat cut deep and I couldn't tell what was rain and what was blood.

My shrieks did nothing to slow the man. He ignored me, obviously not concerned anyone would come to my rescue. This terrified me even more, but I found my howls were stuttering beneath the onslaught of mud and pain. My wrists burned beneath my restraints and my eyes rolled wildly behind the strip of dirty cloth.

After a few minutes I went from screaming to gasping for air. My body felt like a soaked, beaten piece of meat. Rocks rose beneath me as I was pulled and soon my ribs began to scream as they rolled across them like a fragmented washboard. I don't know how long I was dragged. I did my best to focus on just getting air into my lungs, one mouthful at a time. I began to shiver, the never ending rain snapping its icy teeth across my body. My shirt was soaked and torn, my jeans spotted with mud that weighed me down like an anchor.

My brain sparked with blinding pain, sharp flashes with each tug of the chain. Thunder rumbled overhead and I heard something inhuman roaring in the distance.

Jesus Christ, I thought, exhausted, terrified, *what nightmare have I awoken in?*

And then suddenly, we stopped.

I gasped in grateful relief as I felt the chain give a little. I heard it clank to the mud as the big man grunted with effort. I heard the creak of rusty hinges and then the sound of a massive door opening.

I wanted to get up and run, take these brief seconds of distraction and bolt, but I just didn't have the strength. My body was a useless mess of bruises and discomfort and it was all I could do just to lay there and breathe.

I was suddenly hauled to my feet. I gasped as strong hands clutched me and dragged me forward. I tripped over myself and blindly reached out so I wouldn't fall. A yank on the chain steadied my unsteady feet and I felt the air change around me. The rain ceased and a thick humidity now clung to my skin.

The mud changed to hard floor beneath my feet and I realized we were entering some kind of building. The cloth around my eyes offered no glimpse as to where we were headed and so I pitifully allowed myself to be pushed along, praying I wouldn't fall and smash my face open.

As we walked, the noise began to grow around us. I could hear distant screams and cries followed by angry yelling and the clash of metal. A whirring sound beat above my head like the rotation of a giant fan and my nose was assaulted with the stench of stale sweat and unwashed flesh.

"Please," I begged, stumbling forward, "please just let me go. I don't belong here, this isn't right!"

Heavy hands shoved me along and I fell into a fit of sobs and pleas. The chain dragged along the floor behind me like an iron snake and its coils echoed along the walls as we continued our march.

Where were we going? What did this man want with me? Where the hell was I?

My mind spun and twisted, trying to make sense of everything. I was supposed to be dead, my worries and existence left behind in the echo of peaceful nothing.

Jess, I suddenly thought, throat tightening, *Jesus Christ, where was Jess? Was she here?*

Suddenly, my captor stopped me. I stood motionless, chest heaving, waiting, heart racing.

The chain around my throat slithered to the floor and I let

out a hesitant sigh of relief. With bound hands, I reached up and rubbed the raw skin around my throat. My fingers came away warm and wet.

I felt hands fiddling around the cloth blinding me and suddenly, that too was pulled away. I blinked, rubbing the back of my hands across my eyes, letting my vision return to me.

We were standing in an empty cement room, lit by a single yellow bulb that hung from the ceiling like a rotten tooth. The walls were stained and dirty and the filthy floor was slick and slightly wet. I turned around to look at the door we had come through, but only saw the opposite wall of an empty hallway.

"What do you want?" I begged, shrinking before the massive man who was now advancing on me.

The man suddenly cocked his fist back and slugged me across the face. My head exploded with pain and I crumpled to the hard ground, blood spewing from my nose. I hit the floor hard and my breath left me in a gasp.

"Ee quiet!" the man growled around his mutilated face.

My brain swelled in my skull and I fought back unconsciousness. Blood dripped from my face onto the floor and I blinked sluggishly at it.

I heard the clank of chains and suddenly I was hauled to my feet. The massive man bound my wrists and then threw the end over a beam that extended across the ceiling.

He pulled on it and I felt myself stretched into a standing position, my arms restrained over my head like a dangling punching bag. My feet scraped across the floor as I fought to adjust myself to relieve the sudden pain in my shoulders. I found my balance and stood helpless before my captor, clothes in rags, body beaten and bleeding.

The man fastened the end of the chain to a metal loop in the floor behind me and then turned towards the door.

"What the FUCK do you want with me?!" I suddenly screamed, shaking in my restraints.

The man paused and glanced over his shoulder.

"Where am I!?" I yelled, chains rattling.

The man grunted, then turned away and walked out the door, leaving me in horrified isolation.

I screamed at him, furious and frightened.

"What are you going to do to me?" I whispered to no one, my voice quieting, tears blooming in my eyes.

Minutes, hours, days…I don't know how long I hung there. It could have been seconds or years. Every labored breath felt like an eternity. Every twist of the chain a lifetime of pain. My shoulders burned, my ribs ached, and my hair hung in tangled clumps across my bloodshot eyes.

What nightmare had I fallen into? What twisted sickness was this?

I didn't know and the fear that came with that was the worst. My stomach knotted and my legs shook with the effort to keep myself standing, relieving the pressure on my arms.

My mind swam and I began to drift, a blurry haze filling my head and contorting color and images. I don't know if I was dreaming or projecting terror upon my reality, but it shook me to the core. What was going to come through that door? What suffering awaited me? What was this place?

Drool leaked from my half-conscious mouth and I blinked as I heard a new sound enter the room. I raised my eyes, searching for the source.

The room was empty.

The sound came again, a slow slurping sound, wet and thick.

Wincing, I craned my head to look at the ceiling and what I saw paralyzed me with absolute disgust and repulsion.

A massive slug was crawling across the ceiling towards me, its bloated body at least two feet in length. A scream rose in my throat as I realized that it was dragging something behind it.

The slug was protruding from the burst stomach of a man, whom it dragged behind it like a dead shell. The man's eyes were open and lifeless, a look of pure agony stretching his long dead features. His arms and legs hung limply into the open air as the slug slithered itself closer to me.

Strands of slime dripped across the dead man's skin and fell to the floor in gooey puddles. The pale brown stalks of the slug lazily extended from its head like living pendulums, turning to stare down at me.

I shrieked and shook my chains, fear ripping up my throat in a scream. I could only watch as it came closer and closer until finally it reached the crossbar and began to inch its way down the length of the chain.

"Help me! Jesus Christ someone HELP ME!" I howled, shaking my bindings and pulling myself as far away as I could. Slime the color and consistency of mucus began to drip down the iron links and I felt it coat my hands.

The dead man, the host of this creature, gazed down at me with glazed eyes, his hands weakly brushing across my face as the slug slithered closer.

"Stop it! STOP IT! GET AWAY FROM ME!" I cried as the enormous mollusk began to wriggle down my arm, its gelatinous body engulfing my skin.

Suddenly, the man hanging from the slug grabbed my hair, his eyes snapping to life.

"Take this from me! PLEASE! FREE ME!" He gasped, his

face swinging inches from mine. I shrunk away from his grasp, mind spinning, fear coiling in my chest like a burning serpent.

"Get off of me! Leave me ALONE!" I screamed. I cocked my head back and slammed my forehead into the nose of the man. I was rewarded with a howl and then a sickening sucking sound that filled the room.

On the verge of hysteria, I watched in revulsion as the force of my blow knocked the man backward, his body pulling away from the tail end of the slug embodied in his stomach.

With a squishing sound, like a plunger slowly being pushed into a pile of wet shit, the man ripped free of his captor and fell to the hard ground where he lay motionless, mouth agape in a silent, final scream.

I didn't have time to vomit, though my stomach begged for it as the slug above me began to glide over my hair and then face.

My skin was coated with syrupy ooze and I felt it drip down my neck as the twisting body of my new oppressor wrapped around my eyes and then mouth. Squirming darkness filled my senses and I opened my mouth to scream but it was flooded instantly with warm slime.

In seconds, I was out of breath and my lungs hammered against my ribs.

You're going to die if you don't so something! my mind blared, every alarm ringing with furious urgency.

The slug tightened around my face, coiling across my throat like a noose. Its soft skin pressed in on me, squishing my nose and lips under its flabby coat of mucus.

DO SOMETHING!

Internally shrieking, I did the only thing I could.

I opened my mouth and began to eat its flesh.

My teeth dug into the slug, tearing away thick chunks like

rotten jelly. With nowhere to eject the chewed meat, I gritted my teeth and swallowed. Warm liquid was pouring across my face in gelatinous curtains as I sunk my face back into the gored slug. Black blood squished between my teeth as I ripped another hole in its body, choking the slimy strips down my throat without even chewing.

I gasped for air, my progress allowing the slightest of air pockets. As soon as I gasped, the hole filled with an avalanche of guts and blood.

Keep...eating...

Howling, I went in a third time, furiously plunging my snapping jaws into the creature, filling my mouth with its squirming insides. As my teeth clamped down and I ripped my head backward, I felt a rush of air as the giant body tumbled off my face and onto the floor.

Immediately, my body rejected what I had consumed, a sudden heave in my stomach. I leaned over the wounded slug and vomited down onto its face, body shaking, eyes bloodshot and tearing.

Without waiting, I raised my foot and brought my boot down over the slug's head. With a satisfying pop, the mollusk exploded like a bubble of stinking pus. I flinched and turned away as my body and face were coated with its insides, the payoff to my violence.

I wiped my eyes across my suspended shoulders and then spit on the dead slug, gritting my teeth.

"Not today, fucker," I hissed.

Suddenly, I heard a slow clap come from the doorway.

I snapped my eyes up and saw a man in his mid-thirties watching me. He had short brown hair and dull green eyes wearing a white button up and loose jeans. He continued to clap as he walked towards me, a slight smile twisting his full lips.

"For someone who doesn't want to live, you sure put up a hell of a fight," he commented, kicking the dead slug off to the side with a disgusted look.

I blinked back the remaining gore on my face, breathing heavy, "Who are you? What the hell is going on? Where am I!?"

The man held up his hands, silencing me, "Stop, stop, stop. Slow down. Take a breath would you?"

I gritted my teeth, twisting in my chains, but remained silent. I was exhausted, confused, and felt anxiety burn hot in my chest. Whatever misery awaited me, I wanted to know why it would be inflicted.

The man leaned against the wall to my right, watching me. After a moment, he spoke, his voice controlled and authoritative. "My name is Danny. I'm in charge of the orientation process here. You're obviously confused, as most are who find themselves in your position."

I shot a look at the dead slug in the corner, my mouth a thin line across my face.

"What I'm about to tell you may come as a shock, but I want you to be patient and listen to me without going into hysterics. Got it?"

I nodded.

He crossed his arms, his eyes never leaving mine, "You're dead. You killed yourself. Do you remember?"

Ice shot through my veins, a sickening reminder of my act. My stomach knotted and I felt like I was going to throw up again. Of course I was dead. I knew that. But why was I here? Wherever THIS was...

Danny continued, "This is the Black Farm. This is where

God sends the souls who have ended their own lives. Do you understand?"

My mouth was dry, my tongue a dry sponge around my teeth. "N-no..." I croaked, "No this isn't right...there wasn't supposed to be an afterlife...everything was just supposed to end."

Danny outstretched his hands, "Surprise!"

"What is this place?" I asked, dread coiling around my throat.

"The Black Farm," Danny said, sounding like he had recited it a million times. "It was created by God eons ago. The Devil and God couldn't stop arguing over where to send you people, you Suicidals. A life of eternal damnation seems like a harsh punishment for a moment of weakness, right? So they created the Black Farm, a middle ground to send those poor souls who ended their own lives. And then they put The Pig in charge and forgot about us for a while."

"The Pig?" I asked, not sure I wanted to know.

Danny nodded, "The Pig is our god here, in a way. God...king...ruler...tyrant...call him what you like. But it is the authority over our little reality. When God put it in charge and then turned his back on the Black Farm, The Pig saw an opportunity."

My mind was reeling, the onslaught of information overloading my brain with impossibilities.

Danny pressed on, "The Pig wanted to create a life of its own, mirroring the creation of Earth and God's children. But The Pig isn't pure, it contains not an ounce of holiness within itself. And so, its attempts at creating human life where..." Danny gestured to the dead man on the floor, "Atrocities. Its creations, its experiments came out mutated, twisted, evil.

They roam the Black Farm, killing, raping, murdering…they are sin incarnate, hateful things with black, monstrous intentions."

"What the fuck…" I wheezed, staring at the dead man, then at the slug.

"The Pig let its creations wander free, unexpectedly pleased with the horrors it had produced. It watched as they tore the place apart, shaping it into the nightmare you see now. The more carnage and destruction they caused, the more The Pig's vision began to focus. It started creating worse and worse mutations, finally molding the Black Farm into its own dark fantasy born of a hunger for evil and carnage.

By the time God took notice of what The Pig had done, it was too late. The Pig's hold over the Black Farm is cemented. So instead of destroying it and unearthing an age old argument between the Devil and Himself, God lets The Pig have its way here. Just so long as it doesn't fuck with the other afterlives."

"N-no," I whispered, unable to believe what I was hearing, fear ripping apart my insides with cold claws. "This can't be what happens to us after we die…it…it just can't…"

Danny shrugged, "Eh, you get used to it." He pushed himself off the wall, a dark fire suddenly in his eyes, a malicious grin turning his lips. "You get used to the torture his creations will inflict upon you…the way they hunt you, prey on you, catch you. They'll kill you over and over again, each way worse than the last…and then you'll wake up and it'll start all over."

Danny's face was inches from mine, his breath hot on my face. I leaned away, eyes bloodshot and wide. "Stop it…stop saying those things…this isn't real…it can't be."

Danny lightly slapped my face, "Oh, it's real. But before

you're committed to a lifetime of agony, you have a choice to make."

My eyes met his.

"You can always feed The Pig."

"W-what does that mean?"

Danny began to circle me, "You can let The Pig devour you, consume your sin and wickedness. Once it is finished with you, it'll decide what to do with you."

"Do with me?"

Danny's fingers traced my chains, "It'll either send you to Hell or it'll release you back on Earth for another chance at your pathetic life. It all depends on how you...taste."

"What the fuck kind of choice is that!?" I cried.

Danny grinned, "Your only choice. Or you can just stay here with me...with us. Forever."

I felt my mind groaning under the mental stress and physical exhaustion. Feed The Pig? Get sent to Hell? Stay on the Black Farm? What kind of options were those? What if I chose The Pig and was sent to Hell? What awaited me there? What awaited me *here?!* Questions collided with one another in a cocktail of madness and I found myself quivering under the weight of it all.

I just wanted to die.

I just wanted to fucking die.

Suddenly my eyes went wide, a rush of foul air pulled past my lips, "Jess. Where's *Jess?*"

Danny went back to leaning against the wall, saying nothing, his face revealing no answer.

"Where's Jess!?" I yelled, leaning towards him, chains cutting into my wrists, "Where is she? I have to see her! Let me see her, PLEASE!"

Danny slowly shook his head, "She has her own choice to make, Nick."

"Let me see her!" I howled, thrashing about. The thought of her trapped in this place crushed my willpower, destroyed my imagination with scenarios of her own suffering. What was she enduring? What torment was she going through?

I pictured her alone in a room like the one I was in. I imaged the slug-man paying her a visit. I could almost hear her terrified shrieks, see the fear and confusion in her eyes.

No, no, no, *NO!*

I needed to be there for her! I needed to help her! Part of the reason she was here was my fault! I hadn't tried to stop her from killing herself, hadn't insisted we found another way to ease our pain. If I had just steeled myself, been strong for the both of us…

I felt tears form in my eyes. I hadn't done any of those things, not seriously. I was more than willing to join her in death, just give up and make the sadness disappear. And now look at us. Look at where we had ended up.

I gritted my teeth, "Get me out of these fucking chains."

Danny snorted, "You sure about that, Nick?"

Tears rolled down my face, "I'm not going anywhere without Jess. Fuck The Pig, I'm going to go find my girlfriend."

Danny came and stood before me, arms crossed, "Can I just ask you something first?"

I trembled in my bindings, staring at him, cheeks damp.

"Why do you give a shit about her now? If you really cared about her you wouldn't have let her kill herself."

Fire exploded in my chest like a spark hitting gasoline. I lunged forward, snapping my jaws in Danny's face, missing by inches as he jumped back, a surprised look on his face.

"I've made my choice," I snarled, panting, "Now release me."

Danny smiled. "Got some life left in you after all. All right tough guy, I'll release you. But know this…maybe Jess has chosen to Feed the Pig, taken her chances. Maybe she's already gone. Maybe she's burning in Hell. Or maybe she's been returned and is weeping over your dead body."

"Tell me," I growled, "Just tell me where she is, you bastard."

Danny suddenly stepped forward and grabbed me by the throat, eyes alight with hatred, "Let me make something perfectly clear to you, fucker. Once you go out there, into the Black Farm, there are things that will rip you apart piece by piece. They tell me that Hell is worse than here…but not by much."

I struggled to free myself from his grasp, but he tightened his grip, leaning close, his voice like gravel. "And when you're being torn apart, I want you to remember that I offered you a choice."

And with that, he released me. I sputtered and sucked down oxygen as he reached up and freed me from my chains, the iron falling to the floor in a heap. I almost fell over as the pressure and strain left my aching muscles. I leaned over and gasped, feeling the knots in my shoulders loosen. I rubbed my bleeding wrists and stretched my arms, steadying myself.

Danny came and stood by my side, "Now get the fuck out of here. I have others to see."

I gave him a poisonous look, every ounce of me screaming to punch him, but I didn't. Instead, I took one last look at the dead slug and walked out the door.

A hallway stretched in either direction, lined with similar doors leading to rooms like mine. I chose left, my feet echoing off the wet cement, heart racing in my chest. I had so many questions, all knotted around a nest of growing fear. Distant screams crawled down the hallway behind me and I hurried along my path, away from it. All the rooms I passed were empty, dashing any hope of immediately finding Jess.

What if she had fed The Pig? What did that even mean? What was The Pig?

As I approached a large closed door at the end of the hall, I realized those questions could wait. For now, I needed to find Jess and make sure she was safe.

And what do you plan to do if she isn't?

I placed my hand on the cold door before me and braced myself.

Whatever I have to.

Muscles straining, I pushed open the heavy door and stepped out into the Black Farm.

3

Instantly, cold rain assaulted my vision and I raised a hand to shield my eyes. I heard the door close behind me but paid no attention to it. What lay before me defied any sense of understanding and I felt my breath leave my lungs like a hurricane.

To my right was an impossibly massive industrial building. Its size dwarfed me as my eyes roamed the hundreds of feet it occupied. It was structured like a barn, but the red wood was interwoven with sections of black steel. It was as wide as it was tall, towering towards the gloom above and scraping the heavens. An array of spires extended from the roof of the structure, wide and circular. Billowing from the towers were great plumes of dark smoke, lazily exhaling from open ducts and disappearing into the overcast sky.

Coiled around the smokestacks were titanic slabs of pink, organic matter. As I squinted, I realized that it appeared to be human flesh, slotted gills cutting into the twisting abominations. At the ends of the snake-like creatures were elongated human heads, their jaws protruding from their disjointed faces like a dog.

The eyes in each head were completely white and wide, tainted only by bloodshot spiderwebs that spread like lightning across a cue ball. Their skulls were devoid of hair and their nostrils flared in the rain like twin caverns.

The size of them almost stopped my heart as I watched them writhe and thrash in the storm, never detaching from their spires. I followed their fleshy, tube-like bodies and saw that they protruded from the walls of the giant barn.

The sound of clashing metal and blazing furnaces echoed across the muddy plain towards me and I thought I could hear the scream of my fellow humans.

That has to be where The Pig is, I thought to myself, chest thundering.

I tore my eyes away and I was met with an expanse of dirty plains, the grass dead eroding from the soggy soil. In the distance I could make out other shambled structures, smaller than the barn, but impossible to tell for sure.

To my left was a wooden fence, sloppily constructed and running along the length of a thick forest. The trees were tall and sturdy, their branches fanning to form a smothering canopy of leaves. The woods pressed in close and I saw nothing but darkness from inside.

Assessing my options, I looked to the sky. I noted the strange red gashes in the clouds, reminding me again of gored flesh. The strands of maroon drool hung from the eerie edifices, dancing in the wind like tattered fabric.

Where do I go? I thought to myself, blinking against the gale, an icy wind slashing rain across my skin.

Where the hell would Jess go?

I wiped my eyes, trying to make up my mind when I saw something moving towards me from one of the distant structures.

It was tall and fat, a gray smudge on the horizon.

I cupped my hands to my face and tried to make out what it was.

I felt fear slam into my gut.

It was one of those creatures, one of The Pig's creations, like the one that had dragged me here.

And it was sprinting right for me.

My decision was instantly made and I quickly hopped the fence to my left and bolted for the tree line. I heard a roar boom across the sky, an animalistic snarl of rage and hunger.

Feet churning the soaked earth, I thudded through the muck towards the trees, pulse racing. I chanced a look over my shoulder and saw the vaguely human-shaped monster now on all fours, spraying clumps of mud as it drew closer. It was still far off, but the rate at which it was approaching dumped panicked adrenaline into my veins and I sprinted through the tree line into the forest.

The sudden darkness was immediately apparent as I crashed through the snagging underbrush. I couldn't stop, wouldn't let myself stop, terror pushing me deeper and deeper, my breath slowly becoming ragged.

I didn't know where I was running, didn't dare look behind me, plowing forward with a prayer on my lips. Branches scraped across my arms, rocks rose to trip me, gloom and dripping moisture clouded my senses, but I didn't slow.

Behind me, I heard something roar again, vicious and sinister, cutting through the foliage like an ax.

And it was close.

Chest burning, muscles turning to stone, I heard the crash of wood behind me and the thunder of heavy feet pounding the soil.

"Shit, shit, shit!" I cried, desperately looking for some place to hide.

An earsplitting cannon blast boomed through the woods and I heard the massive shudder of creaking wood as a tree came thundering to the earth just a couple dozen yards behind me.

It's going to catch you.

Suddenly, a root found my boot and I went sprawling, smacking my face into the unforgiving ground. Stars exploded in my head like fireworks and the breath was knocked from me. My body ached and my lungs clawed for oxygen. I clutched my sides, gasping, rain and blood washing across my skin.

The ground vibrated as the predator grew closer, cracking the sky with another guttural roar. Strands of wet hair scraped across my forehead as I turned to look for something, anything, to hide.

At the base of a great tree, amidst the coil of roots and knots, lay a natural burrow in the trunk, just an arm's length away. Gritting my teeth, I pulled myself through the claws of the undergrowth. My muscles quivered in protest, stone and vine reaching to pull me back.

Wood splintered and I could feel through my grasping hands just how close the monster was. Grunting through my teeth, body soaked in sludge and sticking leaves, I slid my body to the tree and into the open hollow.

Darkness swarmed me as my body tumbled inside, the interior unexpectedly spacious. I rolled to the side, away from the entrance, and held my breath, slamming my eyes closed.

Seconds later, something huge rocketed past my hiding place, snarling and crashing through the underbrush. I waited with agonizing trepidation, fully expecting it to slow and come barreling into my wooden cove, teeth gnashing and eyes wide. But it didn't.

It never slowed its charge and I exhaled a gentle hiss as it tore past the tree. I listened to the crashing branches, slowly fading away from me, growing more and more distant. Finally, mercifully, I was alone in silence.

"Hello."

I screamed, despite myself, the tiny voice rattling me in the small space. Clawing myself back against the rough bark, I spun and gazed deeper into the hollow to see I wasn't alone.

A small boy in a filthy red onesie sat against the far wall a few feet away. Stretched across his face was a plastic devil mask, completely covering his features except for two huge blue eyes that stared back at me.

"What the FUCK? Who are you!?" I gasped, placing a hand over my sputtering heart.

The boy didn't move and I noticed his eyes were bloated, unnaturally round and jutting from the red plastic like neon water balloons.

"I'm hiding," the boy responded calmly, idly tracing a padded foot in the dirt.

I forced myself to calm, sensing no immediate threat. "You scared the shit out of me, kid."

He just looked at me, almost bored.

"Are you hiding from that...that thing?" I asked, pointing outside.

He shook his head. "No...I'm hiding from Pudge. He doesn't like me very much."

I adjusted myself against the tree. "Who's Pudge?"

"It's what I call him cause he's a big fatty. He's always trying to kill me. I don't know why. I didn't do nothing to him."

I blinked. "He...wants to kill you?"

The boy looked at me like I was stupid. "Are you new or something mister?"

I nodded. "Yeah, actually."

The boy groaned behind his mask. "Great, more dumb Sky Sludge."

I held up a hand. "Sky Sludge?"

The boy pointed outside, "Yeah, Sky Sludge. That's where you all come from. That red drool in the clouds? You drip out of it and fall to the ground. Then the Reapers come and bring you to Danny."

I shook my head, confusion twisting my brain into knots. "You mean the...the cuts in the clouds? We come out of that?"

"Yeah, after you kill yourself, you big dummy," he said, his voice muffled beneath the plastic, "Don't know why you'd want to come here. Suicidals are so dumb."

"Wait," I said, "you're not...one of us? What are you then?"

The boy snorted, "I'm Pig Born."

Alarms began to ring in my head. "You didn't...you're not...human?"

"No, dummy."

I swallowed hard. "Danny said your kind are evil, that I should stay away from you."

The boy grunted. "You should, Sky Sludge. We'll cut you up and eat you down."

I eyed him cautiously. "Then...why aren't you?"

The boy looked at me like I was a slab of hung meat, "Eh...too big. You'd probably kill me."

The matter-of-fact tone in which he said it shook me, the casual way he confronted violence and death.

"Who's Pudge?" I asked again.

A hatred filled the child's eyes, "He's a big fat cow who's hunting me. I'd be an easy to kill. Not as hard as some of the other Pig Born."

I ran a hand over my mouth. "I'm sorry to hear that."

"What do you care? I'm Pig Born. If I was bigger, I'd kill you."

I held up a hand, "Look, I'm not going to hurt you. I'm searching for someone. My girlfriend, Jess. She came here with me. I need to find her, make sure she's ok. Have you seen her? She's about my age with short blond hair. Pretty."

The boy snickered, "I bet Muck has her. He loves pretty things. Always touching his pee-pee."

The news turned my stomach. "Who's Muck? Where can I find him?"

The boy shook his head, "Stay away from Muck. He's worse than Pudge. He's mean, mean, mean. If he has your girlfriend, just hope he kills her quick so she can come back somewhere else. Somewhere away from him."

My heart burned. "Jesus, kid, help me out here. Where is he?"

The boy adjusted his mask before replying, "Stupid Sky Sludge. You always think there's some way out. You always think you can out-smart this place." He leaned forward. "Well, you can't. This is the Black Farm. And it will rip you to shreds over and over and over again. Just accept it like the rest of us. If your girlfriend was smart, she would have fed The Pig." He waved a hand outside. "And if she hasn't…there's nothing you can do for her."

I suddenly felt angry, a sharp twist in my chest. I leaned forward and grabbed the kid by his collar, hissing in his face, "Listen, you little shit, if you think I'm going to give up on her then you are sadly mistaken."

The boy seemed unaffected by my outburst. He didn't struggle as he leaned into me. "Haven't you already, though? Isn't that why you're here?"

I stared into his enormous eyes for another second and then pushed him away, letting out a disgusted snort. He was right. As much as I hated to admit it, he was right. But that didn't mean I was going to give up. As fucked up as it was, this was a new reality with new problems and I damn well wasn't going to let Jess face it alone. I needed to find her.

The boy brushed himself off and crawled to the opening. I watched him, feeling disgusted with myself and with the situation I found myself in. What I wouldn't give to go back. I sighed and felt a weight settle in my chest, a dawning realization of the horrific position I found myself in. My life had gone from sad to survival.

Sensing my change in attitude, the boy looked back at me before scampering away. He pointed out into the forest. "Muck is that way. He lives in a big hole by the Temple of the Pig. You'll know it when you see it."

I smiled a little, eyes meeting his, "Thanks, kid. Good luck to you."

The boy spat at me, "Fuck you. I'm telling you where Muck is so he can rip you apart. See you around, Sky Sludge."

I blinked as the boy scrambled off into the woods, disappearing from sight.

What a little bastard.

I leaned out of the hollow and scanned my surroundings. Nothing but dark, dripping forest. I listened for signs of danger and realized that I couldn't hear anything but the splatter of rain on the leaves overhead. No bugs, no birds, nothing.

You don't know this place, I reminded myself, *you don't know its rules; you don't know its cycles.*

It was an unnerving feeling, one I found hard to fathom. Questions about the Black Farm began to crowd my tired mind. Does it always rain here? Is there night? How big is this place? Is there a way to get out? If I killed myself here, would I wake up in those clouds, about to fall to the earth from that red drool?

As I attempted to come up with answers, I realized that one thing was very apparent. I was thirsty, deathly thirsty.

Well, my biological body still acts the same, I thought to myself, *that's something at least.*

I slowly crawled out of the tree, eyes scanning for signs of life. I stayed on my belly and slithered to a large plant a few feet to my left. Water pooled in its expansive leaves and I greedily lowered my lips and sucked up the moisture.

Sighing, I wiped my face and crawled to my feet. My clothes were tattered and filthy, clinging to my skin like glue. Rain seeped through the dense canopy overhead and I raised my face to it, letting it wash away some of the muck.

"Muck," I said out loud, "Got to find Muck."

I knew it wasn't much to go on, but it was all I had. In truth, I had no way of knowing if Jess was even here. Maybe she *had* chosen to feed The Pig like Danny said. But what if she hadn't? What if this monster, Muck, had taken her?

But I had to do *something.* I realized I needed some kind of destination, something to work towards. It was my lifeline to hope and I knew if I lost that, I was as good as dead. Well…whatever dead meant here at least.

Checking my surroundings one last time, I began to trudge in the direction the boy had pointed. I tried to make as little sound as possible as I walked, each step carefully calculated. The last thing I needed was something chasing me again.

Time stretched before me, filled with agonized tension. I never slowed, the forest remaining eerily quiet except for the rain. My body begged for sleep, but I ignored it. Every second I wasn't searching for Jess was another second she could be suffering. I focused on the image of her face, her shining blue eyes, her precious smile. My chest swelled and I suddenly missed her more than anything. As bad as things had gotten, we had always been together. Together through the end.

Her separation from me was jarring, something I hadn't expected. I had grown so used to her always being around, always being close. Not knowing where she was, what she was doing…it dug into my chest like a mournful termite.

"Please let her be safe," I whispered, climbing over a downed tree.

I stopped suddenly. Who was I talking to? God?

I trained my eyes to the heavens, "If you're up there…if you can see me here…please…help me find her. She doesn't deserve this."

Rain slithered overhead and spat into my face. I shut my eyes against it. It was the first time I had seriously prayed since killing myself. I didn't even believe in God, didn't know what I expected, but I knew I needed help. My reality had been upended, all rational thought and understanding destroyed. The Black Farm was proof of that. If I was going to face this place, I needed to reassess what I truly knew.

The answer came back depressingly stark: *You know nothing. You're a newborn in some fucked up place created by bickering, omnipotent entities. No one hears you, no one can help you. This reality is as cruel and violent as the one you left.*

I balled my hands into fists and opened my eyes to the sky. "Just once," I growled, "Please, fucking *help me.*"

Without waiting for an answer, I plowed deeper into the forest.

I don't know how long I walked, the sky never changing. The gloom that filtered through the green continued to exhale rain in icy gusts, my body growing cold beneath it. The woods never changed, a constant expanse of towering forest and muddy undergrowth. I soon realized I was lost, the environment melting together like repeating pictures. My limbs ached, the exhausting experience I had gone through tugging me to the earth. I wrapped my arms around myself, begging my body to stop shivering, the rain coating my clothes and skin.

Eventually I collapsed, unable to take another step. I thudded against a tree and sat there gasping, rubbing my muscles back to life. My eyes drooped and my mind whispered for sleep. I rested my head against the trunk of the tree and fought against it as best I could, but I could feel myself losing the battle.

Don't you dare sleep while Jess is out there, I thought, *don't you dare.*

Despite my best efforts, I closed my eyes and fell into a light sleep.

Something cold slithered across my mouth, jolting me awake in an instant. My eyes snapped open and I immediately reached to slap away whatever was on my face but froze. A woman's face was inches from mine, one hand over my mouth, a finger to her lips urging my silence. Once she saw I wasn't going to scream, she slid her hand off my mouth and pointed behind me.

I craned my neck to look behind the tree I had been resting against, confusion crashing like waves into my already tired psyche. In the distance, my eyes found the source of my hurried silence.

A cluster of people was slowly walking through the woods, clothed in red hooded robes that obscured their faces. I counted twelve of them, their procession slow and almost reverent. They were in a single file formation and the head of the group swung something from a chain in front of him like a pendulum. I squinted and realized it was a skull. The top of the head had been caved in and filled with burning coals.

The air sizzled and filled with reeking smoke as I continued to observe the strange congregation. They didn't look towards me or my silent companion as they marched, the leader gently swinging the hollowed out head before him, causing thick trails of smoke to curl around them.

Jesus, I thought, *it's like some kind of twisted incense.* As if to prove my point, the twelve began to slowly sing, a deep murmur, their voices somber. Whatever I was witnessing was some kind of religious ceremony, a chilling procession I wanted no part of.

The woman suddenly tapped my arm. I turned to her and really saw her for the first time. She was about my age, her raven black hair short and curling to her chin. Her eyes looked like lifeless holes in her skull, marbles of dull brown appraising me above a worried frown.

"Come with me," she whispered, motioning away from the eerie scene before us. I took one last look at the twelve hooded figures and then followed the woman away from them.

She was quick and careful, her feet carrying her through the underbrush with practiced skill. I tried my best to mimic her silence, but I soon felt like a bull in a china shop, seemingly snapping and tripping over every branch and rock. She shot me an irritated look once or twice at my blundering volume but said nothing.

She took us down a long slope and after a little more walking, I noticed the trees were thinning. The overcast sky slowly began to unfurl over the receding canopy and the ever present rain drenched my skin with increased vigor. I shivered but stayed close to the woman, wondering where we were going. She obviously wasn't…what had the kid called them? Pig Born?

As we pressed on, a new noise began to cut through the rain. It sounded like the crash of waves against a beach. Curious, I picked up the pace, urging the woman to press on.

Finally, through the trees, I spotted a stretch of white running the length of my vision, left to right. The crash of waves was apparent now and I bolted past the woman, heart racing. Was this the way out of the Black Farm? Was this person leading me to some secret exit?

"Stop!" the woman cried as I overtook her, but I paid her no attention.

I burst through the trees onto a sandy beach but immediately skid to a halt, eyes growing wide, a shiver running through me as I gazed out on the scene before me.

A vast ocean stretched to the horizon, black waves curling and foaming along the shore like rotting tongues lapping at the sand.

But that wasn't what chilled me to the core.

It was the three towering monsters in the ocean, their figures soaring to meet the clouds. They looked as if they were made of stone, and each one had strange glyphs and patterns lining their human-shaped torsos, arms, and legs. The glyphs glowed neon blue and pulsed as if illuminated by the beating of a colossal heart. The human similarities ended once my wide-eyed gaze reached their heads.

Driven deep between each of their stone shoulders was an immense cross, the metal crossbeams shining in the rain. Hanging from the arms of the crosses were thousands and thousands of wriggling people, their screams echoing across the dark waves towards me.

The stone titans waded through the ocean, the water rising to their waist. Their long cracked fingers skimmed the surface as if feeling for movement or currents.

I realized my mouth was hanging open as I observed these mountainous entities, their gigantic forms impossibly imposing despite being miles from shore.

Suddenly the woman was at my side, yanking me back into the woods and off the beach. I tripped and stumbled, unable to tear my eyes away from the chilling giants in the ocean.

Once we were a couple trees deep, the woman let go of me and slumped against a tree, breathing hard and shaking her head.

"Are you an idiot?" she asked, her voice harsh. "What is wrong with you?"

I pulled my eyes from the partially obscured beach and looked down at her. "What the hell are those things?"

She cocked and eyebrow at me and then snorted after a moment, "Oh I see…you're new here aren't you?"

I sat down against a tree across from her, still recovering. "Huh? Oh, yeah, I am. I seem to be getting asked that a lot."

The woman sighed, "I'm just not used to seeing new people.

Muck gets most of you right out of the gate. Puts you in his Needle Fields."

I winced, "Do I even want to know?"

The woman smiled sadly. "Hopefully you'll never have to. I'm Megan, by the way."

I looked at her, taking in those empty brown eyes, the nest of black hair. I returned the smile. "I'm Nick."

Megan dug into the pocket of her torn jeans. "Shoulda fed The Pig, Nick."

I turned my gaze back to the tree line. "I can't. I need to find someone. My girlfriend, Jess. She...she came here with me." I felt Megan's eyes on me and I exhaled heavily. "It wasn't supposed to be like this. There wasn't supposed to be an afterlife. We just wanted...we just wanted to sleep in darkness together, forever."

"How romantic," Megan said, pulling something from her pocket.

I shot her a sharp look, "You don't know what we were going through."

Megan tossed me something and I caught it, turning it over in my hand. It was a brown, slightly squishy rectangle that looked like packed dirt.

I cocked an eyebrow, holding it up.

Megan nodded with her chin. "Eat up."

I snorted, "This is food?"

"That it is. Best I can do. And you're welcome by the way."

As I inspected the strange substance I realized I was starving. I sniffed the brown bar and then took a hesitant bite. It was surprisingly tasteless, the consistency like taffy. I devoured it in seconds and felt slightly better.

"Thanks," I said, wiping my mouth.

Megan inspected me curiously. "What makes you think Jess didn't feed The Pig? If she were smart, she would have."

"She's here," I answered, "I just know she is. I can feel it in my gut. I have to find her. She needs me. This place…"

"It's awful, isn't it? Trust me, you haven't seen the half of it. There are things here that you can't even imagine."

"You mentioned Muck. I've heard that name before. Some kid in a devil mask told me that he probably had Jess. I'm looking for him."

Megan shook her head. "Stay away from that monster. I was caught by him…a long time ago. Thankfully he ended up killing me. But the time I spent in captivity…" She trailed off, wrapping her arms around herself, face growing pale.

"So you understand why I need to find her. That woman has suffered enough in life, I can't leave her alone in this nightmare."

Megan sighed, "If she has indeed chosen to stay here, then she could be anywhere. But Muck…he'd be a good place to start searching. I'm warning you though…"

I held up a hand, "I know, I know. I can't do *nothing*, though. There has to be some way for us to get out of here."

Megan pointed to the ocean, "Yeah, they thought so, too."

I turned to look at the lumbering titans in the black water. "Who? Those monsters?"

"No. The people hanging from the crosses," she said sadly. "They tried to swim out of the Black Farm. Thought that maybe the horizon held some kind of escape. Idiots. You can't get away; we're all trapped here. The Black Farm is an island separated down the middle by the forest. You can't escape; you can only hide."

"What are those giants?" I asked.

Megan wiped a strand of wet hair off her face, the rain continuous. "They're called Keepers. There's thirteen of them in total, all roaming the waters surrounding the Black Farm. Anyone who tries to brave the ocean gets taken by them and hung on their crosses, doomed to swing by the neck for eternity, never dying."

"Jesus," I muttered, remembering the screams.

The moment stretched and the silence grew between us. I rolled my head back and stared into the sky. I spotted a red split in the clouds, a growing abyss that gaped like a bloody mouth. I watched in horrified fascination as strands of red drool stretched from the corners and extended towards the earth.

"Oh my god," I whispered, eyes growing wide. Megan turned to stare up with me. Motionless bodies began to fill the tubes of swaying ooze, and then one by one fell from the jelly onto the beach. The bodies slammed into the sand, ten, twenty people, spraying grit into the air. They lay there, motionless, eyes shut like they were dead.

"That's how we are reborn into the Black Farm," Megan said somberly, "Come on, we need to move. Reapers will be here soon to bring them to Danny."

But I was paralyzed, disgust and fear rooting me in place. One of the bodies rolled on the beach, down the gentle incline towards the water. The waves rose and covered the person, pulling him into the ocean with dark intent.

Immediately, one of the cross-headed giants turned to face the shore. It began to walk, long strides pulling immense gouts of water along with it. As it got closer, I began to hear the screams of the people chained to the cross upon its shoulders.

Megan was on her feet, looking worried. "Come on, Nick, let's go. Now."

"Where the fuck am I?" I whispered before Megan grabbed me and dragged me back into the woods.

4

I wiped moisture from my face as we slunk through the woods, keeping a vigilant eye out for any signs of movement. I still had so many questions, but Megan silenced me with a look anytime I opened my mouth. She seemed to have a destination in mind so I crammed the inquiries down my throat and pressed on.

For a while, we didn't see anyone, the two of us focusing on remaining as quiet as possible as the constant rain bled through the expansive canopy overhead. I could feel myself growing tired, but felt like stopping would be too risky until we found shelter.

At one point, we saw a group of people slinking through the undergrowth, distant smudges of pale color blinking between the trees. Megan pulled me down and we hid until they were long out of sight. They looked like Suicidals, but the risk wasn't worth exposing our position.

The sky never changed its gloomy hue as the hours ticked on. It felt like we were stuck in time. Or maybe time didn't exist here. I wiped wet strands of hair out of my face and pulled my eyes to Megan who had noticed me staring up into the green canvas.

"What are you doing? Come on!" she hissed.

I walked close to her and whispered, "Where exactly are we going?"

She stepped over a log, eyes forward. "You want to know where Muck is, right?"

I pushed a scraggly bush aside. "Well, yeah, but I thought you said to stay away from him."

"I did. But if you want to find your girlfriend, it's the most logical place to start."

I suddenly stopped, "Why are you helping me?"

She turned to face me, an exasperated look on her face, "I'm just showing you how to get out of this forest. Once we're out, I'll point you in the right direction, ok?"

"But why?"

She took a step towards me, her guard dropping slightly, "Because I hate this place. I hate what it does to us, to Suicidals. If I can make this nightmare somewhat more tolerable for you…well…that seems like a good way to fight back. If finding Jess brings you some kind of happiness, despite the misery that surrounds us…" She trailed off, looking at the ground.

I put my hand on her shoulder, "Thank you."

She shrugged it away and started to walk again, "Come on. We're almost out."

After another couple minutes, I began to see gray light through the trees ahead of us. Megan put a finger to her lips as the trees thinned, begging caution. I nodded and crouched low, the tree line growing before us.

Megan took my hand and pushed me to the ground, then did the same. We slid on our stomachs in the dirt and brush until we reached the edge of the forest. She wriggled close to me and began to whisper in my ear, but I didn't hear her.

My mouth was wide open, my eyes bulging from their sockets, the vision before me a twisting nest of chaos and impossibility.

Hanging in the sky, amidst the red gashes in the clouds, was what looked like a dead sun. It flickered and blinked like a sputtering black light. Thick trails of venomous darkness dripped from its mass and fell like rain across the horizon. I tore my eyes from the heavens to be greeted by an immense mountain to my left, the snowy peak kissing the sky. I traced the titanic formation to its base and then ran my eyes across a hilly plain to finally end at a beach that ran parallel to us on my right. In the distant waters, I spotted a Keeper pulling itself across the waves, its cross-head towering towards the clouds like a skyscraper.

"Hey Nick, you with me?"

I closed my open mouth, feeling the weight of sensory overload scatter my mind. I wiped the rain from my face and blinked, turning to Megan.

"I-I'm good," I whispered. That dead sun pulled at my attention like strings on a puppet. I traced the black that dripped from it, shaking my head.

"Megan, what is that?" I asked.

She followed my eyes to the sky, the black broken orb dangling just below the cloud cover. "A long time ago, before I was here, The Pig tried to mimic God and his creations. What you're seeing is its attempt at conjuring a star," She wriggled closer, her voice dropping. "But The Pig is evil…that shell of a sun is all it could summon. It just sits there, like a boil in the sky, dripping its infectious innards into the ocean. That's why the water is black."

I let her words wash over me, the cracked, splintered sun filling my head. It was horrible and wondrous at the same time, its alien construction birthing both awe and disgust. Just what were the limits of The Pig's powers?

Megan directed my attention to the mountain, its colossal slopes rising sharply like the blades of a razor,

"Muck lives at the base of the mountain. You'll know you're getting close when you hit the Needle Fields."

"What are those?" I asked, not sure I wanted to know the answer.

Megan shook her head. "You'll see when you get there. Best you just get through them as quickly as possible. Can you see those tiny spires along the base of the mountain?"

I squinted in the gloom and strained my eyes. I thought I could make out...something, a scattering of thin vertical lines littering the very edge of my sight.

"Those are the fields. You make it through those and you'll find his hole. You can't miss it. Once you see the Temple of the Pig, you'll know you're close."

I began to feel a suffocating weight choke me. "How the hell am I supposed to do this..."

Megan shrugged, looking downcast, "I'm sorry, Nick."

My eyes absorbed the expanse before me, the shoreline, the black ocean, the Keeper, the dead star, the great mountain and its snowy peak...I sighed.

"She's out there somewhere...I can feel her."

Megan smiled sadly, "I hope you find her."

I turned to her. "Do you have to go?"

"I'm afraid so. I don't dare go near the Needle Fields."

I frowned, "Where can I find you when I retrieve Jess?"

Megan grunted at my optimism. "Most of us Suicidals hide in the forest. That's where I'll be."

"Until next time, then," I said grimly, "and thank you."

As she crawled to her feet, we froze in unison as something shook the foliage behind us. I met Megan's eyes, wide and terrified as the earth beneath us began to vibrate, the sound of thunderous feet racing towards us. Branches snapped and dirt flew as something of great weight crashed from the wall of undergrowth.

"Run!" Megan yelled, pulling me to my feet, her voice hysteric; our cover was blown.

But it was too late.

My breath was knocked from me as something tall and meaty slammed into my chest. I went sprawling, vision swimming, gasping for air. Megan was screaming and through the distortion of shaking color, I saw someone advancing on her.

Our assailant was naked and covered in ugly scabs that peppered his flabby rolls. A burlap bag was pulled over his head, hiding his features save for a single bloodshot eye that glared at us through a crude cut in the cloth.

I tried to stand, but I was so shaken I found that I couldn't. The naked man had Megan by the throat, lifting her off her feet. Her eyes rolled wildly as she choked and fought to free herself, but it didn't do much good.

Groaning, I managed to pull myself to my knees just as the fat man slugged Megan in the face, knocking her unconscious. Blood erupted from her nose as she went limp in his grasp.

"Leave her alone!" I cried weakly, standing.

The man grunted, his breath rippling the sack over his head, and dropped her. He turned, his one visible eye settling over me. I took a step back, his revolting state shaking me. He stepped towards me, his size terrifying. He was tall, his meaty legs like twin tree trunks. His belly quivered and sloped away from him, stopping just short of his exposed penis.

"J-just leave us alone," I begged weakly, fear rising in my chest.

The man howled, a guttural animalistic cry that made my knees shake. In one quick motion, he leaped forward and tackled me to the ground, his immense weight pinning me beneath him.

I screamed, pushing, clawing, slowly being crushed under his bulk. Something slammed into the side of my head and I felt all the fight drain from me. Stars exploded like dynamite in my head and pain shot through my body like an electric volt.

Another blow and I was out cold.

I was swimming in painful darkness. I could hear myself breathing but couldn't seem to find my eyes. A sour, earthy aroma filled my nostrils as I tried to move. I couldn't. My head was pounding, a knotted fist of pain pulsing through my skull. Slowly, everything began to come back, the world filling like a swirl of dirty paint.

I groaned and heard a dry rattle escape my lips. I found my face in agony and willed my eyes to flutter open. A dim brown light filled my sight and slowly bloomed into dirty yellow. I turned my head and saw that I was in a cage.

No, no, no, my mind cried, panic waking once again.

It looked like I was in a cave, a fire crackling in the center of the hollowed out space. The ceiling was low, nine or ten feet high, its dirt packed walls lined with similar cages to the one I was in. They were filled with bones, pale white skeletons lying motionless against the bars.

Heart racing, I sat up, pain shaking my head. I placed a hand on my brow and wiped dirt and sweat from my skin, hand trembling. The entrance to the cave was directly across from me, a dark hole that burrowed away from the cages lining the walls.

The fire pit cast shadows across the cave floor, stretching and pulling my eyes to soak in this new horror. A crude bench sat against the wall by the entrance, dull metal tools catching the light and sparking my already burning imagination.

"What is this place?" I croaked to myself.

"Nick?"

I turned to look at the opposite wall and my heart slammed to a halt. Megan was chained to the floor, a loop of metal coiling around her throat to connect with a spike that had been driven into the packed earth beneath her feet.

She had been stripped of her clothing and sat huddled against the wall, tears pouring from her terrified eyes.

"Megan!" I cried, standing in my cage and pressing my face against the cold bars. "Are you ok?!"

The firelight reflected in her wet eyes as she shook her head. "N-no…no I'm not. He has us Nick…he has us."

"Who!? Where are we!?" I hissed, watching the entrance with caution.

"Muck," Megan sobbed, bringing her knees up and hiding her nakedness. "He got the drop on us…" She started to become hysteric, her voice rising, "Nick, he's going to hurt us! He's going to hurt me!" She grabbed the chain around her throat, throttling it, screaming now, "I can't do this again! I CAN'T!"

My heart was pounding, her cries igniting my own fear. I tried to shush her, begging to keep her voice down, but she was lost in her own terror. My fingers traced the iron I was contained in, searching for a door, a weakness, anything. I could feel my heart throbbing in my throat, an urgent drum fueled by Megan's all-knowing terror.

Her cries ringing in my ears, I traced a thick chain coiled around a seam in the cage. I grasped it, pulled on it, but it was no use. I was locked in, helpless to await whatever horror this place had in store for me. A bead of sweat trickled down my cheek and I wiped it away, searching the floor for something, anything to pry the chain. But all I found was barren dirt, empty of use.

"Don't bother," a voice called from my left.

I spun, searching for the source. A man hung on the wall opposite Megan, naked and chained in a similar fashion. He was old, his face worn and sporting a filthy gray beard. His skin was tight against his bones, stretching across a beaten ribcage. His dull eyes met mine and I swallowed hard. He looked like a corpse.

Megan quieted, turning her attention to this new inhabitant of our dismal prison. Her face was stained with silent tears, her lip quivering.

"Where is he?" she asked.

The man blinked slowly. "I don't know...but he'll be back...he always comes back..."

"There has to be a way out of here!" I cried, rattling my bars, unwilling to accept my position.

The man snorted, his mouth pulled into a humorless smile to reveal broken teeth, "There's no way out of here, son...not until he's done with you."

My knuckles turned white as I gripped the iron. "Don't say that..."

The man shook his head sadly. "Just pray he gets bored of

you quickly. Pray he kills you. Pray he doesn't stick you in the Needle Fields."

I licked my lips, shooting a quick glance at Megan. "What are the Needle Fields?"

The old man started to cry, "Acres and acres...endless..."

"Tell me!" I shouted, heart racing.

He was sniveling now, hope long since taken from him. "Rows and rows of needles as thick as your finger. He drives them into the earth like stakes and then impales you on them, one on top of the other like pieces of meat..." His eyes went wide. "And then he leaves you there for days...bleeding...dying...begging for death...sometimes you starve...sometimes the elements kill you...sometimes Pig Born come to feed..." he collapsed his head onto his shallow chest, weeping.

I felt an icy hand reach into my body and squeeze the breath from my lungs. I stepped away from the bars and realized my hands were shaking. I turned to Megan and saw she was crying silently, her nakedness a grim reminder at how helpless we were.

Suddenly, the man's head shot up, eyes bulging, "He's coming...he's coming!"

Megan began to thrash in her chains, howling, her hysteria sparking a contagion in me. I collapsed to the ground and pushed myself into the far corner of the cage, huddling into myself. I trained my eyes on the tunnel.

It wasn't long before a naked, obese man entered the dim space. It was the same man who had attacked us in the woods. The burlap bag shuddered over his head as he sucked in wet breaths, his bloodshot eye roaming around the cave from the cut in the cloth.

As soon as Megan saw him, she began to shriek, a deep bellowing recognition that shook my skull. I heard myself whimpering, my unknown fate spooling out in my imagination like bloody film.

The man, Muck, walked over to the old man chained to the wall. Without slowing, he grabbed him by the face and ripped his head from his shoulders in one brutal motion. My mouth dropped open and I felt a scream burning up my throat but nothing came out. Muck tossed the decapitated head into the fire pit and turned away from the corpse as blood erupted from the stump like a bubbling brook.

Unaffected by the violence, Muck rubbed his massive stomach, wiping his hands across the greasy folds as if to rid himself of the act. Megan's screams were constant, but the massive man didn't seem to notice. He walked over to my cage and stared down at me.

I felt my bladder release as his looming nudity pressed against the bars, molding his stomach around them.

"Pretty man," Muck grunted, his voice a guttural snarl. "I like."

"P-please," I croaked, a mess of tears and terror, "Please don't hurt me. I haven't done anything to you…"

Muck reached down and grasped his flaccid penis, squeezing it tightly, "Let's see how the man feels."

He reached out and snatched a ring of rusty keys that had been hanging against the wall. He fumbled with them for a moment before selecting one, working the lock. As the chains slid away, I began to scream, a helpless cry that tore at my throat like burning coals.

Muck opened the cage door and reached inside, grabbing me by the throat. With a grunt, he dragged me across the dirt and into the middle of the cave, his footsteps like thunder. I dug my hands into the earth, kicked and screamed, my body dumping adrenaline and horror through my blood stream like a broken dam.

This isn't happening, my mind screamed, *Jesus Christ this isn't happening, please God, not this.*

With a thud, Muck dropped me and grabbed my pants, tearing them away with a sickening *r-i-i-i-p!* My heart was racing, I tasted bile on my tongue and every ounce of my being begged to wake up.

Muck flipped me onto my stomach with a sharp kick. I gasped, eyes bulging as pain crunched through me. I wanted to gag but found I didn't have the breath. My eyes watered as I sunk my fingers into the dirt, vision swimming as Muck got down on his knees behind me. Through my blurry eyes, I saw Megan across the cave, screaming for all this to stop.

I tried to get up, but something heavy thudded into my shoulders and I went sprawling back onto my stomach, heaving. My nakedness was terrifying, my thighs scraping roughly into the earth as Muck held me in place.

"Don't do this," I gasped, spittle exploding from my lips, "Please Jesus, don't do this to me."

A great weight settled over me and I felt meaty fingers pry my legs apart. I struggled and squealed, the dawning anticipation crushing me with overwhelming horror.

Hot breath blasted on the back of my neck as Muck settled himself into position, one hand pressing my shoulders to the ground, the other fiddling with his now erect penis. I gritted my teeth, world shaking, fingers clenched into fists.

And then Muck began to rape me.

I squeezed my eyes shut, my mouth stretched into an empty

scream. I felt like I was being torn in two, the burning heat splitting me in half. I scraped my teeth across the floor and pounded my fists into the dirt, feeling Muck's great weight rock over me again…and again….and again…

Until it was over…

As he pulled himself off with a satisfied grunt, I felt darkness press in around me. I couldn't move; pain was driven deep inside me like a blazing stake. I vomited into the dirt, feeling the hot bile pool around my cheek.

The world swam and all I knew was pain.

I became dimly aware that Muck was dragging me over to Megan. I sucked in the puke-soaked air and blinked dimly in a growing haze. I felt myself tossed to the ground where I lay motionless, my brain begging to shut off. Muck came into view and I watched as he grabbed Megan by the hair and dragged her to her feet.

She bit at him, clawing and scratching, knowing what was coming. Effortlessly, Muck stood her up and slammed her against the wall with one hand. He was already bringing his dripping cock back to life. I watched all this from the floor, broken and bloody, begging to die.

Muck positioned himself behind her and sniffed along her neck as he spread her. I turned away, shutting my eyes, quivering.

Suddenly, a hand was pulling my head up and I was staring into Muck's infected eye through the bag.

"Watch!" he growled. I tried to pull away from him, squeezing my eyes shut tighter, the fight drained from my corrupted body.

"Watch!" he howled, shaking my head in his hand. I tried to

open my eyes, but my brain wasn't working, pain shutting my systems down one by one into darkness.

Snarling with frustration, Muck dropped me and went to the bench by the cave entrance. My head collapsed to the dirt where I lay, watching, as Megan curled into herself, sobbing, lost in her own terror.

Then Muck was back, pulling my head up again. I blinked in agony and saw he had something in his hand.

It was a long thin knife, the blade glinting in the firelight.

"Watch!" Muck repeated, bringing the knife towards my face. I tried to pull myself away, a cry finding its way to my lips.

The tip of the blade extended closer and closer to my right eye and I was suddenly lost in hot fire as Muck sliced my eyelid off, the knife twisting expertly through my skin. I howled, the scream shaking my already exhausted body, blood pouring into my eye and down my cheek.

And then he cut off the other one.

He dropped my head and pressed a thick hand into my face, turning my now exposed eyes towards Megan. I whimpered and sobbed, my nose soon soaked in my own blood as it poured from my face.

Satisfied, Muck tossed the knife aside and went back to Megan, stroking himself in anticipation. I lay beaten and watched him work her over through my bleeding eyes. Drool and blood leaked from my lips onto the floor, pooling around my face. My chest rose and fell with labored agony as Megan's screams echoed around me.

At some point, I passed out.

When I awoke I was back in my cage. My damaged eyes burned and I felt blood dripping down my thighs. I didn't move, letting my miserable existence slowly bloom back into focus. My mouth tasted like copper and dirt and I was terribly thirsty. I didn't want to move for fear of igniting my resting pain. But I knew it was there, waiting for me.

I didn't hear Megan screaming and hoped, horribly, that she had been murdered and reborn somewhere far from Muck's cave. I tried to blink, but found I didn't have the capability anymore. Tears flowed down my cheeks. What *misery* was this?

In the dirt, I cried quietly. How could I make this stop? What did I have to do? At that moment in time, I gave up hope entirely. I would never find Jess. I would never know happiness again. My life had been a steady march toward worse and worse fates, why should it stop now? I was going to stagnate into a husk, a walking corpse who would be victimized and brutalized for the rest of time. I couldn't fight back against such evil, against such violence. Not when such horror opposed me.

I felt the familiar pangs of suicide rattle my mind. If I had the strength, I would have laughed. A lot of good that had done. The worst part was that all my earthly problems were still very present in my mind, a chuckling reminder veiled by the passage of death. Every mistake I had ever made, every drop of sadness, every heartbreaking event…they were all still there. With the added weight of the Black Farm and my unforeseen future here…hopelessness didn't even begin to describe the ocean inside me.

Added to that was the knowledge that this time there was no escape, no end, nothing. I was damned to suffer at the hands of my own choices forever, waiting for them to tear me apart over and over again.

And knowing Jess might be going through the same thing…

What evil had I done to deserve this?

You're no saint, a dark voice hissed from the empty holes in my mind, *you know what you've done. What you've thought...*

I gritted my teeth through the pain. *Shut up...shut the fuck up.*

But the voice continued: *You never wanted children...you never wanted a family. That's why you never married her, isn't it? You were too afraid to commit, to start something real. You wanted her unwavering devotion, but were too selfish to give her the same.*

"That's not true," I said out loud, lip quivering.

Oh yes, it is. You can't hide from me. I know all there is to know about what goes on up here. When Jess miscarried your son, you were relieved. Oh, how you were relieved.

"You don't know what you're talking about," I whispered fiercely, "I died alongside that child."

Your sadness wasn't brought on by the baby's death...it was brought on because you saw what it did to Jess. It tore her apart. And THAT made you sad. It made you sad because she couldn't be the person you wanted her to be. You're a piece of shit. You deserve this place. You didn't want a child, you wanted your girlfriend's attention, her love, her everything. You were afraid the baby would take her away from you. Well I hope you're happy, you miserable fuck, because she DID give you her everything, all the way unto death.

"Stop it!" I screamed, sitting upright.

I winced as my body exploded in pain, my head rocking as stone fists pummeled at me from the inside of my skull. I pressed my palms flat against my temples, tears flowing down my blood stained cheeks.

The voice didn't respond.

"Nick?" a weak voice called.

Groaning, I turned toward the source and saw Megan, now hanging, limping from chains on the wall. Her naked body was a mess of bruises and cuts, her face swollen and bleeding. Her chest rose and fell with quivering effort as she looked at me through sweaty, clotted strands of bloody hair.

"I'm here," I called to her, "Still here..."

She shifted painfully, "Don't you leave me alone...don't you leave me here..."

I gripped the bars and pulled myself to my feet, body screaming in protest. My legs trembled and I sucked in hot breath as a gaping halo of fire engulfed my backside. Finally, I was able to stand straight.

"Where is he?" I asked.

"I don't know...not here...but he told me he was coming back...soon..."

The thought of reliving the hell I had just endured shook me to my soul. I couldn't take another round of brutality. Both physically and mentally. I would break like a splintered twig in the dead of winter.

Megan whimpered, a pathetic sound that reminded me of Jess during those last days together.

"You have to kill me," Megan begged. "Please...it's the only way out of here."

I just stared at her, miserable.

Her head fell to her chest, sobbing, "Don't let him hurt me anymore, Nick...please...I can't...I can't..."

Suddenly, footsteps echoed down the tunnel towards us. Heavy, deliberate footsteps. Muck was returning. Megan immediately fell into a state of broken hysteria, pleading, screaming, weeping as our oppressor came into view.

I slunk to the ground, crawling towards the back of my cell.

My heart was racing, my body howling, and my mind rocked with the terrifying anticipation of what awaited us.

Muck didn't even look at Megan, instead marching to my cage, his pale, fat gut bouncing past his bloated waist. His one eye gazed hungrily at me from the cut in the bag that covered his head. As he unlocked my cell, his tongue slid across his greasy lips and a sound like glee escaped his mouth.

"Don't," I croaked weakly, holding my hands out in front of me as he advanced on me. He knocked my arms aside and grabbed me by the back of the neck. His fingers dug harshly into my skin as he dragged me from the cage, detonating every slumbering pain I hadn't yet awoken.

He tossed me to the floor in front of Megan and then went to his bench. With his back turned to me, I desperately began to crawl towards the entrance, pulling myself through the dirt one panicked breath at a time. My heart was thundering against my bruised ribs, horror ripping through me. When Muck turned back around, I was halfway to the tunnel.

He stared at me for a second and then angrily snatched something from his bench. He stomped toward me, bleeding hostility. I howled as he grabbed a fistful of my hair and slammed my face into the dirt, stunning me.

In a daze, I suddenly felt needle-like agony press around my thighs, then knees, then calves. With what breath I had, I screamed as I looked down and saw Muck wrapping my legs tightly with barbed wire, binding them together. The razor sharp teeth sliced into my skin as he coiled the wire around itself, securing me.

When he was finished, still ignoring my cries, he took me by the arms and pulled me back toward Megan. He tossed me at her feet in a heap where I lay gasping. A second later, he chucked a hammer down to me. It landed in a puff of dirt, the particles floating into my exposed, lidless eyes and bringing with it fire. I pressed the back of my hand against the exposed sclerosis and fought to regain some kind of control.

"Hit her," Muck's gurgling, raspy voice called down to me.

I rubbed my eyes vigorously, not even registering his instruction.

Muck kicked my bleeding legs. "Hit her."

I slowly reached out and gripped the hammer, its rusty head a grim weight in my hands. I dragged my eyes up to meet Megan's and my own torment reflected back at me. I couldn't do this. I refused to. We had both suffered so much already...

If I could have stood, I would have tried to end her pain with one swift blow to the head, freeing her from this nightmare. But the barbed wire kept me on the ground, biting me, gnashing at my flesh.

I turned my head and saw Muck behind me, his massive, ruined cock in one hand, already stroking it in anticipation. I clamped my teeth together and tossed the hammer aside in defiance.

With a frustrated growl, Muck stormed away from me back to the bench. I knew more pain was coming, but I didn't care. I wasn't going to hurt Megan for his own sick pleasure. It was the only freedom I had left.

From the way Megan began to sob, I knew Muck was returning with something especially nasty for me. I pushed my face into the dirt and awaited whatever sentence this monster had chosen.

I felt a weighty foot stomp down between my shoulder blades and my breath was instantly crushed from my lungs. I snarled and cried, heart a wild drum in my chest as Muck grabbed my left arm and extended it. He stomped down on my hand and pinned me in position, his slobbering, angry grunts dripping down onto my head.

Then he began to saw my arm off at the shoulder.

My world creaked and shattered as pain beyond anything else ruptured my howling body. The hacksaw easily churned through my flesh and began to screech against bone, each pull of the blade darkening my vision.

With a sickening tear, Muck ripped the last strands of skin away as he pulled my arm from my shoulder. He tossed the useless limb into the fire pit behind him. Through my screams, I smelled my own flesh cooking.

Muck took a burning stick from the fire and readjusted his position over me. Then he stabbed the wound, the fire licking at my gushing nub. My back arched as new agony greeted me, a sick popping sound announcing the cauterization of my severed limb.

Just when I thought it was over, he picked the hacksaw back up and began to severe my other arm.

I launched into absolute hysteria and before the gnawing teeth even hit bone, I passed out.

5

Back in the cage. I was becoming sickeningly familiar with its dirty angles and hard edges. I was on my back, lost in my own world of growing hell. The stumps jutting just inches from my shoulders were an alien nightmare, a shocking terror that filled my lungs with howls of fear. Upon waking, I had screamed and wriggled, lost in myself, unable to cope with the absence of my limbs. I could still feel them, could still feel my fingers reaching out to press against the ruined flesh.

Megan was gone. Her shackles were empty, a trail of blood staining the dark dirt that led towards the vacant tunnel. I was alone in the silence.

My eyes *burned*, drying out in the open air. Tears ran down my face, a desperate attempt to bring moisture to them, but I knew I was already severely dehydrated and soon my eyes would shrivel up like snake skin.

My thoughts returned to me in my broken state. They came creeping in like darkness over the setting sun. They bared their teeth and sliced at me with sharp claws, pounding across the shores of my mind like frothing waves.

Helplessness…pain…they weren't just words anymore. They were all I knew. They filled every crack of me, poured down my throat, drown me in their cold, unflinching assault. I didn't have the strength to feel sorry for myself. I didn't have the energy to dissect each thought. I just lay bound in barbwire and listened to the screams inside my head.

At some point, I tried to focus on Jess, to let her image fill my mind with a desire to break free from this hell…but it was useless. She wasn't here. And if she was, there was nothing I could do to help her. What could someone like me do to protect her from such evil? I couldn't even protect her from my own selfishness.

She's better off without you, that voice whispered, *she deserves someone better than you. She deserves someone who will commit to her. Someone who actually wants a family. Someone who respects everything she gives to them. But not you…no…*

I shut my eyes then remembered I couldn't.

If you had actually wanted that baby then maybe you would have handled the loss differently. Maybe you could have related to her agony more. Maybe you could have fucking actually been there for her. Maybe you wouldn't be here.

"I was there for her," I whispered.

No, you weren't. You completely disconnected. Sure, you were a shoulder for her to rest her head on, but it wasn't real. Not in the way she needed you to be. You were more concerned about getting your girlfriend back to paying attention to you. And when that didn't work, you got sad. Oh, poor Nick, no one's wiping his ass for him.

"That's not how it was," I hissed weakly.

Once you realized she wasn't getting better, you let your own selfish sadness take over. You let it pull you down into the same pit she was in. But you did it for you, you selfish fuck. You deserve this cage. You deserve this pain.

The words bounced off the inside of my skull and I let them die. I gritted my teeth and turned my head to the side, chest hitching.

"I-I'm sorry…" I whispered, "I'm so sorry…"

"You should be."

I jumped as Muck's voice cut through the silence. I whipped my head around and saw him watching me through the bars. I hadn't even noticed him approach. His pasty, fat stomach squished around the iron, the bag over his head fluttering as he pulled in wet air.

"Kill me," I begged, my body squirming on the floor as I wriggled towards him. "Just fucking kill me."

Muck snorted, "No."

I turned my head towards Megan's empty chains. "What did you do to her? Where is she?"

Muck was fiddling with something in his meaty hand, "Took her to the Needle Fields. Bitch broke like a dry twig. Found her a nice place next to the rest of you Suicidals."

What remained of my heart broke. "Why are you doing this to us? What did we ever do to you?"

Muck just stared, still fumbling with whatever he was holding.

"Look at me!" I suddenly cried, wriggling my mutilated body at him. Every nerve screamed in protest, bolts of lightning shooting through my spine. "I'm nothing! I'm NOTHING! JUST KILL ME!"

Muck tossed something into my cage. It landed with a *thump* in front of my face. It was dark and resonated warmth. It looked like a piece of meat. I recoiled immediately, the barbs around my thighs licking hotly at my skin.

"Eat," Muck instructed, "Eat or I fuck you."

I knew that wasn't an empty threat. I knew he would do it. The recent memory tore through my sudden aggression and I collapsed back into shuddering fear. I tried to pick up the meat but only wriggled my nub, the ghost of my hand just that. My eyes were burning in the dust, but it barely registered through the other pain.

I inched my face to the meat and sniffed it.

Please don't be human, I thought.

I closed my teeth around the warm cut and bit down. The meat was tough, impossibly tough, and I gnawed uselessly at it. Vile grease coated my tongue and I gagged, recoiling from it and spit the taste from my mouth.

"Eat!" Muck growled, "Eat and stay strong. Can't have you starving on me. Not my pet."

His words chilled me and I turned away from him, slinking my body towards the far side of the cage, "I can't. I-it's too tough. I can't chew it." With my back to him I couldn't see his reaction, but I could feel a sudden heat emitting from where he stood.

"Then we will give you sharper teeth," He snarled, throwing aside the chain and pulling the door to the cage open. Before I could even scream, he was on me, his rough hands dragging me across the floor and over to his workbench.

I felt like I was slowly being run over by a train, every bump and scrape of dirt causing my bleeding, broken body to flare and howl. I didn't know how I was still alive, the familiar black sparking dangerously around my vision as my senses screamed. I begged for the darkness. I prayed to the black.

God…please kill me.

Muck leaned down and gripped me by the throat, hauling me up and slamming me across his bench. I screamed as he bent me over backward across the lip so that I was staring up at him, my bleeding feet dangling inches from the floor.

He reached behind my head and snatched up a pair of pliers. With one fat finger, he pried open my mouth, his naked body pressing against mine, holding me in place against the bench.

The hard metal clinked against my teeth as he lowered the pliers into my mouth. I thought I would begin to vomit blood I was screaming so hard. But my cries were nothing compared to when the grips wrapped around a molar and Muck began to pull.

The pain was immediate and overwhelming. I gagged as blood began to squirt from my tearing gums. My head rattled as my molar was pulled free with a sickening crack, filling my mouth with the warmth that ran down my throat. I tried to stop Muck, but he moved on effortlessly to the next tooth.

And the next...

And the next...

And the next...

I stayed awake for the entire operation, drinking down mouthfuls of my own blood. When the final tooth was pulled free, I ran my tongue across my ruined gums, quivering as it was met with jagged edges and empty craters.

Muck grabbed my head and pushed it to the side, allowing me to empty my mouth of pooling saliva and thick blood. I coughed and sputtered, my mouth alive with prodding agony. Muck pulled me back into position and I realized that my torment wasn't over.

He tossed the pliers aside and snatched up a handful of screws. He pulled my jaw apart and selected two of the screws. I begged for darkness as he fit the sharp tips in my mouth along the backside of my flaring gums.

Then he pressed them through like he was pushing nails through a cupcake. I felt them pass through my flesh and poke out past my lips at an angle. My screams were met with more pain as the sharp tips nipped at my lower lip and chin. Muck selected another two and continued his torment.

As I thrashed, body bound with barbed wire, a thought came crashing through the red: *He's replacing my teeth with screws.*

It was such an awful, shocking moment, an accumulation of everything I had suffered up until this point that I vomited. The bile rocketed past my new teeth and splashed against Muck's bare chest. An amused chuckle escaped the bagged man's head, his one visible eye appraising me through the hole in the cloth as he continued his work.

Muck's pace never slowed, his hands working with careful precision and cruelty. I don't know how many screws jutted from my mouth by the time he was finished. My mouth and jaw felt bloated like a million hot fingers were digging and scraping around my sensitive ruin.

Again, I begged for darkness. I begged for this to end. My head swam and I didn't know why I was still awake. Every ounce of my being howled for some kind of relief, but I knew that I wouldn't find any here.

Muck tossed me to the ground and I fell uselessly. My face bounced off the floor and my new teeth came shooting into my shredded lips. Gasping, I watched as Muck went and picked up the piece of meat he had offered me earlier.

He tossed it at my face and pointed, "Now eat."

I didn't know what his game was, why he was insisting I consume this slab of cooked flesh. Did he just want to see me struggle in pain some more? Of course he did. This monster got off on suffering and violence.

As if to affirm my thoughts, Muck grabbed his penis as I wriggled my face toward the meat. My mouth was in a permanent gape, the rough screws rising from my gums like fractured rock formations. The sharp barbs pressed into my thighs, my seared shoulders cracked from the movement, and I sobbed as I settled my new teeth around the meat.

I tried to bite down, but the slightest touch was excruciating. Snot mixed with blood that mixed with tears. I tried to bite down again, but my mouth screamed in protest.

I looked up towards Muck with shining eyes, blood dripping from my chin, "I con do ih!" My words came out a garbled mess and pushed more oozing liquid from my mouth.

Muck stared down at me. I twisted into myself, crying, broken and humiliated. Muck let go of his penis and shook his head.

"Eat! You have new teeth! EAT!"

I just lay on the ground, staring at nothing as tears rolled down my mutilated face. I sobbed wet, broken cries that trickled from shattered lips and floated up into the dim oppression. I could feel myself shutting down. I could feel the many afflictions my body had endured wring both mind and muscle, shoving me into a darkness I accepted with open arms.

I prayed it was death. Whatever death meant here.

But as I was pushed into the subconscious, I knew my end wasn't here. Not yet.

What...what was that? Sound...yes...soothing sound...gentle...so gentle...and so cool...something cool on my face...licking me...running down my cheeks...no...rain...it was...rain...washing the blood and grime from my mangled face...

If I had eyelids, I would have opened them. Instead, the world swam back into focus, a blurry twist of gray and brown that rushed towards me as my brain re-entered the hell I was encased in. I was on the ground, outside the cave. My cheek pressed deep into the mud as I groggily took in my surroundings.

The entrance to Muck's cave was behind me, an empty cut into a blank cliff face. I could see the fucker, walking towards me, the bag over his head molding his features in the rain. I became aware of something around my neck, a tight coil that pressed in on me like an iron snake. I pulled my head to the side and saw a chain leading away from my throat.

A leash.

I tried to move my aching body, but the barbed wire around my thighs halted any progress with a sharp reminder of their presence. I went to wipe rain water from my eyes, the heavens gutting themselves in spectacular fashion, but the ghost of my arms passed through me. I would never get used to that.

And so I lay, like a beaten worm in the soggy earth as Muck reached me and took hold of my leash. He shook it a few times and I recoiled, alerting him of my awareness.

"Let's go visit the new ones, eh? I'm getting low on Suicidals."

Without waiting for a response, Muck began to drag me through the mud. I gagged as the leash tightened on my throat, the hard angles digging into my sensitive flesh. I started to cry out but immediately regretted it as the jutting screws filling my mouth sliced across my scabbed lips.

Gasping, choking, we began the long journey back.

As I was pulled along, struggling to sneak air into my body between jerks of the chain, I began to become more aware of what was around me.

Spires rose all around us, looming, sharp things that extended from the ground like needles. Shoved through these spikes, rising dozens of feet into the air, were impaled bodies. The finger-thin poles were stained with decades of blood, rusting their surface with an ugly blackish tint. The people, my fellow Sucidals, hung like meat on sticks, motionless, their eyes wide with agony. Most were dead, but I spotted a few rolling eyes, lost in misery, staring at everything and nothing. How long they had been there was impossible to tell.

Rows and rows extended before us across the expanse of the field like human cornstalks. There had to be thousands of them, frozen in their last moments of suffering. I was dragged past one such spire and I noticed a man, probably my age, still alive. My burning eyes met his and he focused on me for a split second before rolling back into his own nightmare. The ones that were alive didn't scream, didn't make a sound. They could only focus on their inevitable death, willing their bodies to give in to the pain and blood loss, freeing them back into the Black Farm.

As Muck dragged me further, a horrible stench began to invade my nostrils. It was a sharp, burning smell and it didn't take long for me to find the source.

In the middle of the Needle Fields was an absolutely titanic pile of dead bodies, slowly burning, one atop another. Thick, ugly smoke rose from charred flesh, the rain and wind carrying the aroma of death with it.

Hundreds and hundreds of people formed the small mountain, individual victims to Muck's torment. How many had this monster tortured? What had he made them endure? How long had they been kept alive until pain or starvation took them? How many had been nailed to the earth in the Needle Fields, left alone to their own misery until their bodies gave out? Was I looking at my eventual future? Was Megan out there?

Was Jess in that pile of discarded bodies?

The weight of violence before me caused my mind to shudder, gloom pressing in through the cracks of my fraying sanity. I felt myself slowly slip into an unaware lull, the rain beating down from the pregnant clouds shushing me in my pain. Gray swirled across my unblinking eyes and I lost myself in it.

I don't know how long I was dragged. Every second felt like an eternity I wasn't part of. The iron around my throat allowed minimal oxygen intake and my head felt bloated and compressed at the same time. The Black Farm began to drip dull color and the gray that flirted in my vision pressed in deeper.

At one point, I became aware of screaming and forced my eyes from the mud. We were traversing across small foothills, the earth rippling out before us. The dead grass rolled away from me like a dirty rug and in the distance, I spotted the coast. I could see the outline of a Keeper on the horizon, its giant cross rising in the rain to kiss the clouds.

I let my head roll to the side and heard the distant screaming again. As water rolled across my agonized eyes, I spotted the source.

Dozens of people were being herded away from us, their naked, trembling bodies lined with bloody stripes. Their captors, a smattering of twisted Pig Born, kept them together with the snap of hungry whips. They were guiding the Suicidals like sheep, howling and laughing at their victims suffering. The Pig Born were similar in biology and shape, their bodies tall and bent at unnatural angles. Their arms extended from their pale bodies like wriggling snakes, looping and coiling in the air. In their hands they held wicked-looking whips that never stopped licking the Suicidals.

Where were they taking them? What were they going to do with them? I slowly realized they were leading them towards the far off coast, towards the Keeper. Were they going to make them swim? Was this a game to them? Try and see who can make it the farthest before drowning or being abducted by the bizarre titans?

My eyes rolled backward, catching a glimpse of the rotting sun in the sky, a broken orb of dripping darkness. I felt a connection to it, an understanding. It too was shattered, an incomplete creation just like me. And now we both bled our poisons into the world.

I lost myself again, the Needle Fields and herd of Suicidals growing further and further away. The gray swallowed me back into its jaws and I gratefully accepted it.

At some point, I became dimly aware that we were back in the woods. Roots and rocks cut into my exposed skin, but it was nothing compared to the burning around my throat. I could feel my neck rubbed raw by the leash, blood dripping across my black and blue chest. I began to realize that pain was something you could never become accustomed too. It was everything to me at this point and it made sure I was acutely aware of that.

The dripping canopy overhead dimmed an already dark sky and I burrowed into my own mind as much as I could to escape the constant scrape of undergrowth. Muck never slowed his pace, never stopped, never so much as glanced behind him to see if I was still alive.

But he knew I was. Somehow, he knew.

Another period of miserable affliction passed under the

gray. My armless body was slowly covered in mud, leaves, and grime that stuck to my open wounds like parasites. I felt like every bone in my body was bent and broken, the constant teeth of the barbed wire gnawing at my thighs. The screws protruding from my wrecked gums jabbed and bit with every bump and tug. I was sure I was leaving a trail of dirty blood in my wake, a red carpet to my eventual demise.

And then we were through the woods, hours, days, years later. I didn't know. I just became aware that the rain was beating harder against my face now and the blanket of green overhead had vanished.

I could hear Muck become excited as we got closer to wherever we were going. A new noise echoed in the distance, a great clang of metal and gears like working, shifting machinery. I let my head fall to the side and I spotted the colossal barn I had seen after I was released into the Black Farm.

The two towers that jutted from its construction were still wrapped by those human looking worms. Their size dwarfed us, their squirming pink bodies constricting along the wood and metal columns. Their elongated faces turned to stare down at us from a distance, their white eyes infected with bloodshot veins. Jaws like a dog extended from their necks, snapping loudly in the gale. Lightning flashed behind the towering barn, across the two towers forever billowing rancid smoke, and the creatures howled.

As they gazed out on us, I watched in horrific disgust as one of the monsters began to gag, a nauseating retching sound that filled the sky. The creature leaned its slick, smooth neck towards the earth and extended its jaws, its milky eyes bulging. Out of its mouth rolled a twisted, curled body. It fell the remaining twenty feet to the earth with a thud, splashing in the mud.

The snake-like creature readjusted around its smoke stack, reverting back to its watchful gaze over the cathedral-sized barn. The ball of flesh that had been evacuated slowly began to move and then stood, rising up on two legs.

Its head was smashed and mangled, its form vaguely human. Its naked stomach was half torn open to reveal a nest of tiny, dead arms that spilled out past its waist. The creature opened its busted mouth and let out a shriek, raising broken fingers towards the sky in exultation.

As I watched, pieces began to click in my head.

I had just witnessed the birth of a Pig Born.

An especially hard jerk on my leash whipped my head back in a blaze of pain and my thoughts were cut short. I winced and saw that Muck was leading us back to the concrete structure I had been contained in shortly after my arrival.

To my left, as we approached the building, I saw a flash of color that drew my eye. A large, obese man in overalls was walking in the opposite direction of us, a small red body slung over his shoulder.

With a slow dawning recognition, I realized it was the boy in the plastic devil mask I had met earlier, his red onesie now soaked with blood.

The child's head had been eviscerated.

Pudge finally caught up to you, my scattered mind observed, the name pulled from the conversation I had with the boy. It felt like a lifetime ago.

The Black Farm gets us all...

I noticed other Pig Born huddled around the entrances of the building before us, waiting for new Suicidals to emerge after their interview with Danny. Just like I had. When the crooked abominations saw Muck, they began to back away, snarling and spitting insults at us through disfigured mouths. Each one was a different shape, each one sprouting unnatural mutilations.

Muck ignored them and pulled me to a door along the side, flinging it open with careless abandon. Gloom leaked out from a dark hallway, a faint echo of human screams washing into the rain and mud outside.

Muck entered, dragging me along with him. The cold cement floor felt like silk against my battered skin compared to the terrain outside. How long had it actually been since I had been in this very hall?

Time was an impossibility here and I soon gave up trying to calculate it as we began to pass empty, barren rooms. From somewhere down the hall, I could hear Danny, his voice bouncing along the grim interior.

Suddenly, Muck stopped and the leash mercifully loosened against my throat. For the first time in what felt like years, I sucked in lungfuls of dirty air, drinking it down greedily. Blood sluiced from my skin, a mess of angry red drops that stained the floor.

We were standing in front of an open door that exposed a room much like the one I had been held in. A man was slumped unconscious in a chair before us, his head resting against his chest. He was bound, his hands tied behind his back. A single bulb flickered over his head like the last remains of a dying hope.

Muck leaned down to me, pressing against my wire wrapped legs. "You go and have a bite of him. Wake him up. I need a good wank."

I barely had the strength to breathe, never mind wriggle my armless body across the floor. I rested my head against the wet concrete, unable to respond to the order.

Muck grabbed a fistful of hair and leaned in close, the bag over his head unable to filter out his rancid breath, "You go in there and bite him up or I'm going to plug you again."

My already ruptured lower half flared at the mention of another round with this monster of a man and I raised my head, exhausted. Taking a deep breath, I slowly began to wriggle towards the bound man, pulling my broken body along the floor an inch at a time.

As I got closer, I saw the bound man begin to stir. Already I could hear Muck masturbating behind me, his breath wet and lustful. I was now at the bound man's feet and I slowly lowered my head towards his naked foot, the screws jutting from my ruined mouth scraping along the man's unaware skin.

And then I bit down.

The reaction was immediate. The man in the chair bolted into consciousness and a howl escaped his terrified lips. He jerked his now bleeding toe away from my makeshift jaws and recoiled at the sight of me.

"Get off of me! Stop it!" the man screamed. He kicked out at me and his heel bounced off my skull, crunching it into the hard floor. I let out a howl as stars exploded across my vision. I heard Muck release a loud moan and I knew he had just finished, the sight of my agony pushing him to the brink of pleasure.

Without pause, Muck suddenly jerked me away from the bound man, back towards himself and the doorway. The air was squeezed from me and I coughed violently as I was pulled back to my captor. Without slowing, Muck took us from the room and back down the hallway from where we had come.

Confused at the sudden departure, I looked behind us in a haze of misery.

Danny was marching towards the room we had just left, a look of seething fury on his face. Our eyes met for a split second and I saw him freeze, moments before entering the room we had just left.

Recognition bloomed across his face and the anger drained from his skin. His eyes became emotionless as he realized who Muck's pet was. Who I was. As I was dragged towards the exit, Danny followed our retreat with his eyes. He showed no sympathy, no pity.

He simply gazed upon what the Black Farm had done to me.

Muck burst through the exit door, back out into the rain. My mouth pulsed with intense pain, the blow to my head rattling some of the screws loose. Blood poured from my chin and I stared miserably up at the sky. The clouds boiled over one another and I saw a few of those red gashes in the gray, their hanging drool floating high above the earth.

And that's when an idea bloomed from the blackened soil of my exhausted mind. As Muck pulled me along the length of the building, muttering angrily to himself, I extended my tongue. Upon quick inspection, I realized that three of the screws embedded in my gums were loose enough to wriggle free. Wincing, tears flowing from my wide eyes, I crunched my jaw together and muffled a shriek that erupted in my throat. The three long screws fell onto my tongue, the tiny ripples filled with torn flesh.

Taking a deep breath, I opened my mouth and filled it with mud. The soft earth was cool against my mangled mouth and for a split second I felt relief. When the sensation passed, I balled the mud against my cheek, mixing it with the three screws.

I chanced a quick glance at Muck and saw he was still marching us forward, his back to me.

This was it.

My way out. My escape from this monster.

I swallowed the clump of earth. As I felt it pass my tongue and into the back of my throat, I constricted my neck muscles. The clod, now halfway down my throat, came to a screeching halt as the screws buried themselves into the soft sides of my esophagus.

The pain was a brilliant flair that shook my entire body, but I gratefully accepted it. I fought against my gag reflex, a desperate attempt to rid the blockage, my chest heaving. The ball of mud easily blocked any oxygen to my brain and I fought against a rising panic, a natural reaction to the horrible sensation. My lungs began to burn and blood dripped down my throat. My vision swam and I felt a great weight press against my chest as the seconds ticked by. I had to remain calm, had to die in silence so Muck wouldn't try to resuscitate me.

The world bled to darkness and my body bucked and squirmed for air, my brain thundering against my skull.

I was dying…

Again. And this time, there were no second thoughts.

So close, I screamed internally, *just a little longer and you're free from this torture!*

Through the growing haze, I could tell the ball of mud was disintegrating. I strained my neck muscles even tighter, burying the sharp screws deeper in my throat, closing off any growing opening.

And that was all it took.

The black roared in on me and I felt myself begin to float out of my head...

Away from the pain...

Away from Muck...

Into the heavens...

6

Nothingness…
No pain…
No sound…
No sight…
I was everywhere…and I was nowhere. I could feel space expand around me, coils of silent black shimmering into the eternal. Pain…suffering…the words floated through my soaring mind and I couldn't pin meaning to the strange, alien concepts. This was death…and this was life. This was everything…and this was nothing.

The nothing didn't last very fucking long.

Something exploded violently across my body and I screamed, face bouncing off hard angles. The darkness still had me and the sudden force did nothing to push it away. Pain splintered through my aching limbs and I gasped down air, mind blaring with furious urgency.

Had it not worked!? Where was I?!

Open your eyes…just open your fucking eyes, Nick!

I could feel a slight drizzle coating my back, the rain softly whispering against my soaked shirt. In the black, I reached up and rubbed my aching head, willing my brain to focus.

My arm…my hand…I could feel my hand!

Groaning, I pulled my eyes open, blinking for the first time in what felt like eons. I raised my hands to my eyes and saw all ten fingers wiggling before me. I cried out in relieved joy, sitting up and examining the rest of me.

I had both my arms, my teeth, and my legs were no longer wrapped in barbed wire. I had done it, my God, I had fucking done it! I wrapped my arms around myself, tears pouring from my eyes. I rocked on the floor as my cries turned into mad laughter, an exaltation of bitter freedom.

"Fuck you!" I screamed into the sky, howling now, my mouth split into a wide smile, "Fuck you, you miserable BAS-TARD!"

After a moment, I calmed myself, lowering my voice and taking in my surroundings. I had been reborn into the Black Farm. I didn't know where I was or what was around me. All I knew was that I wasn't Muck's prisoner anymore.

I looked around and saw that I had fallen into some kind of shack. The rotting wood ceiling above my head now sported a Nick-sized hole from where I had tumbled from the clouds. Through the busted wood, I could see the dripping gash in the clouds where I had been spat. I gave it the finger.

Gritting my teeth, I stood slowly, making sure none of Muck's torture had carried over into this new body. Once I was sure I was ok, I looked around the room. A creaky wood floor grumbled beneath my booted feet and barren walls stared back at me. In the corner of the shack was a pile of rusted machinery and chains. To my right was an array of buckets, all of them filled to the brim with an unsightly substance.

And resting against the wall next to the buckets was an ax.

I stepped towards it and picked it up, the weight agreeing

with my grip. I inspected the head and felt something rise in my chest like hot coals.

Hatred.

Pure, uncut hatred of everything that crawled in this miserable place.

I hated the rain, the mud, the evil that infected every creature, the lumbering Keepers in the ocean, Danny, Muck, the kid in the plastic devil mask...and most of all...

...most of all I hated The Pig.

I hated The Pig for twisting this nightmare into what it was. I hated it for birthing the torturous monsters. I hated it for what it stood for. I hated it for giving me a fucking choice. What kind of deity desires to inflict such suffering on those who have already suffered so much? What kind of monster was The Pig? What did it want from all this? Why did it allow such hellish conditions?

"Fucking sadist," I spat, knuckles going white against the long ax handle.

Armed with fire and freedom, I decided to restart my search for Jess. The weapon in my hands gave me an unexpected confidence, gasoline for the burning in my heart. I had suffered so much, gone through hell...I wasn't going to let that happen again. At least not without tearing something apart.

The door before me was closed and I decided it was probably time to see where exactly I was. Hefting the ax, I went to the door and as I placed my hand on the handle, I froze.

I could hear something in the distance, approaching fast. Whatever it was, was yelling. I pressed my ear to the wood and listened.

"Sky Sludge! Going to get me some Sky Sludge!"

I quickly stepped back, feeling my heart begin to beat against my chest. Something had seen my rebirth into the Farm. Something was coming to get me.

"Not this time," I muttered darkly, positioning myself against the wall parallel to the door. As the rapid footsteps approached the door, I hoisted the ax and planted my feet. My heart was racing and a thought slammed into my anxious, murderous mind.

You've never killed anyone before, Nick.

Suddenly, as the door exploded inward, I smiled.

Not a fucking problem.

I spun just as the Pig Born entered the shack. Its misshapen eyes went wide as they traced the ax, now flying towards its face.

The blade plowed into its slobbering jaws and severed the top half of its head in one stroke. Its bloated, naked body crashed to its knees and fell forward. The floor pooled quickly as spreading gore expanded around its still body.

"Eat it, you fucking FREAK!" I screamed, bringing the ax down again, "Weren't expecting *that,* were you!?" With each word I slammed the blade into its lifeless body, the spray of black blood coating my face, arms, shirt.

I cackled, voice rising into a mad roar. I hacked and split its body into pieces, the ecstasy of the kill fueled by righteous revenge. When I finally stepped away, slumping against the wall, I was sweating.

I let the ax fall, chest heaving, and observed my work. The Pig Born looked like diced rot. I spit on it, gritting my teeth, and wiped my face clean from its splatter.

"Fucker."

I wondered if there were any more coming. I didn't hear anything but the pitter-patter of rain, but that didn't mean I was safe. I ran a wet sleeve over my face, clearing it of gore, and snatched the axe back up. Now that the blade had been bloodied, I felt like I had a chance here. These monsters could scream just as loud as us Suicidals. And I intended to hear those howls again.

Leaving my ruined opponent behind, I stepped out into the open air. It looked like I was in some kind of small shanty town, make-shift huts and fences littering the dead earth. I turned around, taking it all in. There were maybe twelve or thirteen such structures, all varying in shape and size. Who built these? And to what end?

I hugged the wall of the shack I had exited and crept to the corner, peeking around the side. When I was sure the coast was clear, I dipped low and trotted to the next shambled construction. I didn't know where I was going, what my immediate plan was, but I pressed on nonetheless. I just wanted to get somewhere I felt remotely safe. If that was possible. And Jess…had to find Jess. It was a distant hope at this point, a dying star in a sky filled with growing darkness. She was my lifeline. She was the willpower behind every step.

I crept to the next building, a long stretch of rotting wood that looked like a stable. *What the hell would they stable here?* I thought. After quick reflection, I decided I didn't want to know. I plastered myself against the side and slunk to the corner, a repeat of my steady progression.

When I got to the corner, I peeked out and spotted the ocean, its black waves rolling soundlessly not far from my position. Three Keepers were visible on the horizon, like lumbering statues plastered across a muddled painting.

I also spotted the dead sun, its cracked frame eternally leaking its ebony guts onto the world below. It was a great distance away, a dime shaped shadow hanging just below the ever gray sky. Judging from what I had seen of the Black Farm, I guessed I was on the side of the forest where Muck dwelt. Just the thought of my former captor set my teeth on edge and caused my heart to flutter.

I dug into my memory and remembered that the forest cut the island in two, one side with the dead sun and the mountain, the other with that massive barn where The Pig resided…and whatever else lurked in those rolling foothills.

I wiped the rain from my eyes and squinted towards the horizon, with my back to the ocean. It didn't take long to pick out the distant peak of the great mountain, a sharp triangle jutting towards the heavens. I knew that below that mountain, across the many dozens of miles between us, were the Needle Fields and that fucking cave. I made a mental note to keep my distance, the rising summit a sharp warning sign.

I decided to make my way up the coast, keeping the mountain to my left. I remembered Megan mentioning something about a temple on this side of the forest. I didn't know anything about it, other than the name she gave it: The Temple of the Pig. Probably not somewhere I wanted to go, but if I stuck to the shadows, maybe I could discover something about Jess.

Why are you so insistent on finding her?

I froze, that sneering voice a quiet whisper from the back of my mind.

You don't really love her, Nick. You know you don't, so why keep on with this charade?

"Shut the fuck up," I growled quietly. "You don't know what you're talking about.

A chuckle. *She's just the next step in your selfish life. When you get bored of her, you'll move on. It's so easy for you to move on isn't it, Nick?*

I clenched my fists. "Go back to wherever you came from."

The voice ignored me, *The people in your life...they're just conduits you expend for your own pleasure. You surround yourself with people you can use. Just like Jess...what did you use her for again?*

"I love that woman," I hissed. "I would do anything for her."

You love what she provided you. She gave you confidence...she made you feel like a man. But there was one thing she gave you that you didn't want. Do you remember what that was?

"Stop it..." I begged, chest suddenly hitching, "Just leave me alone..."

Ahhh...it was the baby, wasn't it? Yes...your unborn son. That wasn't part of the plan was it...oh no. That little bastard would have taken Jess's purpose from you. Her affection. Her love...her affirmation.

I closed my eyes, clutching my head. "Shut up, just shut the fuck up!"

When that little fucker died, when you got the call that Jess had miscarried...what was the first thing you felt?

"STOP IT!" I screamed, voice bouncing off the sky.

You felt...relieved.

"That's not true!" I cried, falling to my knees, tears brimming, "I...I..." my hands dug into the muddy earth, searching for an answer.

I stared at the ground, teeth clenched and face wet with grief, "Goddamn it...that's not who I am. That's...that's..."

The only reason you killed yourself was because the last remaining conduit of your existence had already decided to. You had already burned out all your other conduits...and without them...who are you, Nick? Just who the fuck are you?

I shook my head, eyes squeezed shut.

You're nothing. Nothing but an empty shell of an incredibly selfish human being. And god FUCKING forbid you have to come to terms with that.

I could feel something peeling away inside of me, something that I had felt for a long time. What lay underneath made my stomach churn, my head spin, and bile slide up my throat.

I saw myself for the first time. What I really was. How I treated people...how I acted...why I did the things I did. I saw the decisions in my life and the way they always benefited me. I surrounded myself with complacent, caring, good human beings who knew how to sacrifice their own comforts for me. And I had abused that...I had taken their kindness and wrung every last drop of it from their willing hands.

And as I grew older, those people eventually left my life.

Everyone except Jess.

The last barrier between myself and facing what kind of person I really was. I had been relieved when the baby died. I had been relieved because the stripping of myself would have come much sooner than this.

But now...when faced with the poisonous human being I was...I still fought against it, still pushed away from the burning mirror. Confronting my life in this new light, this sick, selfish light...

I wanted to scream and bury myself in the dirt. I wanted to place a gun to my head and blow my brains out over and over again. This wasn't the person I had seen myself as...this wasn't who I imagined I'd grow up to be.

How could I turn into such a bastard?

There's still hope, a new voice whispered from the opposite corner of my mind, *there's still hope, Nick.*

I suddenly opened my eyes, hands muddy at my sides.

"Is that why I've been so hell bent on finding Jess?" I whispered to myself. "Am I trying to save her to prove something to myself? Have I really subconsciously known this whole time what kind of asshole I really am?

Only if you're looking for her for the right reasons, that voice cooed.

I looked down at my hands, fresh tears trickling down my rain washed face. "I want to find her because I love her."

My voice shook as a cold wind caressed my face. "I want to find her because she deserves better than what I've given her. She gave me everything...she gave me everything she had..."

I trained my eyes to the heavens. "She doesn't belong here. She never did anything to deserve this kind of fate..."

My chest hitched and I continued to gaze into the clouds. "How could you send her here? How could you do this to someone so good?"

I wiped my soaking hair from my eyes. "Please...God...just help me get her...show me where she is...just this once...not for me...but for her. Please..."

My words were carried off in the wind, the sky remaining a silent sheet of rain and gloom.

A sudden fire burned deep in my chest and I felt my mouth twist into a snarl, "No?"

I picked myself up, gritting my teeth, and turned away from the sky.

I would do it alone.

I continued through the broken town, keeping my eyes

peeled for movement. The ocean off to my right was a soft chorus in the distance, the black water a dark sliver in the corner of my vision. How many Suicidals were like me? How many were still free from the oppression of the Pig Born? How long could I last like this before another monster caught me? I thought about those people I had seen, the herd driven by whips and snarls towards the ocean. How long could I last? How many of us were here? How many Pig Born? Was hope even a thought, an idea?

"You're not going back to that," I whispered to myself, edging along another shack. "I'll plant this ax into my own skull before I get taken again."

And what happened if I did do that? Would I be reborn again into the Farm, my soul pulled up into those red gashes in the sky? It had happened once, I didn't see any reason to doubt it happening again. I looked towards the overcast curtain above me and spotted several of the red slices, clean cuts of hanging vermillion drool dangling like saliva from angry jaws. In the distance, I could see bodies falling from them, perhaps new souls cast from the heavens for the first time. Or maybe they were like me. Collected and thrown back into this hell, forgiveness wrenched away and replaced with eternal consequence.

I reflected on the Pig Born I had killed. What happened to it? Was it dead forever or would The Pig regurgitate it back into its hellish world? Would those snake creatures coiling around the smokestacks vomit it up? Could anything truly die here? Were we all trapped to torment one another forever?

There had to be a way out of this. The Black Farm had rules to the way it worked…and rules could be broken. And what of The Pig? Did it simply enjoy torturing us? And what WAS The

Pig? Where did it come from? Why had God put it in charge? Who created The Pig?

Lost in thought, I didn't hear a door to my left open until a voice called to me.

"Hey! Pssst!"

I spun around, ax raised and eyes searching. My heart drummed in my chest and a sudden urge to run overwhelmed me. Before I sprinted for cover, I saw that a young man was waving me over towards one of the shacks. He stood in the doorway, hand urgently beckoning me. He looked like a teenager, a swath of thick black hair pulled across his face.

"Get over here or they'll see you!" he hissed.

I immediately jerked my head around, going on full alert. Who would see me? Where were they!? I didn't see anyone, but the sense of panic the kid had written across his face was infectious. I sprinted towards him, feet clacking up the wooden steps toward the shack. The kid stood shoulder height, his deep, dark eyes meeting mine.

"Come on, man, let's go inside," he pressed, grabbing me by the arm, "They'll come if they see you out here."

His touch ignited something inside of me and I batted his hand away. I grabbed him by the throat and slammed him against the wall, bringing my face close to his, my voice a guttural snarl.

"Who are you? What are you doing here?"

The teenager grabbed me, trying to free himself from my grip. "Hey dude, chill! I'm just like you, I'm a Suicidal! It's cool!"

He began to choke as I tightened my grip. "Listen, kid, I've been through some shit." My face was inches from his now, "and I don't trust easily."

A new voice boomed from inside the shack, a rumbling growl, "Well maybe you should start."

I cocked my head toward the voice and found myself staring down the end of an impossibly sharp iron pole. It looked like it had been ground down to form a needle-like tip that now rested inches from my right eye.

Holding the pole was an imposing, dark skinned man. His eyes held violence in them and I slowly let go of the kid. But I gripped my ax even tighter.

"We're on the same side," the man said, still leveling his weapon at me. "We got enough out there trying to kill us. Let's not make it worse by doing their job for em, ok chief?"

"We're not going to hurt you," the kid said, rubbing his throat.

I shot a look at them and then cautiously nodded, "All right...all right..."

I took a slow step back and raised my hands in submission.

The big man lowered his pole and brushed past me, shutting the door. The rain outside threw itself against the wood and in the distance thunder chuckled darkly across the horizon.

The kid pulled me deeper inside the hut. It was a fairly small, empty space with a tiny fire pit formed at the center. Soft flames danced in the still air and I was drawn to it like a moth. The warmth was welcome and I hovered over it, keeping a watchful gaze on my new friends. I raised my hands over the fire and the kid joined me, smiling.

"It's the little things, right?" he said, flicking his hair out of his eyes with a quick jerk of his head. His pale skin was peppered with pimples and his tattered shirt fell past his waist over a pair of skinny jeans.

I didn't respond as I seized up the kid's friend who looked

much more intimidating. The man was probably in his late forties, a dark cut of hair hugging his scalp. He wore long dark pants and a flannel shirt that was unbuttoned to reveal rippling muscle.

"I'm Kevin," the kid said, rubbing his hands together over the fire, "Good to meet you, man. I heard you fall from the sky and came to get you but I saw the Pig Born first." He looked at the bloodied ax now resting against my leg, "Guess you took care of him, huh?"

"Always trying to save people," the big man behind us rumbled, "Gets you into nothing but trouble and it always will."

"Who are you people?" I finally asked.

The man propped his pole by the door and peeked out through the cracks in the wood. "Name's Trent. We're Suicidals just like you. Obviously."

"Is this the first time for you?" Kevin asked, "First time in the Farm?"

I felt something twist inside of me, "No…I know what this place is."

Trent joined us by the fire, towering over me. "Good. Hate having to explain eternity to new folks."

Kevin sighed, "We just have to make the most of it, Trent. We've done good for a while now."

Trent snorted, "Good…ain't no fucking good here, Kev."

Kevin turned to me, ignoring the negativity. "What's your name? How long have you been here?"

"Nick…I'm Nick."

Kevin slapped me on the back, startling me. "Glad you're with us, Nick."

Trent went towards the back of the shack, rummaging around on a table I hadn't seen before, his voice carrying over his shoulder. "Swear to God. You the most cheerful fucking emo kid I've ever met."

"How long have you been cooped up here?" I asked, clearing my throat.

Kevin shrugged, "I don't know, man. Times kinda screwy here. We've been here a while, though. No one really makes it this far out so we don't see many Pig Born. Or Suicidals for that matter."

"Got lucky getting dropped here," Trent said, turning back to us and holding something out for me. "Most of us get dropped on the other side of the forest closer to The Pig and that big-ass barn."

I took what he was holding and examined it in my hands. It looked like the squishy brown brick Megan had offered me in the woods.

"Eat it, man, first one is free," Trent said tossing another square to Kevin. "You stick around and I'll show you how to make these. Bout the only edible thing we've been able to cook up."

"Thanks," I said taking a bite, realizing just how hungry I was.

Trent nodded and took a seat on the floor, resting his head against the wall. "So what's your story, chief? How long you been here?"

I followed his example and sat against the opposite wall, now cramming the food in my mouth. I swallowed and sighed.

"Not long. But long enough to see how horrible it is."

Kevin took a seat next to Trent, crossing his legs out in front of him. I almost laughed. Three people just sitting around a campfire, swapping stories. I ran a hand over my eyes, exhaling.

"How bad was it? When you died again?" Kevin asked.

I met his gaze with dead eyes. "Muck got me."

Trent let out a low whistle, "Shit, man..."

The recent horrors began to wash over me and I wrapped my arms around myself, "Look, I don't want to talk about it."

Kevin nodded understandingly. "Of course, dude, we won't press any further. I'm real sorry about that though. Trent and I have been fortunate enough to not encounter Muck...but we've heard stories."

I shifted uncomfortably. "What about you two? What's your story?"

Trent snorted, "Why's it matter? We're all here now...ain't no fucking way about it."

Kevin just stared straight ahead, a far off look on his face. I let the seconds drag out, becoming more comfortable in the silence than exchanging stories of personal suffering. I began to clean the blade of my ax with my shirt, listening to the crack of the fire.

Kevin broke the silence, his voice soft, "I killed myself over a girl...seems so stupid now..."

Trent shot him a look, an eyebrow cocked like this was the first time he was hearing about this. I looked up from the ax and saw Kevin fiddling and staring at the floor.

"I had a crush on her since freshman year. Her name was Amanda. Didn't really talk to her much though. She was popular, pretty, hung out with the jocks...you know the type. But something about her just captured me in a way I had never felt before. I was a pretty angry kid, held a lot of hate in my heart."

He looked up at us and I saw he was struggling. "My dad used to beat the shit out of me. My mom let him do it. It kind of tainted my outlook on things. Everything I did seemed to emit a violent reaction from him. I started wearing eyeliner and shit to school so people wouldn't see my black eyes, my bruises. Grew my hair out. I did anything I could to hide what was happening at home. It was embarrassing. I didn't know anyone else who had abusive parents and so I started to think there was something wrong with me."

Kevin's voice began to shake, "And then I saw Amanda. She was like an angel. I fell in love with her from a distance. It's stupid I know, but I couldn't help it. Everything about her was perfect. The way she smiled, the way she laughed, the way she'd toss her hair. Hell, even the way she sneezed was cute. I could feel something happening to me the more I paid attention to her. It blocked out all the shit I was dealing with back home. It made things easier. I knew that no matter how bad it got, I'd get to see her the next day. I wanted to talk to her, let her get to know me. Who knows, right? Maybe she'd feel the same way."

The shack was dead quiet as Kevin continued, his voice strained and growing weak.

"Well, finally one day I got up the courage to talk to her. It was at lunch and she was surrounded by her friends, but I didn't care. It had gotten to the point where I couldn't hold it in any longer. I walked right up to her and asked her out. And you know what she did?"

I stared at the kid, shaking my head slowly.

A tear escaped down Kevin's cheek, "She didn't even acknowledge me. She didn't look at me, didn't respond, nothing. All her friends were laughing while I stood there shaking. I couldn't believe it.

She was the only thing keeping me going at that point. After that day I had nothing to hold onto. Nothing. Everything else in my life was misery. She was my one hope for happiness. And as it turns out, I wasn't even worth of a response. Do you know what that's fucking like man? To be in love with someone and have them not even acknowledge your existence?"

Kevin's hands were balled into fists, his face stained with sadness, his voice a harsh whisper, "It fucking hurts, man. It fucking *hurts.*"

Trent and I made eye contact and then turned away. Neither of us knew what to say. We were all here for a reason. Something in our lives had pushed us into this hell. And yeah...Kevin was right...it did hurt.

Trent reached out and patted Kevin's shoulder, "Take it easy, chief."

Kevin wiped his eyes with his sleeve, forcing a laugh, "I'm sorry, guys. Jesus, look at me."

"Don't sweat it," I said softly.

Kevin shot me a smile, "I've just never told anyone that before. Feels good to get it out, you know?"

I watched the fire dance before me, "Sure, kid...I get it."

In the distance, something screamed.

I ignored it.

7

We sat for a while, listening to the rain and thunder have its way outside. I got lost in the constant drumming against the fragile shelter, the droning splatter of rain mixing with the steady crackle of the fire. My mind wandered and I hugged my knees to my chest, eyes glazed over and trained on the dancing ribbons of flame.

After some time, Kevin finally spoke up.

"So, Nick…what's the plan?"

I pulled myself out of a semi-trance and ran the back of my hand across my face. "What do you mean?"

Kevin poked at the dying fire with his shoe. "Where are you headed? What are you going to do now that you've been reborn?"

I sighed, tension leaving my body in a rush. "I don't know, man…I'm looking for someone, but all my leads have dried up."

"Who are you looking for?" Trent asked.

I pulled the ax into my lap. "My girlfriend, Jess. She came here with me."

Kevin furrowed his brow, "Jess…Jess…"

"She's out there somewhere," I muttered. "I know she is. I

met someone who thought she'd be in Muck's cave, but she wasn't."

Trent cocked an eyebrow at Kevin. "Wasn't that girl we ran into named Jess? The blond girl who was looking for someone? Remember? In the woods?"

Kevin snapped his fingers. "Oh yeah! I knew I recognized that name!"

I sat upright, gripping the ax. "Was she about my age?!"

Trent nodded. "Yeah, and short. Thin too. Looked scared as hell. Said she was looking for someone."

I stood up, heart racing. "Was she ok? Which way did she go!?"

Kevin and Trent exchanged wary looks before Trent continued, "Look man...we were only with her for a little bit, before...before..." He looked to Kevin for support.

Kevin shook his head, eyes on the fire. "They got her man. I'm sorry."

"Who!?" I practically shrieked.

"They call themselves The Hooves of the Pig. Crazy radical religious cult that has a temple by the mountain. They worship The Pig and all it does. They're a bunch of whacked out Suicidals; been around for a long time now. It's an all-male society. They capture women and use them during 'prayer'. I'm sorry, man. There was nothing we could do. They were having some kind of procession through the forest when we ran into them. As soon as they saw her, they sprang on us. They slugged Trent pretty good and shit...I'm no fighter. They dragged her off to their church."

I sat down hard, my breath leaving me. My mind was spinning, the influx of information overwhelming me. I was conflicted between joy and horror, oil and water mixing in my gut and churning nausea like butter.

Jess. She was out there. I was right. She had stayed and was looking for me. My heart ached at the thought of it, of her scrambling through this nightmare all alone. But who were these people, these crazy pig worshipers? What did they want with her? Were they hurting her? I felt my hands tighten along the length of the ax.

I remembered my time with Megan when she had first found me. We had seen some kind of procession through the woods, a gaggle of hooded figures chanting as they marched. They had to be part of this group, these Suicidals who called themselves The Hooves of the Pig.

"What are they going to do with her?" I asked, feeling my blood begin to boil.

Trent looked at me apologetically. "Look chief, these people are fucked in the head."

My voice grated like iron. "Tell. Me."

Trent sighed, "Shit, man…they take women and make them breed with Pig Born. They think it's the closest humanity will get to mirroring The Pig in all his fucking evilness. Most of the children die at birth, along with the mothers, but a few have survived. They keep them at their temple, treat them like royalty. If I had to guess, I'd say your girlfriend was taken to breed."

I felt my throat turn dry. "Jesus Christ…"

"They're insane," Kevin said softly. "There's nothing we could have done. I'm really sorry, man."

I turned to him, "Well…there's something *I* can do." I felt a deep rage stir in my chest like a forgotten ember stirred by a summer wind.

I swung the ax over my shoulder, voice a rumbling growl.

"I'm going to get my girlfriend back and hurt anyone who gets in my way."

Trent held up his hands, "Whoa, whoa, hold up, man. You'd be walking to your death. There's way too many of them. They'd slaughter you before you even made it to the front gates of their temple."

I jabbed a finger at him, "If you think for a second that I'm going to leave her there, you got another thing coming. Now get out of my way."

Kevin stood by Trent's side, concern riddled across his face. "Nick, please, there are smarter ways to do this."

I gritted my teeth, that ember glowing in my chest. "They could be raping her right now. Every second I wait is another second she has to suffer."

Trent put a hand on my shoulder and gazed intently at me. "Look chief, I get it. You're hurting right now. You want to go out there and let that anger loose. But cool the fire for just a second and listen to me. There's another way to get in there."

"I'm listening."

"Approach them like you want to join them," Trent said. "They accept recruits all the time."

I looked at Kevin. "Will that work?"

He shrugged, "I don't know, dude. I've never tried. But it's a way better plan than going in swinging. I don't know how many exactly there are…but I know there's enough of them that they'd stop you before you could save her."

I chewed on my lip, torn. Every ounce of me was ignited with a desire to kick the door down and start chopping. But behind the raging emotion, I knew it was a stupid idea. They were right. I'd be cut down in seconds. I had no idea what I was walking into, where they were keeping Jess, or how many there were. I exhaled, frustrated.

"Fine…where exactly is their temple?"

Trent patted my shoulder, "Good man. I still don't encourage this, but I'm glad you're not charging in crazy. Start walking towards the mountain, back toward the Needle Fields. I'm assuming you're familiar with that area?"

I nodded grimly.

"Ok," he continued, "just stay on this side of the forest with the mountain in front of you. Can't miss the place. It's big."

I looked at both of them, gaze lingering on each of their faces. "All right…thank you. I guess I'll go then."

Kevin held up a hand before I could leave. "Hold on, dude. One more thing." He shot a look at Trent who nodded.

"What is it?" I asked.

Kevin looked hard at me, "If you can get her and make it back here, we'll be waiting. Trent and I have been building a raft. We're going to try and get past the Keepers. We're going to try and escape this place. We have room for two more."

I took a step back. "What? Are you serious?"

Trent crossed his arms. "Dead serious. No one knows what's out there. No one knows what lies beyond the ocean if anything. And so we're going to find out. We've been working on this raft for a long time now. That's why we're here in this busted ass town. Finding materials isn't easy, but we've made a lot of progress." He saw my disbelieving look and snorted. "Hey, it beats the hell outta waiting around for something to kill you."

"You'll never make it past the Keepers," I said, "And when they DO catch you, you'll swing from their crosses forever. You really think it's worth risking that?"

Kevin planted his feet. "We have to try. There's a reason those Keepers are guarding the water. Did you ever think of that?"

I shook my head. "No...actually I didn't."

"Exactly," Trent exclaimed, "which is why we're going to find out. So if you actually manage to get your girl, then come back here and hook up with Kevin and I. We won't wait forever, though. Ok?"

I turned it over in my mind and then nodded. "Ok. Ok, we will. Thank you, both of you. I really appreciate this. I should probably get going now, yeah?"

Trent slapped my shoulder. "Hey, good luck to you, chief. I hope you find what you're looking for."

Kevin held out his hand and I shook it. "Best of luck to you, dude. We'll be waiting."

I shifted the ax across my shoulder and dipped my head to both of them before going to the door and throwing it open.

Rain darkened my hair and pulled it down to hang across my eyes as I marched out onto the soggy earth. My boots squished in the mud and a cold wind slapped across my face. My shirt was soaked in seconds, the fabric rippling and clawing away from my body. I squinted through the downpour, trying to cut through the gloom. The gray obscured my view of the mountain and so I started walking from memory.

I prayed nothing was stalking me, the steady drum of rain covering any sound of monstrosities sneaking up on me. I passed through the shanty town with ease, slinking from corner to corner until I was past the frayed construction. Ahead of me lay miles of open land, rolling foothills, and dead grass as far as the eye could see. I knew behind the veil of water the temple waited under the shadow of the mountain.

I hefted the ax in my hand, the wood slick. How exactly did I plan to do this? What if these religious freaks didn't let me join their ranks? What if they turned me away? I set my jaw, my resolve turning to stone. There was no way I would let them. I didn't care what I had to say or do, I was getting inside. And then I could start looking for Jess.

I summoned her face in my mind and held onto it. Where was she right now? Was she safe? I imagined her lost in the woods before Trent and Kevin found her. She must have been so scared. How long had she been looking for me before she was taken? How long did I have? Or was it already too late? Was she already suffering at the hands of these people?

I didn't want to think about it but forced myself to stay centered on that. It fueled me, a spark on my heels as I trudged through the dreary landscape. Every bruise on her body, every cry from her lips...in some way I was responsible for that. I needed to make it right, needed to rip her out of this cycle of fear and hopelessness.

I don't know how long I walked. At some point, my lungs began to burn and my legs quivered from exertion, but I pressed on through the storm. Ever so slowly, the peak of the mountain began to grow on the horizon, pushing through the sheets of rain to stare down at me.

Up above, the slimy trails of red ooze fluttered in the wind, dangling from the crescent cuts in the clouds. I watched one of the ooze trails, slightly off to my right. As I marched, I saw a body fill the gelatinous tube and slowly slide towards the teardrop exit. It looked like a man my age.

When he reached the end, he slipped through the crimson substance and tumbled to the earth. I traced his descent, wondering whether it was someone new or merely a reborn Suicidal. He landed about two hundreds yards ahead of me, his body disappearing behind a timid foothill.

As I drew closer, I saw that something had already reached the man. It was a Pig Born. It was slowly wrapping the unconscious figure with chains. The Pig Born looked very much like the one who had taken me to Danny.

It hadn't seen me yet, my presence masked by the rain, and so I ducked low and began to circle around the duo. As I walked, a thought popped through the bog of my cautious mind.

Kill that thing. Don't let it take another.

I paused, the Pig Born now a couple dozen yards to my left with its back turned to me. It was securing the chain around the man's throat.

It's an abomination. Cut it down.

I gave in to the voice and took my ax in both hands. Staying low, I rushed the unaware monster, heart racing, anticipation like gasoline in my veins.

When I was directly behind the mutilated creature, I raised the ax above my head and brought it down into the base of the Pig Born's skull. The blade thudded deep into the rotting meat and I felt the edge split bone.

With a surprised howl, the ruined creature spun, clawing at the base of its neck where my ax remained. I quickly stepped back, grip lost, watching with grim satisfaction as its eyes widened in pain. It fell to its knees, still screaming, its jaw extending beyond human capabilities.

Black blood poured over its bloated, pale flesh as it stared at me, its strength fading.

I booted it in the face as hard as I could.

Gurgling, the Pig Born tumbled backward and the force of

the ax meeting ground was enough the drive the blade deeper, forever silencing the monster.

Surging with righteous pleasure, I kicked the corpse over and yanked the ax free. I turned to the unconscious man and saw he was actually much younger than I originally thought. Rain bounced off his face as I turned away from him.

Black blood seeped around my boots, diluting in the mud. I surveyed my victim unsure what exactly I should feel.

And then I embraced the violence like an old friend. I wrapped myself in my murderous action, draping the warmth it brought me over my shoulders and grinned into the storm.

I could get used to this feeling.

I left the man where he lay, knowing I couldn't help him any more than I already had. I pressed forward and soon he was lost behind me in a torrent of rain and dim gray.

After some time the rain let up a little, reducing to a gentle trickle and I bounced my gaze between the growing mountain and the gashes in the sky. I didn't want any unexpected company falling on my head.

The broken sun sat miserably to my right, a dark reminder of how poisoned we all were here. I wondered what the creation of it must have looked like. How did The Pig do it? Did it simply sit in its massive barn and summon it? Did The Pig once roam the land along with all of its creations?

I wrapped one arm around myself, shivering as I walked. The wind was getting colder and I felt myself begin to shiver. My boots sunk deep into the earth, each step costing me more strength than I wanted to expend. Somewhere on the plains, I heard the howls of other Pig Born and I sharpened my awareness as best I could. To my left the forest grew, emerging from the horizon like a green strip of cloth. I readjusted my course and re-centered the mountain before me.

As I walked, casting occasional glances ahead of me, I saw something on the snow capped peak. I was still a couple miles from it, but the sudden contrast immediately captured my eyes.

It was a flash of blue light, blinking once, twice, and then vanishing. It was a mere pinprick of color, but enough to stand out against the stark white summit.

"What was that?" I muttered to myself, watching for another flash. When none came, I continued on, new questions rising in my mind like zombies from the grave. I shook myself free of their claws and buried them back where they belonged. I had enough to worry about right now.

Soon Muck's Needle Fields came into view. From this distance it looked like an iron cornfield, the sharpened steel rising high into the sky. I turned my path away from it and headed for the other side of the mountain.

My legs were burning like fire when I finally spotted The Temple of the Pig. It sprang from the background, emerging from the mountainside like an optical illusion.

It was enormous, resting at the base of the mountain opposite the side where Muck's cave was. It was built entirely from rock, four carved spires poking into the gray sky like the ends of a pencil.

Its crude walls rose dozens of feet into the air, the long rectangular design not quite symmetrical, almost as if it had been formed from clay by clumsy hands. At the front of the temple, resting above the colossal twin doors, was an impeccably carved pig head. Rain sloshed into its ears and exited through the mouth creating a natural waterfall that splashed across the shallow steps leading up to its entrance.

I observed all this from the peak of a small foothill, weighing my options carefully. As I considered what my next move was, I spotted a trio of cloaked figures emerge from the temple. I crouched to one knee, feeling exposed, and watched nervously as they descended the stairs and turned my way.

I scrubbed rain from my eyes and felt my heart begin to race. I knew what I had to do, I knew I needed to interact with these people in order to get inside…but even so, I felt fear tickle my senses with a cold finger. I had no idea what awaited me behind those walls. What if they saw my true intentions? What if I was captured again, held against my will and tortured for their pleasure?

The three figures continued to approach, smudges of gray across the long plain, slowly growing larger with each anxious breath. I knew I was exposed, I knew they could see me. I gritted my teeth. This was probably the best chance I'd have. I needed to confront them, ask for admission. I prepared the words on my tongue and strolled down the hill to meet them. I kept the ax slung across my shoulders. No need to part with my weapon yet.

If the three hooded men felt threatened by my approach, they didn't show it. As we grew closer, the man in the middle lowered his head and met my gaze from fifty yards. I held his eyes until the four of us stood a handful of feet apart.

I waited for them to speak first.

"What are you doing here?" the man in the middle asked. His eyes were dull and matched the shade of his short gray hair.

I blew rain off my lips. "I heard this is where Suicidals pledge themselves to The Pig."

The two flanking the older man kept their hoods drawn low, but I could see them exchange a look. The gray-haired man spread his arms. "You heard correctly. Is that why you've come?"

I nodded, "Yeah. What a place, huh? Pretty wild. Inspiring, really. I feel like I've been waiting my whole life to experience something like the Black Farm. It's incredible what The Pig has done. I want to be a part of that." I had no idea if what I was saying would ring true with these three, but I figured honesty tainted with soft lies was my best bet at getting on their good side.

The man in the middle crossed his arms, his face giving away nothing. "You know what we do here?"

I shrugged, "I've heard talk."

"And you want to be a part of that?"

I grinned with confidence I didn't feel. "Absolutely. You guys are doing something special in there. And I want in."

The man appraised me with cold eyes. "We get a lot of requests from Suicidals. And a lot of those requests are for the wrong reasons. They come to us seeking protection and shelter. Is that what you're after?"

I rested the head of the ax between my feet and cracked a smile, "Do I look like I need protection?"

The man didn't seem impressed. "So, shelter then?"

I raised my face into the rain, "From what? A little rain? Don't make me laugh."

The man exchanged a look with his companions and then cleared his throat. "The Temple of the Pig is a holy place and the next step towards realizing what The Pig intends for us. Becoming one of us is no easy task and requires multiple checkpoints that you must pass along the way. It's not as simple as a yes or no. First, you must meet with Ryder, our leader, so that he may witness your true intentions. Then, if he accepts you into the fold, you will travel with the other new recruits to pledge yourself to The Pig. When your elder returns you to the Temple, you'll take the oath and begin an apprenticeship until your elder clears you to become one of us. Do you understand?"

I mentally exhaled. "Yeah, I understand."

The man stepped towards me suddenly and grabbed the ax handle, his face inches from mine, his eyes buzzing. "And let me be clear. This isn't some casual decision to make. If you're serious, then prepare yourself for some very serious shit. Got it?"

I forced myself to smile. "Got it. I'm Nick, by the way."

"Peter," he said with rocks in his voice. "And as of now, you won't be needing this." I screamed internally as he pulled the ax from my grip. "That's not going to be a problem, is it?"

I let him take it. "Not at all."

"Good. Now, let's return to the Temple. There are introductions to be made."

I motioned ahead of us, keeping my tone light, "Lead the way, Peter."

This felt too easy and it made my skin crawl.

As the four of us turned back toward the Temple, I tried to suppress the feeling of dread that dripped down my throat and pooled in my stomach. My heart told me this was how I found Jess, but my mind screamed madness and caution. The silent, nameless two flanked my sides as Peter led us across the plains towards the base of the mountain where the colossal stone temple awaited.

I focused on remaining loose and non-threatening. I held my head high and walked with a sure step, eyes locked on the back of Peter's head. If I had any hope of pulling this off, I needed to remain confident in my lie. It wasn't easy.

"Who built the temple?" I asked as we walked.

Without turning, Peter responded, "Eons ago, the original seven bonded together and presented their vision to The Pig. It rewarded their dedication with the temple you see before you. Ever since then, our numbers have grown and we seek out new ways to honor what we have been gifted with."

The looming structure grew out of the sheets of rain, morphing detail and texture the closer we came. I searched for doors, hidden windows, something that might be useful later on, but none were apparent other than the twin gates at the front.

This wasn't going to be easy.

Staying cool, I turned to my hooded companions. "You guys must feel pretty special, huh? To know that The Pig accepts you and rewarded your religion with such an impressive token."

They didn't even look at me, water dripping from the edges of drawn hoods.

"What's The Pig like?" I continued. "What's it look like? Does it speak to you?"

We were almost to the stone stairs leading up to the expansive double doors. Peter turned his head without slowly. "You ask a lot of questions, Nick."

"I'm just curious," I said offhandedly, "and excited. I've wanted this for a long time now."

We were walking up the stairs now and Peter pulled his hood over his head again, "Best save them for Ryder."

I shut my mouth and looked up, the enormous stone pig head vomiting rain above us. Tiny waterfalls lapped at my boots and slithered across the slick stone. I hugged myself as

I realized we were going to walk directly under the cascading tide.

Peter went first, his form lost for a moment as he passed through the pillar of falling water and then I was under. I gasped as a shock of freezing cold engulfed my body, the icy rain drenching me in a current of power. I hurried through the frigid column and ran a hand across my face, clearing my vision.

Peter was waiting for me, his back to the closed doors. Before I could say anything, he was suddenly toe to toe with me, his eyes hostile and his voice dangerous.

"Now understand this, *Nick*. You are a pet I've brought home to show my master. Act accordingly or I swear on the Pig Born I'll make you regret it. Do you understand me?"

I swallowed hard. "I understand. You have nothing to worry about." Peter held my gaze a moment longer and then nodded, satisfied.

"Then let's go in."

Peter, along with the help of his two companions, pushed the front gates open. The hinges groaned and creaked and I could hear them grunting under the weight. Satisfied, Peter nodded me ahead and I entered the temple, caution an echo in my mind.

I heard the doors close behind me, but my attention was focused on the crude sanctuary before me. Wooden pews lined the vast space, the shoddy carpentry obviously hewed from inexperienced hands. The floor was made of bare stone, smooth and gray as the clouds outside. Bowls of fire hung from the ceiling, the squirming flames reaching towards an arching ceiling overhead. An altar rested at the head of the church, a granite slab that was draped with dirty cloth.

To my left was a set of stairs that twisted down and out of sight, but shadows moved along the walls and my imagination conjured monsters to match. I wondered if Jess was down there.

A handful of hooded figures sat in the pews, hunched over in what I assumed was prayer. None of them turned to see who had just entered their church, the noise of our arrival washing over deaf ears. The place smelled of dirt and ash, a film of filth coating the walls. I felt it on my skin and caught myself wiping my hands on my pants.

"Wait here," Peter said, placing a hand on my shoulder. "I'll tell Ryder you're here. He'll want to see you right away."

"Ok."

My other two companions circled around me and joined the others in the pews. They kept their hoods up and heads down. With the absence of windows, the bowls of flame cast shadows that gave the small congregation an almost statue-like quality. They just sat, motionless, like they were waiting for something to happen. I nervously waited, trying to prepare myself for whatever came next. Every part of me screamed to rush down the stairs to my left and seek out Jess. Knowing she might be in the same building as I was eating away at my nerves. I felt my fingers twitching and I forced myself to settle down. If I was going to make this work, I had to be patient.

"What the hell are you doing here?"

I turned towards the voice and saw Danny exiting from a small room to my right. Surprise rippled through me, soon joined by unease. I tried to keep my face neutral as I crossed my arms and nodded at him.

Danny approached me, his dull eyes boring into my skull. "Come to join the ranks?"

I shrugged, my heart inexplicably racing. "If you'll have me."

Danny's face twisted in disgust. "Don't think for a second I'm part of this. I'm only here to arrange a viewing for the new recruits."

"Oh, to see The Pig?" I asked.

Danny's mouth remained bent at the corners. "I don't know why The Pig wastes its time with these morons. But who am I to question?"

I turned my eyes away from him, letting the conversation die.

But Danny wasn't ready to leave me alone. He cocked his head at me. "So did Muck finally kill you? Or did you find a way out of there?"

I kept my eyes away from him. "What do you care?"

Danny smirked, "I don't. I'm just curious."

"Let's just say I found a way out."

Danny took a step closer, "Did you now? Did you have fun with Muck? I've never had the pleasure, but I hear he's quite the entertainer. And judging from the way you looked, I'd say he gave you the royal welcome."

My hands suddenly clenched into fists. "Drop it, Danny."

He grinned, his full lips peeling back to reveal white teeth, "Ohhh, tough guy now? What are you going to do? Huh? You going to hit me? To get back at me? To get back at the Black Farm for what it's done to you? Is that why you're really here?"

My heart was racing now and I knew I was dangerously close to being exposed. "I've had a change of heart. This religion is what I need."

Danny's face became unreadable. "Of course it is."

"Just leave me alone."

He reached out and patted my arm, "Sure thing, Nick. Wouldn't want to mess with you."

"Just try me," I muttered.

Suddenly, Danny sprang forward and grabbed me by the throat, slamming me violently against the wall. His breath was hot on my face and he leaned in close, his voice a guttural snarl.

"You think you've figured this place out, huh? You think you've lived through the worst the Black Farm has to offer? You think you're some kind of badass now? Well let me tell you something, fucker, the moment you think you're in control is the moment this place will destroy you all over again."

I tried to shove him off me, but he only tightened his grip, bringing his face closer, spittle spraying from his lips.

"I don't know what kind of idiot you think I am, but I know you aren't here to join these fucks. So why is it? Are you still looking for that bitch of yours? What was her name?"

"Jess," I growled, forcing fire into my voice, "and you're goddamn right I'm going to find her."

Danny shook his head, voice dropping to a whisper, "What is it with you? Why do you keep going?"

I matched his tone, anger starting to bubble just beneath the surface, "What the hell is your problem with me?"

Danny stared at me for a moment without saying anything before releasing me, brushing his hands against his pants as if to wipe away the contact. "Because you still have hope and that disgusts me."

It was my turn to advance on him. "Why does that scare you?"

His eyes snapped back to me, burning. "Oh...you're *pushing* it right now."

I jabbed a finger, growing more confident, "No, you're afraid of something. What is it? Why does hope piss you off so much? Is there something about this place you're not telling me?"

Danny looked like he was going to throttle me so I quickly stepped back. I was growing tired of people grabbing me. I raised my hands defensively, smiling slightly. It felt good to put Danny on edge.

"Hey, relax. I guess I'll find out for myself. And Danny?" I said, "I have all the time in the world."

Danny visibly fought to regain control of his emotions, "There's nothing out there for you but misery. And let me tell you something, Nick. I'm going to be there when you finally break."

I leaned into him. "I've already been broken. But you know what? I put myself back together. You know what's different now, though?"

Danny just glared at me.

"All those broken pieces have *edges* now, fucker," I growled. "Now get the fuck out of my face."

A slow smile began to grow on Danny's lips. The grin lit his eyes and I felt some of my confidence drain. Remaining silent, he reached up and patted my cheek affectionately and then turned and left. His expression hovered like a ghost in my mind and I shivered despite myself.

"Crazy bastard."

8

Peter returned not long after Danny's departure. He ushered me down a hallway, informing me that Ryder was ready to see me. As we walked, I took note of my surroundings, searching for possible exits. We passed a few closed doors, but nothing that looked like it led to the outside. As far as I could tell, the big double doors were the only way in or out of the temple.

More bowls of fire hung overhead as I followed Peter, our footsteps echoing off the plain stone walls. From what I could deduce, I figured we were in the living quarters. We passed a couple people, all of them throwing me a wary glance. Most were in robes, eyes somber and faces grim. They didn't look afraid, but there was a hollowness to them that unnerved me like they had seen things that still whispered from the corners of their minds.

Peter led me around a corner where we stopped before a plain wood door. That ashy smell seemed stronger here and I felt my eyes water.

"Ryder awaits you. Behave yourself and answer truthfully. If it is the will of The Pig, he will see your intentions are pure."

"Ok, thanks," I said feeling slightly nervous.

Taking a deep breath, I reminded myself that I was growing

closer to finding Jess. I reached for the handle and pushed the door open. Immediately, I gagged as a hot wave of stinking air rushed past me. It smelled like decay and burning rot. Gathering myself, I walked inside and heard Peter shut the door behind me.

Sitting before me was the fattest man I had ever seen. He was completely naked and slouched upright on a filthy bed, his back against the headboard. His stomach avalanched between his legs and pooled across his knees, his skin streaked with angry stretch marks.

His face was a bloated mess, a drooping water balloon with eyes and a mouth. A patch of dark hair rested at the peak of his skull like a tiny cap.

Next to the bed was a table littered with bizarre looking food, mostly meat. A fireplace roared in the corner and to my horror, I saw it was littered with charred human bones. My unease grew as I realized there was another person in the room. A woman.

She was chained to the bedpost by the neck, a naked mess of blood and dirt. Her eyes were glazed over, lost in her own miserable existence. Drool dripped from the corner of her mouth and slid down her naked breasts, leaving a trail through the grime that coated her body.

And that's when I realized part of her shoulder was missing. It looked like an entire chunk had been lopped off and blood poured from the open wound.

I physically recoiled at the sight of her and then my heart sank as I realized who it was.

It was Megan.

My stomach crawled up my throat and I had to fight against a tide of emotion that suddenly rose in my chest like a cold moon over an ocean. I clenched my fists and stood there, fighting against anger and empathy that she had been subjugated to such suffering yet again.

The massive man on the bed, Ryder, motioned me forward. As I cautiously advanced, Ryder picked up a small knife from the bed and casually sliced a piece of Megan's shoulder away. He licked his lips and popped the flesh into his mouth like a piece of bloody cheese.

Megan's shriek stopped me dead in my tracks as she leaned forward, howling, shaking in her chains. My heart hammered against my chest and I fought back an overwhelming urge to help her. She had gone from Muck to this. A new nightmare to bring her fresh agony. I gritted my teeth behind my lips. I convinced myself that doing something rash would only get us both killed. Just breathe and be smart.

"Want a bite?" Ryder asked, his voice a bubbling chorus of chuckling fat.

"I'll pass," I said weakly.

Ryder rolled his massive shoulders in a shrug. "Suit yourself."

I said nothing, swallowing my urges.

"Peter tells me you're interested in joining us."

I nodded, face pale, eyes never leaving Megan. She didn't look at me, didn't look at anything. She sagged against her restraints, blood and saliva dripping down her body.

Ryder reached out and tapped her head with his knife. "Does this bother you?"

I swallowed hard, "I guess there's a first for everything."

Ryder chuckled and it sent waves rippling down his sloping belly. "Good answer, I like that. What's your name?"

"Nick."

"Well Nick, what makes you think we want you here?"

The brashness of the question cut through the turmoil I found myself wading through and I stood a little straighter and cleared my throat. "Why wouldn't you want another soldier in your ranks?"

"Deflecting a question with a question," Ryder mused, "Is that why you've come? To become my soldier?"

"If that's what you need me to be."

Ryder ran a finger across his chins. "You know what we do here? How we breed humans and Pig Born together?"

"I've heard some."

"And what do you think about that? Why do you think we do it?"

I tried to remain focused on Ryder, blocking Megan's pain from my mind as best I could. "I think you do it because you want to elevate the human race to mirror The Pig as best you can. I think that it's the best way we can honor it."

"Hmm," Ryder said clicking the blade of the knife against his teeth. "Not bad. An obviously constructed answer, but I can appreciate that."

His eyes never left me as he reached out with his knife and dragged the blade through Megan's shoulder once again. Her screams rattled me to the bone and I felt myself begin to sweat, anger and horror growing hotter in my chest.

Ryder held the flesh on the blade and brought it dripping to his mouth. He slurped it up and lazily chewed, blood dribbling from the corner of his mouth.

Megan's eyes remained on the floor as she wept and I was thankful. I didn't want her to know it was me, watching her and doing nothing. Christ knows I wanted to. As Ryder's lips smacked and slurped down his snack, I found myself loathing the man. It wasn't hard.

"You look like you want to say something," Ryder mused, licking dangerously along the edge of the knife, cleaning the blood from the steel. "Go ahead, don't be shy. Speak your mind."

I tried to swallow the words, but Megan's whimpers brought them to the surface, "I find your choice in edibles rather disgusting."

Ryder seemed unaffected by my comment, now cleaning his teeth with the tip of the knife, "When you grow as hungry as I do, your appreciation for new things expands in unexpected ways. Have you ever eaten human flesh before?"

I shook my head, appalled.

The gluttonous man flicked the knife with lightning fast precision and before I could blink, Megan was screaming and Ryder was extending a chunk of her shoulder for me to take. I stepped away, eyes wide, shaking my head viciously. Ryder shook the streaking meat at me, goading me, a look of sick delight pasted across his piggy face.

"Go ahead, take it. Have a bite. She's delicious."

My stomach rolled. "No, I don't want it. I couldn't."

Ryder grinned, his cheeks balling under his eyes. "Yes you can. Just a bite."

I swallowed hard. "No."

Ryder shifted on the bed, the wood groaning in protest, "Nick….I'm not asking. Eat it." His voice had taken on a dangerous tone that told me I didn't have a choice. He was testing me. He wanted to see how far I would go to be a part of their movement.

I shot a look at Megan who was huddled into herself, clutching her shoulder. Tears fell from her face onto the dirty floor. My eyes rose from her to the piece of dripping flesh that hung above her from the edge of the knife. My heart raced and my pulse quickened as I stepped forward. This was for Jess, everything I did here, every awful horrible thing was for her. I reminded myself of that as I took the slick meat between my fingers.

It was warm to the touch and I fought off the urge to fling it into the corner, away from me. I could smell her skin, the blood and sweat emitting a nauseous concoction that brought bile to the back of my throat.

Ryder urged me on, his face alight, "Go ahead. Slide it between your lips and onto your tongue. Allow your taste buds to ignite with her flavor, completely raw and untainted by fire. It is the purest meat you'll ever consume."

Slowly, I raised the chunk of flesh and placed it in my mouth. I squeezed my eyes shut as I chewed, teeth squishing against the meat, the consistency disturbingly gummy. All I tasted was blood and I gagged once before I managed to swallow it all down, gasping as it descended into my stomach.

My eyes were watering as I opened them to see Ryder beaming from ear to ear, a look of gleeful anticipation on his face.

"Well?! What do you think?"

I steadied my breathing and tried to forgive myself for what I had just done. "A little raw for my tastes."

Ryder clapped his hands together laughing uproariously. "I like you, Nick! You got spunk! I'm a little disappointed in your palette, but perhaps the taste will grow on you, yeah?"

"I hated sushi when I was a kid," I said trying to mask my misery and disgust. "I kind of like it now."

Ryder waved his arms about, "Well, there you go! Maybe I'll have you back in here for a snack now and again."

The thought made me want to retch, but I pushed the conversation back towards the reason for my being there, "Does that mean you'll have me? I can stay and be a part of your temple?"

"I think I'm willing to give you a chance," Ryder said, "if you're willing to learn and abide by our rules. I want to get to know you a little more, Nick. There's something about you…something I can't put my finger on. Something under that spunk."

Yeah, it's my barely controllable urge to murder you, I thought.

"Peter is taking some of the new recruits to The Barn soon. I want you to go with them. I'm going to place you under his watch. He's our longest running elder and I trust his judgment. He will observe your dedication to us, The Hooves of the Pig, and report your progress back to me. After some time, if you've proven yourself worthy, we will induct you as one of us."

I bowed my head slightly. "Thank you. You won't regret it."

"Be sure I don't," Ryder said turning his attention back to Megan. "Leave me now. Peter will take you to your quarters and inform you when they will depart. He will return you to me when he has made his decision."

I bowed again and turned to go, quickly pushing out of the room as Megan began to scream behind me. The door closed at my back, her cries assaulting my ears, and I found myself trembling with helpless rage.

It was then that I vowed to kill Ryder before I left.

The ease in which I made the decision should have worried me, but I didn't have time to fret over the state of my mental being. You can only bend for so long before the inevitable break and when you do, you don't have time to worry about the pieces you lose in the process.

Peter was waiting for me outside the room. His hood was down and the lines of his face were deep with impatience.

"Come with me; I'll show you to your room," he said walking down the dim hallway without turning to see if I was following.

I jogged after him, the sound of Megan's pain fading. I pushed it aside, for now, suppressing the helplessness clawing at my heart. The smooth stone walls twisted and turned, leading us deeper into the crude temple. It was bigger than I had first imagined, a stretching maze of doorways and similar looking halls. I tried my best to keep track of the turns we made until finally, we stopped before a simple wooden door.

"This is another brother's room, but he's away for a little while. You'll stay here until he returns," Peter said.

"Ryder mentioned going to see The Pig. When do we depart?" I asked.

Peter sniffed, "Aren't you eager? Can't say I blame you though. Going to see The Pig…there's nothing like it. I'll let you know when we leave, don't worry. As for now, you're free to roam the temple. The only area off limits to you is the basement. Do not go down there."

"Is that where you breed the Pig Born and humans?" I pressed.

Peter nodded. "Among other things. Ryder has put you under my watch which means he trusts you enough to keep you around. Which means I'll offer you the same level of trust. Don't break it. You break my trust and you're out, understand?"

"Sure."

"Good," he continued, "now feel free to get some rest before we leave. Or if you'd like you can head back to the sanctuary for some quiet reflection. Up to you. I'm not going to dictate your every action, but I will be watching."

"I'll behave," I lied.

As I turned to open the door, Peter placed a hand on my shoulder, "Nick. This road before you is a long one. You've been placed under my care I want to make sure you reach the end. I was hard on you earlier because I had to be. If Ryder has given you his blessing…know that you have mine as well."

I don't want your fucking blessing, I thought, pasting a smile to my lips.

"I appreciate you saying that, Peter."

He offered me a small smile before turning and leaving. I exhaled for the first time since I arrived. This was going to be harder than I thought. If Jess was here, she would be in the basement. The one place I wasn't allowed to go.

Wonderful.

I opened the door in front of me and walked into my new living quarters. A single bowl of flame ignited the room, casting shadows over every surface. A small bed was shoved into the corner and sitting beside it was a small desk and chair. The floor had some kind of grass rug draped across the cold stone. I padded across it and went to the bed, sitting heavily, fatigue returning in my isolation.

I dragged my hands over my face, allowing the tension to drain from my shoulders. I wondered how long I could keep this charade up. There were a lot of them and only one of me. I wished I still had my ax.

I heard a muffled cacophony of voices outside my door, but the conversation passed further down the hall and disappeared. Who exactly were these freaks? What had they gone through to buy in to such barbaric rituals? What morals had they been stripped of?

Men need purpose. When they are denied or stripped of that, what remains is an aimless shell of anger and violence. Instead of working to gain back their purpose they build something new in which to define themselves. This new platform regrows the ego and straightens the bended knee. It poisons the mind with contempt because now they define themselves as self-made and they look upon their past purpose as a chain that once held them back. Violence and aggression curl around this new heart and whispers domination into every beat, filling every vein.

Men with self-created purpose is a dangerous thing and I felt its jaws all around me. I stood up, shaking the feeling out of my fingers. I didn't want to be a part of this farce. I wanted to grab something sharp and go hunt for Jess. She was here, just beneath my feet. What was she doing right at this moment? Was she crying? Screaming? What were these monsters making her do?

"Stop it," I whispered, pacing, "you can't think about that. It's just going to make you do something stupid. Be patient. Don't get caught. Stay focused. It won't be long now."

After twenty minutes of fidgeting I decided to go back to the sanctuary. That's where I had seen the stairs leading to the lower level. Maybe I'd piece together something that could help me. Mind set, I opened the door and began navigating the twisting hallways back to the entrance. I passed a handful of robed figures, all lost in some kind of philosophical conversation. I paid them no attention and they returned my interest in kind.

The walls and doors began to blend together, a wash of

gray stone and dim light. I took a wrong turn somewhere and had to double back. After another ten minutes I finally exited the labyrinth and entered the expansive sanctuary. I spotted a few men huddled over the pews in silent prayer and I quietly went to the back of the room and stood by the massive double doors. I gripped the top of the pew in front of me and tried to act inconspicuous. No one seemed to pay me any attention. I watched as a group of three walked to the front and knelt down in front of the altar, placing something on its flat surface. I tried not to focus too much on what it was. The three joined hands and began to pray, their whispers rising like smoke toward the ceiling.

I turned my head and looked to my left at the stairs leading down to the basement. It was nothing more than a square hole carved into the floor. Wide steps led down into the depths, twisting out of sight at a sharp right angle. No noise came from below. I didn't see anyone guarding the entrance, but my imagination conjured what lay around that corner halfway down.

I slid my hands along the pew, inching closer. My ears were tuned to pick up any noise that might be coming from below. I don't know what I expected, maybe the howl of women or Jess screaming my name, but the dark hole remained silent.

I quickly surveyed the room to make sure no one was watching me. My heart was galloping in my chest and a trickle of sweat caressed my spine. Should I do this now? Would I get a better chance?

My knuckles turned white against the pew and my eyes darted across the sanctuary, fighting internally with myself.

Go, go, go, do it! She's down there! No one's looking!

I bit my lip, breathing hard. NO! It's too soon! They'll catch me!

I ground my teeth together, frustrated and torn to the brink of madness.

GO YOU COWARD!

I took a step towards the stairs.

The second I did, the massive twin doors behind me groaned open and I quickly spun on my heel and made like I was exiting the temple. I pushed past a group of men coming inside, shaking water from their hair, and walked out into the rain. The waterfall cascading from the pig head above soaked me instantly and I shuddered and hurried down the stairs, gasping for air at my close encounter. I reached the bottom and as my boots touched earth, I leaned over and placed my hands on my knees, calming myself.

"Jesus Christ, that was close," I muttered. Rain thudded into my back and I slowly stood upright.

"How the hell am I going to do this?" I whispered to the mountain looming before me.

I blinked in the rain as I saw something on the peak.

It was a flash of blue light, just like before, a pinprick that winked out of the gloom once, twice, then vanished again.

What is that?

I shielded my eyes from the rain and squinted at the summit, a triangle slicing into the heavens.

The light never returned.

As new questions rose in my mind, I turned back to the temple. I stared up at the flowing pig head, its great stone jaws vomiting an absurd amount of water. I didn't want to go back inside. I didn't want to be around those people.

So I sat down on the stairs, embracing the rain, and watched the mountain.

I stayed like that for hours, the wind slapping my face with an icy palm. I was soaked to the bone and completely numb when I heard my name being called. I turned around and saw Peter walking towards me, shadowed by two hooded men. He was holding something in his arms and I realized it was a robe. He reached the foot of the stairs and extended it out to me.

"Here, take this and put it on. It's yours now."

I stood up, shivering, and wordlessly accepted it. The fabric was thick beneath my fingers, red dyes weaving between browns. I slipped it on and welcomed the warmth, the heavy cloth immediately bringing my stiff muscles back to life.

Peter shook his head, "Why are you out here? We couldn't find you."

I pulled the hood up to mirror the look of the two men behind Peter. "Just wanted to think for a while in the open air."

He rolled his shoulders at me, jabbing a thumb behind him. "These are the other two new recruits that are coming with us to see The Pig. This is William and Anthony." The hooded figures tilted their heads at me and I returned the gesture. Their eyes looked empty, their age written across their faces in thick lines and wrinkles. I guessed their devotion came with a hidden agenda as well. At that age, I could only imagine what easy targets they were for the Pig Born. The Hooves of the Pig offered not only religion, but protection as well.

"I'm Nick," I said, wrapping my arms around myself. My teeth were chattering and I fought to control the clatter.

Peter had a pack on over his robe and he slid it off and began to pull things out, speaking as he did so. "We're going to start our journey now. Our path takes us across the plains past the mountain and into the forest. Once we're through that, we'll make our way to The Barn. Ryder has set things up with Danny so they know we're coming. Also, just because we wear the robes doesn't mean the Pig Born aren't a threat. Be careful if you spot one. They know not to bother us, but sometimes you'll get a rogue who doesn't care. More dangerous than them though are the Suicidals. There's a group of them that hunts us. They hate everything we stand for. They're cowards, unable to accept the changes that come with new reality. They want us dead. While we're in the woods, be vigilant."

Peter paused and pulled out two thin knives and handed them to William and Anthony, "Take these. You'll need them if the Suicidals find us." The two old men looked at one another before accepting the weapons. Their hands shook and I wondered if they could actually kill someone.

"What about me?" I asked.

Peter flipped his robe aside and withdrew my ax. He handed it to me, eyes hard, "Thought you'd want this back. You seemed rather attached to it."

I tried not to smile as I took it. "Hello again, buddy. Missed you."

Peter didn't release his grip, locking eyes with me, "I'm trusting you with this, Nick."

Jackass.

"You don't have anything to worry about," I said, waiting for him to release it. After a second he did.

Oh you shouldn't have done that, I thought, almost laughing.

"What do we do when we reach The Barn?" one of the old men asked. I thought it was Anthony, but then realized I didn't give a shit.

"I'll fill you in once we get there," Peter said, sliding his pack back on. "And if you three are ready, I think it's time we were on our way."

I slung the ax over my shoulder, but paused, my gaze zipping back to the summit of the mountain.

The blue light was flashing again.

"What is that?" I asked, pointing toward the towering gloom.

Peter followed my finger. The light flashed again, nothing more than spark on the snowy slopes.

"I've seen that three times now. Is there something up there?"

Peter turned warily back to face me, "We call them the Eyes of the World. If you know what's good for you, you won't mention them again."

"Why? Who's up there?"

Peter held up a hand, "Nick, I'm warning you. Don't press it. They leave us alone and we leave them alone. Don't ask me about it, don't ask Ryder about it, and especially don't ask Danny. You want to get on our bad side? Keep probing."

Questions flooded my mind as the blue light flashed once more then went dark. Don't ask about it? Why? What were they afraid of? And what did Danny have to do with it? I decided to keep my mouth shut and store my inquires away for another time.

"Let's go," Peter said taking the lead.

Soggy earth squishing beneath our feet, we turned our backs on the temple and began to make our way across the long stretch of open plain toward the distant forest. As we walked, I couldn't help but feel a twist of sickness in my stomach. I didn't even know if Jess was at the temple, but leaving it behind felt wrong. It felt like I was abandoning her.

You mentally abandoned her years ago.

I shook my head. I wasn't going to listen to that voice anymore. I was here and everything I did was for her. Everything I did was another step toward reuniting with her. One way or another, I would make it happen.

And so I walked.

Peter didn't say much and the two older men trailed behind me, huffing and puffing in the rain. We had to stop a few times so they could catch their breath, but Peter never allowed us to stop for very long. He kept his eyes moving, constantly searching for Suicidals. A few fell from the red slices in the sky, like drops of water from the tip of a needle. The wind carried the roar of Pig Born, but it came from a great distance. Regardless, I kept my ax at the ready.

As the miles trailed behind us, I looked toward the mountain over my shoulder. I shivered as I spotted the Needle Fields, a grim vision stretching miserably over acres of dead land. I put the sight where it belonged…behind me.

The forest grew from a thin line to a green wall and when we finally crossed into its dreary belly, I lowered my hood. We marched through the foliage single file, Peter still in the lead. Behind me Anthony and William crashed along, earning irritated looks from our leader. He seemed extremely on edge, like he was expecting something.

Ten minutes later, I found out what.

Through the trees, we began to hear soft calls, simple hoots and whistles that echoed through the dim interior of the woods. My heart began to race and every tree became a statue waiting to kill me. I heard Anthony and William begin to mutter nervously as Peter hurried us along, a curse on his lips.

Never thought I'd wish for Pig Born over Suicidals, I thought, swallowing hard. We were being hunted. I could feel it. Peter's cautionary warning at the start of our trek came back to me and I gripped my ax. Shadows began to dance from tree to tree, circling us. They were still far enough away that I couldn't make out what they were…but I knew. These weren't monsters. These weren't Pig Born. These were people, human beings just like me. And they wanted to kill us.

To them, you're a part of the problem, I thought, *you're part of the evil that infects this place.*

Peter was pulling out a machete from his robes, shooting us a look. Be ready.

Those are Suicidals out there, I thought, exhaling slowly as the calls became louder. *Those are human beings, just like you, who have had enough. They're tired of being controlled and hurt. They're pissed. They're angry. And they're coming for you, Nick.*

"Fuck," I whispered, voice not quite steady. Back at the temple, plans of death had come so easily. The Hooves of the Pig were the enemy, the ones holding women hostage and forcing pain and humiliation upon them. Justifying their end was easy, almost welcome.

But this…these were just people.

What are you going to do? They're almost on you.

And they were. Peter waved us closer to him and we huddled in a small circle, slowly moving forward, a head turned in every direction. Crunching leaves and snapping twigs grew louder and someone laughed from the trees, a piercing shrill climax of hysteria. It sprouted and icy finger along my spine and I shivered.

"There's six of them, the ones I warned you about," Peter whispered, sweat standing out on his forehead. He seemed nervous. I didn't like that.

"What do we do!?" one of the old men asked. William, I think.

Peter clenched his teeth. "We're going to have to fight them. They're not going to let us through."

"Why!? Who are they!?" the other old man asked, voice trembling.

Peter shot him a look. "Weren't you listening earlier? They're Suicidals. Now pull yourself together, we're going to need you."

The man fell into a fit of babbling panic and Peter abruptly slapped him across the face, bringing a shocked look to the man's wrinkled features.

"Stop that! If we stay together we can make it out of this. I thought we'd be able to slip through the forest unnoticed if I kept our group small. We've done it before. But clearly that hasn't happened. So put some steel in your fucking spine and get ready!"

As the words left his lips, two men came charging us from the underbrush, teeth bared. They were wielding clubs with angry bits of metal sticking out of them. The four of us spun as one, our weapons drawn and at the ready. My heart slammed into my ribs, my throat an oasis, adrenaline pumping like diesel.

Peter blocked a blow with his machete that had been aimed at one of the old men's head.

The clash of weapons ignited me into action and I ducked as the other attacker took a swing at my skull. I could hear the other Suicidals circling around us.

William and Anthony backed away, crying out in fear. I shoved one of them to the ground as a spiked club honed in on his head. As the weapon whistled through air, I stepped forward and slammed the blunt end of my ax into the attacker's stomach. He doubled over, wheezing, and out of the corner of my eye, I saw Peter drive his blade through the other man's throat.

You're going to die if you don't kill them, my mind screamed. *Just do it, they'll be reborn somewhere else!*

The man before me gained his breath back and stood, throwing me a blazing look of pure violence. I knew I wasn't actually killing these people, but the act itself would feel the same. Pig Born were easy; I could rationalize that. They weren't human. But my fellow survivors? People who fought back against this cult of abominations? People who might be looking for their loved ones, just like I was?

They're not people, a cold voice suddenly muttered from a hidden darkness in my mind, *they're fucking obstacles standing in your way. They're walking sacks of blood and meat trying to stop you from getting to Jess.*

I heard the crash of foliage behind me and I knew the other four were coming.

You've come so far. Kill them or you'll never get to Jess.

The man before me charged, howling, club raised.

Something inside me unlocked and I exhaled, my breath tainted with fury.

I stepped into the man, planting my foot like a baseball player and swung my ax with every ounce of strength I had. The blade plowed into the man's face with the force of a bullet train and I felt bone erupt, the force shuddering down the length of the handle. Blood exploded from the contact and my attacker dropped like sack of bricks.

"Nick, DUCK!" I heard Peter yell.

I dropped immediately, feeling something whiz past my head. I landed on the man I had just killed, his blood staining my hands.

I welcomed the warmth.

I scrambled to my feet, scooting backwards, and faced my new foes. Peter stood at my side, one hand on my arm helping me up. Anthony and William had scrambled behind us, their knives discarded as panic took them.

Four bulky men faced us, grinning. They wielded the same nasty looking clubs and began to taunt us with them.

"Going to paint to dirt with your brains," one of them leered, "or maybe we'll take you with us, show you what it's like to live in fear."

Another stepped forward, licking his lips. "You think it's ok to take defenseless women and make them objects in your sick games? Huh? Not so fun when people fight back is it?"

Sweat and blood ran down my face in streaks as I ground my teeth together. Something was unraveling inside of me, a dark blossom of cold anger and hatred. Who the fuck were these people standing in my way? Did they have any idea what I had fucking gone through to get this far?

"Get the fuck out of our way," I snarled.

Another of the four laughed. "Not a chance. You see, we have an issue with you and your whole operation, bitch."

I could see Peter ready himself, chest heaving.

I shook my head at the Suicidals. "I don't want to do this."

One of them pointed his club at me, "No one wants to die, Pig lover."

I bared my teeth, blood staining them. "I meant I don't want to butcher you, mother*fucker.*"

That bought me a second of silence and I took it. I threw my ax at one of them and charged the rest. Peter roared at my side and dove into the fray, blade raised. My ax crunched into one of them, the heavy steel head dancing off the side of his skull, dazing him. I targeted another one and tackled him, bringing us breathlessly to the ground. I heard my victim cry out beneath me, his hands reaching for my throat. I batted them away and drove my thumbs deep into his eyes.

His screams satisfied a primal part of me I didn't know existed.

His face squirt thick gouts of blood as I rolled off the blind man. I got to my knees and punched him in the throat until he stopped moving, my fist numbing in the process.

Suddenly, something hard thudded into my ribs, bringing a howl of pain to my lips. Now on my back, I looked up just in time to dive away as a club came thundering down into the dirt where I had been.

I scrambled to my feet, catching a glimpse of Peter locked into brutal combat, circling a Suicidal. The man who had taken my ax to the head was on his knees, still recovering, hands clutching an angry red spot on his skull. The fourth faced me, brandishing his club for another blow.

I jumped back as my attacker tried to end me, his club reaching for my face. My back struck a tree as the nose of the club kissed the tip of mine. I blinked and the man was swinging again. I ducked and heard the tree take the blow, bark exploding around me. I brought my fist up with all my weight behind it, connecting with the man's chin. I heard his teeth clank together and he stepped back, momentarily stunned.

I stepped towards him and head butt his nose, bringing fresh screams and pouring blood. He waved his hands at me, backing up further, desperately trying to recover.

I stooped and recovered my ax, the handle slick with blood. Gritting my teeth, I swung it into the man's stomach. The blade sank into the Suicidal's guts like warm pudding and I heard him gasp as his insides were pulverized.

I ripped the blade free, bringing with it chunks of meat. Snarling, I buried the wet blade into the side of his neck, ending his life with a sickening thunk!

Before I had a chance to catch my breath, something exploded into me, taking me to the ground. I cried out in pain as a rock crunched into my side, the agony heightened as someone fell on top of me.

I punched out, realizing it was the man who I had dazed. His hands found my throat and he positioned himself over me. He began to squeeze, his fingers like a vice grip. My eyes bulged and I suddenly found I didn't have any oxygen.

My hands reached to claw at his face, drawing long red lines in his skin, but he never stopped squeezing. A vengeful smile lined his lips, his eyes like hot fire. Darkness began to swirl across my vision as I desperately fought to get him off me.

Suddenly, the man's grinning face was flying through the air away from me. Blood gurgled like a waterfall onto my face as the headless stump vomited gore. The now lifeless hands lessened their grip and slid off my throat.

I pushed the headless body off me, sputtering and gasping for air. I wiped my eyes and sat up to see Peter leaning over me. His hands were on his knees, his face a battered, bloody mess.

His machete dripped hungrily from his hands. "You ok?" he asked, sucking in lungfuls of air.

I coughed violently and rubbed my throat. I looked behind Peter and saw the last Suicidal, dead and motionless. The forest was silent.

We had survived.

I lay back down, exhaling. Jesus Christ…what the *fuck*…

I realized my hands were shaking and I squeezed them into fists.

"Nick?"

I closed my eyes. "I'm here....I'm here."

9

My side burned as we pushed on through the forest. Anthony and William were silent behind me, still stinging from the verbal onslaught Peter had delivered after our skirmish. I let them wallow in their self-pity. Those two pussies had almost watched me die while they pissed themselves. Pathetic.

Peter had given me a bandage from his pack that I wrapped around my bloody ribs. Thankfully the skin had barely broken, despite the nasty bruising. I pressed my hand against the wrap, exhaling through my teeth. It sure made walking painful.

As we marched through the miles of silent woods, I found myself thinking about what I had done. More specifically, about the voice that had spoken to me from the back of my mind. That cold, violent voice. After the blood had dried, it retreated back to wherever it had come from, leaving me stunned at the ease in which I had murdered the Suicidals.

You're surviving; you did what you had to, I thought. *Aren't you tired of being a victim? Not just of others, but of the restraints put on you by moral decency? This place is different. The rules are different. There are no repercussions for what you did.*

Murder without accountability. The thought was terrifying…and disturbingly wonderful. I was in a place where the strongest sat on the throne. I was in a world where brute force was the only police. If I didn't like something, I had the freedom to eliminate it.

And that's exactly what I had done.

I realized I was smiling.

Whatever you are, feel free to come back, I urged, sending the thought deep into my recesses of my mind.

I never left, Nick.

I adjusted the ax on my shoulder and hurried after Peter, now a couple dozen paces in front of us and urging speed. We were close to exiting the forest.

And then we'd reach The Barn. I realized I didn't know what to expect once we got there, what was expected of me. The thought of being in the same room as The Pig sent worms of unease squirming in my stomach. The Pig: the creator of all this suffering and violence, the head of this infectious, rotting corpse of a place. The mouth that breathed hideous life into the Pig Born and set them free to torment us, the Suicidals.

And you're going to pledge your allegiance to it.

I shook my head. No, I was doing whatever I had to in order to save Jess. Convince the Hooves of the Pig that I was one of them, gain access to the basement, and pray I could get her out of there…if that's indeed where she was.

What if she isn't?

I shook the thought off like clinging beads of poison. Why would Trent and Kevin lie? I had to believe them. I didn't really have a choice. I wondered if they were making progress on the raft. Did they really think the Black Farm ended beyond the ocean? And what if it did? Would they be able to make it past the Keepers?

They told you to return and join them once you find Jess.

I stepped over a log and thought hard about that. I was so focused on rescuing her that I hadn't given much thought on what I would do after. Were Trent and Kevin right? Was that the way out? Sail the black ocean to the ends of the horizon? What would we see?

It's not a bad option. It's not like you have another plan.

In truth, I didn't. We could run, hide away in the forest and hope the Pig Born left us alone. I snorted. Fat chance of that happening. It seemed like no matter what, they would find us, hungry to torment our existence. How long would we last in the forest? Hours? Days? We would eventually be caught and either be dragged away or murdered.

You can't die again once you find her.

The thought almost made me stop in my tracks. If I died I'd be reborn from the clouds somewhere else, possibly miles from her. And in that time, what if she was taken? I couldn't lose her again. I had to stay alive.

I tightened my grip around the ax.

Everything from this point on is an obstacle. Do what you have to. You've already been judged.

One of the old men behind me tripped and cursed, picking himself up from the foliage, and brushed off his dirty robes. Peter stopped and turned around. He sighed and came to us, putting a hand on my shoulder.

"We're almost through. Anthony, pull yourself together. You represent The Hooves of the Pig now."

"Sorry," Anthony mumbled, adjusting the cloth.

Peter shook his head. "Just keep your heads held high and mouths closed. When we get there, leave the talking to me unless instructed otherwise. And don't go into hysterics, we'll be surrounded by Pig Born. They know who we are, they see the robes you wear. They're not going to hurt you unless you give them a reason to. So stay smart."

We all nodded. Satisfied, Peter turned and we continued. It wasn't long before we broke the tree line, stepping out of the dense gloom into the rain. I pulled my hood up and forced myself to remain calm.

The Barn stood before us, an industrial behemoth. The smoke stacks rising from the roof carved the sky and vomited heavy lungfuls of thick black haze. Panels of steel patched the immense walls, stained with dirt and rust. Extending towards the heavens were the two monstrous creatures, the hairless snake-like worms that squirmed and slithered along the length of the ventilation towers.

As we crunched through the dead grass toward The Barn, I watched in disgusted fascination as one of the creatures lowered its bald, elongated human head and began to gag out a new Pig Born. The new life rolled from the jaws in a mess of slime and mucus. It crawled to its feet and let out a roar of elation.

Another monster to hunt us, I thought grimly.

Drawing closer, I looked to my right at the long concrete building I had first been contained in. The place I had been given my choice. Stay or feed The Pig. How many were in there right now being forced to make that same choice?

As we passed the faceless construction, I watched as a woman stumbled from the exit, her eyes wide and shaken. She looked like she was in her forties, a terrified expression creasing her worn face. Peter ignored her, leading us closer to The Barn.

Still walking, I turned my head and watched the woman sprint for the woods. A roar cracked the sky and I spun my head to see the newly created Pig Born charge her. The woman shrieked in terror, begging for help and scrambling for the tree line. She wasn't going to make it.

I suddenly had an itch to help her. I knew what she was going through right now...what she was about to be exposed to. Torment. Suffering. Death. Endless helplessness.

Not your problem, Nick. She made her choice, just like you.

"Dumb bitch," I muttered, turning my back to her screams as the Pig Born fell on her. The words immediately soured on my tongue and I winced at my own coldness.

Your humanity only holds you back from getting what you want. You had to learn that the hard way. No one saved you from Muck. No one rescued you as he slowly stripped all decency from your mind and body. Why should you save her from whatever choices led her here? Let her bleed. Jess is the only thing you can afford to care about. Destroy everything else.

The woman's screams soon escalated to quivering agony, but I let the rain wash it away. Why bother to be a good person here? Why hold on to morals and compassion? What good would that do me in this place? What good had it done while I was alive?

If you had shown more compassion to what Jess was going through after your son's death, maybe you wouldn't be here. Maybe if you cared as much for others as you did yourself, you'd still be alive.

I clenched my teeth.

"Jesus, make up your fucking mind," I muttered.

Ahead of me, Peter turned and cocked an eyebrow. I shook his inquiry away, adjusting my hood to shadow my face more.

We marched to the gates of The Barn, twin doors of immense size. Peter led our sorry party to the side where a smaller entrance awaited us, hidden by a swath of rust and grime. He pushed the door open and immediately I was hit by a blast of heat. I felt the two old men gasp behind me and I didn't blame them. It was sweltering and I slowly lowered my hood, looking around as Peter led us inside.

We were in a small antechamber filled with Pig Born who turned to stare at us with hungry eyes. The floors were coated with a layer of filth that stunk like the worst kind of decay, and the area was lit by low-hanging bulbs that swayed on naked strings a dozen feet overhead. Another pair of doors blocked our passage and Peter shuffled toward them. I huddled close to the other two in our party and heard my knuckles crack around my ax handle. The Pig Born leered at us, a gross ensemble of gurgling noise. Bloated tongues ran over broken teeth and mucus ran freely down contorted faces.

"They're going to kill us," one of the old men hissed fearfully.

"Shut up," I instructed, fear coiling in my gut. "Don't look at them, don't acknowledge them. Remember what Peter said. We wear the robes; they won't harm us." The words felt like a lie and I scraped them from my tongue.

"There's so many," the other hooded man whispered. "Oh god, this was a mistake."

I turned and shot him a hard look. "Just stay cool. If you go into hysterics, I don't think even Peter can save us."

As if summoned, Peter was suddenly before us, the Pig Born parting to idle in the corners of the room. I felt like I could breathe slightly easier.

"Ok, we're next," Peter said, face flushed. "Just be still and stay calm until we're allowed entrance."

"What's behind those doors?" I asked already knowing the answer.

Peter's eyes turned cold. "The Pig."

The two older men shared a look of pure fear. Peter rested a reassuring hand on their shoulders and leaned in, muttering words of strength to his soon-to-be Brothers. I stepped out of their circle and leaned against the wall, calming myself.

Suddenly I felt someone tap my shoulder. I turned and found myself staring at Danny.

"I really am getting sick of seeing your face," he said, extending a hand.

I looked down at it, "What, you suddenly want to be pals?"

He rolled his eyes, "The ax, jackass, give me your ax. No one goes to see The Pig armed. Not even me. Hand it over."

I gripped it protectively.

He sighed, "You'll get it back when you're done, fucker."

Reluctantly, I surrendered it to him. He turned and collected the rest of our parties weapons, hiding a sneer at their obvious fear. When he had taken everything, he went and dumped them in a box by the door. I made sure to note the location.

"Going to bend the knee today?" Danny asked, walking back to me. Peter and the other two were still huddled away from me in what I could only assume was prayer.

I focused back on Danny. "I have no problem pledging my allegiance to The Pig."

Danny threw his head back and let out a cackle, "Yeah, right! How long do you think they'll buy into your bullshit? Huh?"

I shot a look at Peter to make sure he was out of earshot, then back at Danny. "Oh Jesus, not this again. Why do you have such a problem with me going through with this?"

"Because there's just something about you that I fucking loathe, Nick."

I crossed my arms, unfazed. "Yeah, we've been over this.

Well, let me tell you something, Danny, because I'm getting sick of your mouth."

Danny stepped closer, almost nose to nose now, "Oh yeah? And what's that, tough guy?"

"You're afraid of something," I whispered.

Danny didn't move. "What do I have to fear? I own this fucking shit hole."

My eyes narrowed, "Really? Do you own the Eyes of the World?"

His reaction was immediate. Danny stepped away from me, his face a blanket of shock.

He blinked and then quickly tried to mask his surprise, shaking his head and forcing a smile back onto his lips.

"You have no idea what you're talking about."

I advanced. "Well, why don't you enlighten me then. You sure seem to know what I'm talking about, judging by the way you almost tripped over yourself just now."

Danny jabbed a finger in my face, growing hostile. "Leave it alone. Do not talk to me or anyone else here about that shit. Do you understand? Fuck, what am I worried about? You don't even know what you're saying."

I grinned, "I know that it comes from the mountain. I've seen the lights. What are they?"

Before Danny could answer, a scream erupted from the other side of the doors. It sounded male, but it was pitched so high it was hard to tell. I felt my mouth grow dry as the shriek continued, a belting howl of absolute agony.

The anger melted from Danny's face and he smiled at me, a cold, slimy twist of the lips, "Oooooh...sounds like someone is feeding The Pig."

An icicle of sweat formed along my spine. "What the hell..."

The screams continued, slightly muffled but in obvious anguish. Peter and the other two had their eyes closed as silent offerings fluttered from their lips. They were clearly shaken and I felt the same terror roll through me as well. I had never heard another human being make such awful sounds.

And it kept going...and going...

Danny just watched me, that sick smile still staining his face. "Pretty unsettling, isn't it? Trust me, once you've heard it a couple times, it loses its impact."

I said nothing, trying my best to mentally block out the shrieking. I could tell it was getting to me, worming its way deep inside my mind. It reminded me of the way I had screamed when Muck raped me.

Mercifully, the screams were suddenly cut short and I shivered with relief. I realized I had been holding my breath and I let it out like air from a balloon.

Danny placed a hand on my shoulder. "You ok?"

I shrugged him away, disgusted by his touch. "Let's just get on with this, yeah?"

Danny smirked and motioned to the Pig Born in the corners of the room. They all looked at him as one and he waved them to go inside. Grunting, they obeyed, pushing the twin doors open and disappearing beyond them.

"Clean up duty," Danny said casually. "Sometimes The Pig makes a mess. And it doesn't like that."

Peter approached us, head bowed and hands folded. "Hello, Danny. Are we almost ready?"

Danny rolled his eyes. "Everyone is so impatient today. Yes, give them a minute."

I curled my hands into fists and then released them, the

repetition forcing my nervous energy into action. I had no idea what I was walking into, what this ceremony of allegiance entailed. I just wanted to get it over with and get back to the Temple where Jess hopefully awaited rescue. A very small part of me itched to retrieve my ax and see how many of these bastards I could lay waste to until I was cut down. I shook the lingering thought from my mind and reminded myself that I had a plan to stick to. Still, I hated the waiting. Possible scenarios and horrors ran through my mind unchecked and I concentrated on shutting them out and squeezing my fists.

Danny took notice and snorted, "Jesus, *relax.*"

"First time meeting a godly entity," I said, trying to ignore him. I could hear something massive shifting its weight behind the doors, thunder striking concrete that sent shock waves through my legs.

The two old men were lost in prayer, great beads of sweat rolling down their faces in nervous terror. A muffled squeal echoed beyond the walls, something animalistic and undeniably not human.

"Doesn't sound too happy," Danny mused, "must not have enjoyed their taste."

"What do you mean?" I asked against my better judgment.

"I think The Pig just sent some poor bastard to Hell," Danny grinned, teeth shining.

I exhaled slowly and squeezed my fingers into fists, focusing on the slight pain my nails caused as they dug into my skin.

"Who's in there with The Pig?" I finally asked, breaking the silence. "I thought you were in charge of the new Suicidals?"

Danny nodded, "I am. But there's a lot of you fuckers. You really think I do this alone? Shit, I see a lot of you assholes, but I can't get to everyone. I have help."

"Who?"

Danny shot a look at Peter who cast his eyes to the floor. "Members of the cult you're about to join. High ranking members who have shown their loyalty to The Pig. True loyalty."

I didn't like the way he said the last part and I quickly followed Peter's gaze to the floor. The last thing I needed was for him to catch on that I was bullshitting this whole thing. Even a seed of doubt could make things incredibly difficult and I mentally ripped Danny's tongue from his mouth.

I jumped as the doors opened with a loud creak and the Pig Born filed out, eerily silent. They went and stood back in the corners of the room, not looking at anything and remaining oddly still.

They're terrified, I realized. *Scared shitless of their own maker.*

Danny waved an arm at us towards the open doors. "Shall we?"

Trembling, the two old men linked hands and offered me one which I ignored. Peter nodded to the three of us and turned to Danny.

"Let us begin."

Danny walked us through the doors and I heard them close behind us as we entered the room.

Immediately, my breath was robbed from my lungs and replaced by a choking heat that threatened to sear the inside of my throat. I coughed and blinked in the haze, raising my eyes to the scene before us.

I felt my bladder tighten as the room swam into focus beneath the thick humidity. Twin furnaces blazed in the far corners of the room, roaring infernos that licked between coal black grates. A heavy smoke billowed out of the great iron contraptions and rose toward a ceiling high overhead that was hidden beneath a layer of swirling darkness.

But my eyes barely registered that, as they instead fell upon the sight in front of us.

The Pig.

It was titanic in size, an enormous mass of rolling flesh that loomed before us like a living, breathing nightmare. Its head was the size of a bus, its jaws cracking around teeth the size of steak knives. Its eyes met our own, twin black pits of ebony ink. Fresh blood leaked from its chin and dripped onto the floor, licked quickly by a long, gore-stained tongue that shot from its mouth like a skinned serpent.

It stomped in place, an impatient gesture that sent an earthquake through my feet and up my legs.

I explored its body with bloodshot eyes and saw something growing out of its ribs. Jutting from either side of its ribcage were fleshy tubes that extended outward towards the walls of The Barn. They pulsed and shook with life and I shuddered as something moved from inside one of the long coils, slowly pushing toward the walls.

The sheer disgust of what I was seeing paralyzed me and it took me a second to realize that the skin tubes disappeared out of the walls and grew past my line of sight. As I stared, I felt pieces starting to come together in my mind.

Jesus Christ, those two snake-like creatures wrapped around the smokestacks outside are part of The Pig!

As the fog of fear continued to clog my mind, I suddenly noticed something moving on either side of The Pig's colossal head. I choked back a scream as I realized there were two massive Pig Born standing next to the Pig. They were a dozen feet tall, their charred flesh covered in scabs and infected scars.

Their heads were covered by sacks of bloody skin, a draping veil hiding their features from view. Twisted, knotted muscle lined their deformed shoulders and I saw that each of them held a crude strip of iron as tall as they were, sharpened to a deadly point at the tip.

Suddenly, Danny was stepping forward, his head bowed in reverence, his voice booming but respectful. "I have brought another eager group who wishes to join your herd. Will you allow them to swear their lives to you? Will you grant them the honor of shaping their existence to parallel your perfect vision?"

The Pig stared at us for a long moment, its eyes boring into each and every one of us. As it appraised me, I felt a knot form in my stomach and a fear took hold of me so great that it took everything in my power to remain standing. Under its gaze, I suddenly was acutely aware of every imperfection in myself, a razor sharp point that pierced every flaw: the taste of stale sweat lining my tongue, the coat of dirt that plastered my skin, the grease tangling my hair, the grime beneath my fingernails, everything that made me disgusting in that moment.

Slowly, the Pig lowered its head.

Face grim, Danny bowed once again and motioned for Peter and the rest of us to come stand with him before The Pig. Knees knocking together, I approached, feeling my companions at my sides. Judging from the smell, it appeared as if one of them had pissed himself.

Danny walked behind us and gently placed a hand on our shoulders, instructing us to kneel. As his hand brushed the nape of my neck, I got down and joined the others. Sweat dripped from the mess of hair hanging over my eyes, the heat in the chamber threatening to suffocate me. The Pig's snout was only a couple feet in front of us and I forced my gag reflex under control as it blasted us with blinding heat, its breath rolling over our skin like hot garbage.

"Are you three ready to pledge your existence to the will of The Pig?" Danny asked quietly from behind my shoulder. The two old men were sniveling in fear and Peter hushed them urgently into silence. I focused on breathing through my nose, The Pig's dripping snout swaying before us.

"I am," I said as loudly as I could, keeping my eyes trained on the filthy floor.

"I am," the other two said in unison, their voices cracking.

"Then repeat after me," Danny recited. "I have come from nothing, and I seek reformation."

"I have come from nothing, and seek reformation," We echoed. My heart was throwing itself against my chest, sweat streaking down my dirty face. Here we go.

"My body and mind are broken and shapeless, and I beg on bended knee to be molded into the form best suited to serve," Danny continued. We repeated his words, The Pig watching us silently.

"I wish to become a pillar on which to carry the world. Brand and bathe me in the desires of my God, and accept my fragile state so that I may become a Hoof of the Pig."

As we repeated the words, one of the Pig Born giants moved in front of us, its flesh sack swaying over its face.

I heard Danny take a step back. "Accept the will of The Pig, and let its eternal power wash away any doubt or fear you hold."

"We accept," the three of us said weakly.

The Pig Born raised its iron weapon as The Pig slowly opened its mouth. Unable to stop myself, I looked up, fear a heavy drum in my chest. The Pig Born inserted the makeshift spear into The Pig's mouth and pushed it down its throat.

The Pig stomped its hooves and cannon fire rocked my ears as its dark eyes bulged. Suddenly, with a horrific squeal, The Pig lurched, its body jerking as a spasm rocketed through it. I had only a moment to slam my mouth shut as a wave of hot vomit exploded from the open maw of The Pig and splashed over the four of us.

Immediately, my gag reflex went into overdrive as the warm bile gushed over my face and ran across my chest. The smell was beyond anything I had ever suffered, an acidic rot that dripped of death and decay. I opened my eyes and stared down at myself, the brown sludge swirling with bits of gore from its previous meal. A severed finger slid down my shoulder and plopped onto the floor with a sickening splat.

My stomach rolled and I bit my tongue to keep it in check. Waves of heat emanated from the discharge, warming my skin like a gore-soaked rain. At my side, one of the old men cried out, falling forward on his hands.

He gagged once, twice, then heaved his guts up onto the floor, body going into repulsed spasms.

Without explanation or warning, the tall Pig Born stepped forward and slammed his spear down into the back of his head, killing him instantly.

I felt a bolt of shocked horror rip through me as blood gushed from his head, the spear pulled away with a sickening jerk. The back of his skull was obliterated and I watched as his brains oozed out onto the floor in a wave of sticky gore and bone.

"He was not able to accept the gift," Danny said quietly behind us. "And so he has been cast out, back into the herd."

The Pig had shut its mouth and stood to watch the rest of us, exhaling loudly through its nostrils. Between the stink of its breath and the vomit soaking my body, it took every ounce of willpower to keep gallons of bile out of my mouth. I squeezed my eyes shut, body shivering despite the heat, and focused on settling my revolting stomach.

The old man next to me was crying, but he managed to get himself under control after a few seconds, his murdered comrade motionless before us. I shot a sidelong glance at Peter and saw his face pale, his mouth a grim line. He had been through this before. He knew what would happen. Why hadn't he warned us?

You're being tested.

I turned away as the second massive Pig Born stepped forward and stabbed the corpse with its spear. Effortlessly, it lifted his corpse up and walked it to one of the blazing furnaces where it flicked the flesh inside. The flames roared and accepted the fuel gratefully.

I looked up, waiting to see what would happen next and found myself staring directly into The Pig's eyes.

The blood drained from my face and I felt as if something sharp was boring into my eyes, but I couldn't turn away. The Pig held my gaze, its inky eyes two wells of eternal darkness.

And I saw a malicious intelligence in them.

It was in that moment that I realized something.

This was not a mere animal, despite its appearance.

"Stand," Danny instructed and I felt a hand under my arm pulling me up. My legs almost gave out as I stretched them, the muscles turning to liquid. I placed my hands on my thighs, rubbing life back into them.

"You have accepted the offering, you have been washed in

the desires of your god. Let us go forth and conform our lives to its will," Danny said. "Do you so accept?"

"I do," we mumbled, strands of blood and vomit trailing down our bodies.

"Then it is finished," Danny said, "let us depart."

Without thinking, I lowered my head and bowed to The Pig. It snorted loudly and then we were leaving, a stunned silence clinging to our minds.

As we wordlessly exited the chamber and pushed through the doors back outside into the rain, a single thought wormed its way forward.

You're never getting out of here.

10

None of us spoke much on the way back to the Temple. What we had just witnessed was still ringing in our ears and rattling around our disturbed minds. Even Peter was quiet. The rain washed the vomit and blood from my face as we trudged toward the forest. The Black Farm was eerily silent. I adjusted the ax on my shoulder, grateful to have it back in my hands. Behind us, The Barn shrank, the two coiled monstrosities on the smokestacks watching us with still eyes.

The trees and heavy canopy of green grew before us and we crunched through the underbrush, wading into the belly of the woods. My robe stank, but I was grateful that most of the gore had been erased. I lowered my hood.

"How are you doing, William?" I asked the old man beside me.

He looked at me with bloodshot eyes, "Anthony. I'm Anthony."

I shut my mouth and decided to return to the miserable silence. My iron will and determination had been shaken, a brutal reminder of the hell I was in. How could I possibly hope to overcome such awful odds? I realized that eliminating a couple Pig Born and Suicidals didn't make me invincible, despite how I had felt. I was just one man against an entire world of snarling violence, just waiting for an opportunity to hurt me.

I moved past Anthony and walked to Peter's side.

"Can I talk to you?" I asked quietly, stepping across a snaggle of thorns.

"Sure," he responded, his voice empty of emotion.

"Why did you do that with us?"

"What do you mean?" he asked turning.

"You've already been through that; you've already passed your test. You didn't have to partake, you could have simply watched from the side. So why go through that again? This was our initiation, not yours."

Peter let out a long breath, "I've been doing this for a long time now. I've seen many new recruits go through that. And each time I get down with them, bend my knee right alongside them. I hope that one day, Danny or The Pig will take notice of my constant servitude and dedication. I want to join them at The Barn, permanently."

"Why?"

"I want to rise. I want to help Danny usher in the new Suicidals like my brothers before me have. To be able to witness the birth into this world...in my eyes, there is no greater thing."

I stepped around a tree and turned back to Peter. "What about what you do at the Temple? Breeding Pig Born and humans? Isn't that what you're all about? Isn't that the point of our servitude? To be able to witness the fusion of human and pig?"

Peter sighed, "Yes, of course, and that's a wonderful thing. It is a great honor to be able to be a part of that. The ones that live and grow are a wonderful, beautiful tribute to The Pig. But my heart lies elsewhere. I've been at the Temple long enough that I seek out new ways to contribute to the Black Farm."

I didn't say anything for a little bit, letting the drizzle of rain fill the void. After a moment, I decided to press my luck.

"Do you think I can see it?" I asked.

Peter looked at me, confused, "See what?"

I lowered my voice so that Anthony wouldn't hear. "I want to see the consummation."

I could see Peter turning the idea over in his mind before he answered cautiously, "I don't know, Nick. That's reserved for members only. Just because you passed this trial doesn't mean you're fully one of us yet. I told Ryder I'd inform him when you're ready. This is just too soon."

I could feel impatience bubbling in my stomach and I forced it down, trying to placate Peter instead. "Yeah, I understand that; I do. But, I just want to watch. I know I still have a long way to go before I'm a true Hoof of the Pig. I think I've earned that, no? Without me, we'd all be dead. Those Suicidals that attacked us, I helped you kill them. Anthony and William were useless. If I hadn't stepped up, our corpses would be rotting in these woods."

Peter sniffed, "You got a point there."

"Please," I begged, "I'm not asking for much. Just let me watch the next time they breed."

Peter exhaled heavily and pushed a low hanging branch out of our way, "All right. But don't go telling anyone about this. The other recruits would not be happy."

I tried to suppress the elation I felt. "Thank you."

Peter's voice turned hard, "I'm warning you though, Nick. Just sit in the back and watch. Don't talk, don't even breathe. Once the ritual is complete, you go back to your chambers and tell no one. I'll let the other members know you've earned a viewing."

I drew my fingers over my chest. "Cross my heart."

Peter looked back at Anthony. "Actually, there's going to be a breeding soon. When we get back, change out of your robes and meet me by the basement stairs."

I nodded. "Ok."

We trekked on, falling back into silence. The woods became a continuous, unchanging blur of dripping oak and tangled brush. Anthony remained silent throughout. I almost felt bad for him. The events behind us had clearly shaken him to the core. I felt it, too; the echoes of the actions we had witness vibrated behind my mind's eye. I kept it there though, refusing to let it cloud or falter my step. I focused on putting one foot in front of the other, my destination before me, my mission unchanged.

Eventually, we emerged from the forest and crossed over to the other side. The mountain towered in the distance, its eerie splendor only matched by the dead, broken sun hanging in the sky. The grass crunched underfoot as we made our way back towards the temple, a cautious eye cast up at the dripping crimson tears in the clouds. Only once did we spot a handful of Pig Born but they kept their distance, making their way for the Needle Fields.

Finally, after what seemed like an eternity, we reached the temple. I was almost glad. We walked up the stone steps and under the stone pig head above, the rain water gushing over us as we crossed the threshold.

Peter pushed the doors open and a thick silence greeted us. I scrubbed moisture from my face as Anthony shuffled past me and quickly retreated to his chambers, his eyes reflecting the ghost of his lost friend.

I watched him go and then turned to the sanctuary. I paused, unaware that it was mostly full, the pews lined with kneeling Hooves. Their eyes were downcast, their hands clasped in reverence. At the head of the chamber, standing on top of the altar was a creature unlike any I had ever seen.

It stood about three feet high, its form standing on two human feet. Its eyes shined with intelligence, two black pits sunk deep into a pale skull. Its skin was white, shockingly so. A snout jutted from its face but ended abruptly. I realized that the lower half of the face was pig-like, almost as if it was wearing a mask from the eyes down. A shock of black hair tumbled into its eyes and the creature snorted at me, a blast of mucus misting in the air. It raised its hands towards the ceiling and I saw that its arms ended in hooves.

Peter closed the doors and then turned, his eyes meeting the creatures. Immediately, he dropped to his knees and pulled me down by his side.

"Show some respect," he hissed. "That's a Son of the Swine."

I lowered my head. "What? What is that?"

"That's one of the cross breeds that has survived the birthing. It's one of two that have lived past its first birthday. The Hooves are holding Adoration," Peter said quietly.

I chanced a look up and saw the creature frozen in place, arms still stretched toward the ceiling. It was completely naked and its human feet remained planted on the altar, something completely inhuman swinging between its legs. I turned away.

"This is what we breed here?" I asked quietly.

Peter gave a curt nod. "This is the next step in evolution. This is how we purify the human failings of our race."

I swallowed hard, completely disgusted by the monster before us. The congregation remained rooted in their pews, complete adoration emanating from each one of them.

These freaks actually looked up to this abomination.

"It's beautiful," I lied.

Peter murmured his approval and then leaned into my ear. "Go change. Meet me back here in a couple minutes. They're preparing for another breeding. I'm going to go report our trip to Ryder. By the time you're back, we'll all be downstairs."

I quickly got up and scurried for the hallway, doing my best to remain quiet. I slipped down a corridor and began to navigate back to my room. My ax clinked against the stone floor and I jumped, having completely forgotten I still held it. It was beginning to feel like an extension of my body.

I finally found my room and pushed inside, stripping the stinking robe off and throwing it into the corner. I looked for another, but the room offered none. I adjusted my shirt to make sure none of the vomit had soaked through, and when I was satisfied, I walked over to the small desk in the corner. Someone had left a bowl of water on it and I gratefully lowered my head and slurped half of it down. Sighing, I then splashed the remainder over my face, ridding my skin of the clinging filth. The water dripped back into the bowl, a filthy concoction that I stared at in disgust.

I paused suddenly, catching my reflection in the rippling water.

"You're not looking too hot, Nick," I said quietly, gazing into the gaunt face that glared back.

You're almost there.

I laughed. "Almost *where*?"

The water stilled and I backed away, retrieving my ax from

the bed. It was time. If Jess was here, she'd be in the basement. I didn't want to think about if she wasn't.

Taking a deep breath, I prepared myself.

"Here we go."

I left my room and began making my way back to the sanctuary. I tried my best to suppress the surfacing worries and doubts that were now arriving in mass quantities. I tightened my grip around the ax at my side.

I was slightly surprised no one had relieved me of it. The Hooves were either immensely stupid or immensely confident. I hoped it was the former. If they wanted to take it from me, they were going to have to ask. Until then, it stayed in my hands at all times.

The passageways were quiet and I only passed a single person walking the other way, his hood drawn low. He didn't even look at me as I pressed forward, twisting back the way I had come.

When I eventually reached the pew-filled room, I was grateful to see that it had emptied. The altar stood vacant of the cross-breed monster. I knew where they had all gone.

I walked to the basement stairs and peered down into the darkness, the sharp corner halfway down revealing nothing of what waited below.

Gritting my teeth, I descended.

As my feet echoed down the steps, I began to hear a noise. It was distant at first, but as I rounded the corner, it grew louder. It sounded like chanting.

Bowls of fire hung from the ceiling, casting shadows across the dim depths. As I delved further downward, the stone walls pressed in tight and I fought against a growing sense of claustrophobia.

Finally, I reached the bottom and my boots kicked up dirt as I walked into a large open room with a low ceiling. Pillars of stone rose from the earth and I booted a pebble ahead of me. I could see a mass of Hooves toward the end of the long room, a cluster of robes and drawn hoods. They were sitting down on the bare floor, their backs to me.

I cautiously approached, searching for Peter. As I got closer, I spotted dark holes in the walls, crude passageways that disappeared deeper into the Temple. I could only imagine the horrific secrets that waited at the end of them.

I was about a dozen yards from the Hooves when I froze, the state of their stillness now apparent. They were watching something.

I slid to hide against a stone pillar, heart accelerating.

A single Pig Born stood before the collection of people, a fat behemoth of incredible weight. His stomach sagged over his nakedness, a drooping deluge of pale, scabbed flesh. Its face was twisted and broken, teeth jutting from a broken jaw, tongue lapping at cracked lips. Its eyes rolled in its head, breath coming out in panting gasps. But it didn't move. It just stood there, before the others, waiting for something.

A scream suddenly echoed from one of the dark passageways behind the Pig Born, bouncing off the stone walls and filling the space.

The Hooves of the Pig stirred, an air of excitement sparking between them.

Another scream followed.

It sounded female.

I wiped sweat from my brow and tried to calm myself as the scream grew louder, now accompanied by a rattle of chains.

The Pig Born stamped its feet in excited anticipation and I felt my stomach plummet.

A hooded man emerged from the passageway, a long chain in his hands vanishing into the black behind him. He gave it a sharp tug and I heard a cry of pain from inside. The man reeled in the coiling iron and after a moment, two shackled women exited the hole in the wall.

They were naked and filthy, their shivering bodies trembling beneath the crackle of fire overhead. Tears filled their eyes and horror swelled across their faces as they saw the Pig Born waiting from them.

The first woman was in her fifties, a tussle of gray hair cut short across her scalp. She was bleeding from the nose and she sobbed, covering herself in shame and fear. The man holding the chain jerked her forward and she cried out, almost falling. The second woman caught her and put a hand on her arm, their eyes meeting.

My heart stopped and all sound drained from the room.

The second woman…was Jess.

I slammed my hand over my mouth to stifle the call rising in my throat, tears jumping from my eyes at the sight of her. My knees melted and I heard the ax fall by my side.

Jess looked like absolute hell. Her blond hair was a snarl of filth and her face shined black and blue along one of her cheeks. Dried blood coated her right arm and her left thigh sported a long cut that wrapped itself around her body. Her skin was pale and gaunt and she struggled to stay standing, the chains around her wrists so tight they drew blood.

It was really her…Jess…my sweet Jess.

I felt like I was standing on an island opposite her, the world stripped away to leave nothing but her image before me. Every drop of blood, sweat, and grime staining her skin consumed me, every detail and strand of hair, every breath she took was like a gale that blew heavy across my soaring heart.

Look at what they've done to her. Look at what they've done to the woman you love.

Murder rose inside of me like a demon, a brutal rage that roared like furious hell. My hands balled into fists and I began to shake with the violence screaming inside of me. Sweat dripped from my nose and my teeth screeched against one another as I ground them, jaw popping.

Get. Her. Out. Of. Here.

The hooded man holding the end of the chain was circling Jess and the other woman, the crowd in front of me beginning to murmur their approval. The Pig Born stomped its feet once again and jiggled its dangling cock at them, its passion growing.

Stop this. You have to stop this.

But what the hell was I supposed to do? If I charged in screaming, ax raised, I'd be cut down in seconds. I tapped my fingers against my thigh in a frenzied panic, knowing my time was growing short.

"Fuck," I hissed, maddeningly frustrated, emotions bleeding uncontrollably.

You need a distraction. You have to get them out of the basement.

My eyes roamed the basement as the herd before me began to chant again, the sexual energy rising. My mind threw every possible option across my unsteady judgment, and I countered each with how long I would live if put into action.

And then an idea popped into my mind and I seized it with desperate certainty. I stooped down and retrieved my ax, casting a look at the crowd. The Pig Born was approaching the first woman, running its ruined fingers through her hair, snot and pus leaking from its face. The Hooves were riling it up.

"I'll be right back," I whispered to Jess, never taking my eyes from her shivering body. "Wait for me just a moment longer. I'll get you out of here."

I turned and ran back to the stairs, my heart crashing into my chest like the tick of a clock. I took the steps two at a time, my ax clinking against the stone. Everything had been stripped away once I saw Jess. It was now or never. She was all that mattered.

I reached the top and spun around in the sanctuary, raking my memory for the correct hallway. After a second, I bolted toward one that looked familiar, passing a startled Hoof. As I ran down the passageway, I saw him turn, lowering his hood and eying me cautiously.

They were all supposed to be downstairs. Oh well, it's too late now, I thought, ripping around another corner and spotting the door I had been looking for.

I reached it and allowed myself a single second to breathe. Then I put my boot through the wood, knocking the flimsy door off its hinges.

"Nick!"

I entered the room, dark death hanging above my shoulders like wings. "Hello, Ryder."

His naked mass was just as offensive as I remembered. He shifted his bulk on the bed, propping his drooping stomach up; his flabby back made the headboard creak. The bowl of fire overhead spit shadows over my face as I walked to him, knuckles white against the handle of my ax.

Megan was still chained to his bedside, her arm now completely flayed to the bone, all the way down to her fingers. She looked completely comatose, her skin a sickly white, dried blood pooling the floor where she sat.

She slowly raised her eyes to look up at me, squinting in pain. For a moment, she didn't recognize me, then something like surprise rose to the surface.

"N-Nick?" She asked so quietly I thought I imagined it.

"What is all this about? What are you doing here?" Ryder demanded, his fat face twisting like a squished doughnut.

I stomped to the bed and shoved the head of my ax into Ryder's face, the blade inches from his upturned nose, my voice dripping with vengeance. "Keep your fucking mouth shut, you goddamn pig."

Flustered by my aggression, he snorted, "Listen, I don't know who you think you are, but-"

I pressed the blunt end of the blade into his face, my voice grating like steel. "Open your mouth again and I'll gut-fuck you with this ax."

His mouth dropped open and I knelt down and stared into Megan's eyes, sympathy leaking from my own. This poor woman. What hell had she endured in this room?

"Kill...me..." she begged, voice cracking with effort, "release me...back into the Farm."

I stared at her for another second and then gave a quick nod, "Stay safe."

I raised my axe and swung it into her neck as hard as I could. Megan's expression never changed as the blade severed her head, spraying my knees with a gout of blood.

"No!" Ryder yelled, jerking the chains that had held her. "What have you done?!"

I exhaled thoughts of Megan and inhaled the image of Jess, waiting below. I turned to Ryder, a snarl twisting my lips.

"This nightmare ends today," I growled, "the Temple, the Hooves, and most importantly..." I leaned into him, "You."

Ryder's eyes went wide with shock. "You can't do that! Think about what you're saying! Think of all this place has given you!" his tongue slithered between his lips like an obese worm. "What do you want, Nick? Tell me and it's yours."

I raised the ax over my head, "I want you dead."

He extended his stubby arms to me, panic bleeding into his face. "No! No, we can help each other! Together we can build this Temple into—"

I slammed the blade of the ax into his stomach.

His screams shook the walls and I grinned, ripping the sharp edge toward me and opening up his heaving mass. Coils of gore spilled onto the floor followed by a waterfall of blood, Ryder's face contorted in shocked agony.

I plowed the ax back into his exposed guts, a sickly squishing noise bringing with it a splash of blood that fell like rain on my face.

"You're a big boy," I cackled, "this could take a while." I hacked into his stomach again, further separating the flesh. Ryder began to shake, his cries warming my heart with deathly intention.

I slammed the blade deep into his splitting stomach, feeling something important rupture beneath its sharp bite. More blood soaked my arms and face and I grinned around it, the red staining my teeth.

"Lucky for you," I said panting, jerking the blade free to another scream, "I don't have all day to kill you."

Ryder's eyes rolled in his head, lost in pain, blood leaking from the corners of his mouth. His bulk quivered on the bed like a bowl of trembling lard, splattering the carnage against the walls.

I lifted my ax above my head and hooked the blade around the bowl of fire hanging over the bed. Slowly, I pulled it down and watched as the burning oil fell, splashing with a flare of heat into Ryder's open stomach and across the floor.

Immediately, his pounds of fat began to sizzle, encouraged by the blazing oil. I had turned his body into a human fire pit, and I stepped back and watched him burn. His howls of agony reached a new level as he tried to swat out the hungry flames, but he couldn't reach across his rolling bulk.

"Looks like it's back to square one for you," I said. I was counting on his screams, counting on his bulk to burn and spread, the flames licking at the bed frame and across the floor.

I turned to leave and froze. The man I had brushed past earlier was standing in the doorway, mouth open in horrific shock.

I stared at him, unmoving, my ax resting loosely in my hands.

"W-what have you done?" he asked, paralyzed by the sight of me.

I gave him a smile, the one with the edges, as blood dripped from my face. "Come on, come get yours, cunt."

He took a step back, despite Ryder's dying screams, conflicting impulses written plainly across his face.

I threw my ax at him with all my might. The head struck him in the shoulder and he let out a cry of pain, fumbling against the wall of the hallway. I didn't give him any time to recover. I sprang forward and gripped his face in my palm, slamming the back of his head against the hard stone.

I heard a satisfying crunch, and then he was falling to the floor, leaving behind a streak of red.

I steadied myself and wiped a handful of blood from my face. I could taste it on my tongue, smelled it with every pant of breath. I scooped up my axe, Ryder's screams still roaring behind me.

Time to see if they'd take the bait.

I bolted down the hall back to the basement, upturning every bowl of fire I came across. Even as I reached the stairs, I could still hear the howls of my violent work. I thundered down the stone decline and raced into the gloomy depths of the Temple, wiping blood from my face.

I jumped the last step, hiding my ax behind my leg, the Hooves still splayed out before me, "Stop! Stop everything!"

In unison, the crowd turned, and I spotted Peter's flaring eyes in the mass. The Pig Born had the first woman against the wall, one gnarled hand between her legs. It appraised me viciously, infuriated that I had halted its sexual feast.

I pointed toward the stairs, yelling, "It's Ryder! There's someone in his room killing him! We have to go stop them! Let's GO! NOW!"

Confused rippled through them, and a few stood, shock painting their faces. They looked at one another, lowering their hoods, murmurs snaking between them.

"He's fucking DYING!" I screamed, motioning them forward, "Come ON!"

Peter pushed through the crowd, a sudden urgency in his step, "Follow me everyone, let's see who dare defiles our temple!"

A roar of anger rose from the Hooves and they charged the stairs, a worried desperation shaking away any lingering doubt.

They quickly filed up the stairs, each one eager to be the first to put down the attacker. I knew that each one of them probably saw it as an opportunity to rise in standing, a showcase of dedication to their precious religion. They would be a hero.

As they poured past me, I smiled internally, pressing my bloodied axe against the back of my leg, hiding it in the low light. They thundered up the stairs, Ryder's screams now audible. It fueled the mob mentality, bringing a roar of concern.

A cloud of dirt and dust was all that remained of them, the basement empty. I heard the crash of feet upstairs and I quickly turned to the Pig Born and two women. Jess was on her knees, crying in the corner, lost in the madness of her surroundings. The other one was frozen in place, pinned to the wall by the Pig Born. It ignored me and turned back to her, intent on finishing what it had started. It slid its fingers back between her legs, its diseased tongue lapping at the woman's neck.

I strode forward, bringing my ax around and over my head.

At the last second, the Pig Born turned and I saw something like fear enter its eyes. The blade split its skull down the middle, spilling rot onto the floor, its body dropping like a sack of sand. The woman it had been molesting didn't even scream. She raised her hands over her head, silent cries pouring from her lips.

I severed her chains with a swift chop and pointed toward the stairs, my voice urgent, "Run!"

She stared at me for a moment and then I grabbed her by the neck and shoved her. "Go! HURRY!"

As I turned to Jess, I heard the woman sprinting for the stairs, now audible sobs tearing from her throat.

Ignoring her, I quickly got down on my knees in front of

Jess, cupping a hand under her chin and turning her face to me. "Jess?" My voice trembled as I touched her. Curling into herself, still crying, Jess raised her eyes to mine and I melted.

"Nick?" she sobbed, breathless, unbelieving.

My chest hitched as emotion tore through me like a train. "It's me, honey, I'm getting you out of here."

Fresh tears budded in her eyes and her lower lip quivered, "Nick, is it really you?"

I lovingly stroked her bruised cheek. "It's me, sweetie. I'm here. I've missed you so, so much. I'm so...so sorry..."

Jess leaped into my arms, weeping uncontrollably, her arms wrapping around me, "Oh Nick, I thought I'd never see you again! With everything that happened and all the...the horrible..."

I kissed her passionately, one hand wrapping around her head, filling my world with her. She looked into my eyes as I pulled away, tears streaking trails through the grime on her cheeks.

"Please get me out of here," she whispered, shaking.

I stood up, hefting my ax. "You better believe it." I severed her chains and helped her stand, her legs shaking. I put her arm around my shoulders, her battered body even more apparent now that she was pressed up against me.

These fucking monsters...

"We don't have much time," I whispered urgently, "we're leaving, right now. Can you walk?"

She looked up into my face, her beautiful blue eyes the only color I ever wanted to see again, "Yeah, just help me please."

I smiled down at her, my heart breaking, "I'm never going to let these bastard touch you ever again."

"We'll see about that."

I jerked my head towards the foot of the stairs and saw Peter walking toward us, machete drawn.

"You've been a bad, bad boy, Nick," he growled, voice like rolling thunder.

11

I watched Peter warily, unsure what to do. Jess clung to me and I wrapped an arm around her naked shoulders.

"What have you done!?" Peter yelled, clutching the machete dangerously.

"I'm leaving," I said, listening to the chaos above our heads begin to escalate, "and I'm taking her with me. I won't let you stop me."

Peter took an aggressive step toward me, furious. "Was any of it real? Did you ever have any intention to join us?"

I shook my head. "I don't want anything to do with you sick fucks."

Peter's eyes narrowed. "I took you under my wing. I vouched for you. I trusted you!"

"So what?" I spat, "that supposed to make me feel bad?"

Peter gritted his teeth. "How did I not see this…how is any of this happening right now? Do you know the extent of what you've done?"

"I extinguished a monster," I said, hefting my ax.

Peter pointed a finger towards the ceiling, "It's burning. It's all burning right now. Kind of ironic, isn't it? The world is nothing but endless rain, but you've managed to start a fire in one of the few places it can't reach."

"Get out of my way, Peter," I said, hardening.

Peter shook his head. "Not a chance. While the others try to put out the inferno you've started upstairs, I'm going to snuff out the source right here."

I released Jess and she looked up at me, scared, "Nick...?"

"I have to take care of this," I said, bracing myself.

"It didn't have to be like this," Peter said, advancing.

I stepped into him. "Of course it did."

I swung first, my blade whistling. Peter stepped away and slashed horizontally for my neck. I ducked, heart leaping into my throat as I felt the air sing. I hammered the handle of my ax into Peter's gut and was rewarded by a grunt of pain. He stepped back and I went with him, bringing the head of the ax around, aiming for his ribs.

Peter jumped back as I missed, eyes blazing. Before I could recover, he punched me in the face, hard, and stars danced across my vision. I blinked and had the awareness to bring my ax up, catching the machete as Peter followed through his assault.

"No one makes a fool out of me," Peter snarled, locked in combat.

I leaned into him, muscles straining, our faces inches apart. "I didn't have to."

And then I spat into his face. He retreated immediately, crying out in surprise, hands going to his eyes. I jumped forward and swung low, my ax hungry for blood.

The blade crunched into the side of Peter's knee and I felt bone break. Peter screamed and went down on his good leg, blood pouring from the wound as I yanked the ax back out.

Dirt and dust swirled around us, kicked up in the struggle, and I wiped it from my face and stood over Peter.

"When you come back," I said, panting, "don't try to find me."

Peter stared up at me with venom in his eyes, "I will never stop hunting you, Nick, for as long as we're here."

I planted the ax directly in his face, splitting his skull in two. He went limp immediately, his body collapsing. I stepped on his chest and jerked the blade free, watching as blood and brain oozed out onto the floor.

"Until next time," I muttered.

I turned and saw Jess staring at me, her eyes wide. Without waiting, I reached out and grabbed her hand, pulling her with me.

"Come on, we have to leave right now. I don't know how much longer we have until they figure out I was the one who started the fire and killed Ryder."

Silently, she nodded and we raced for the stairs. I felt the heat on my face as we pattered up the stone steps, an orange hue beginning to paint the walls. The fire had spread quickly and I was grateful for it.

About time something went your way.

We reached the ground level and were greeted by complete disarray and madness. The fire had snaked into the sanctuary and the pews roared with flame, the dancing ribbons reaching towards the ceiling. Smoke choked the air, a burning black haze that settled around everything. I coughed, eyes burning, as the Hooves sprinted about in complete chaos, trying to put out the blaze. One of them kicked the twin doors open, hacking, and a gust of cold air swept through the chamber.

The fire greedily accepted the oxygen and began to spread

even faster. Cloaked Hooves bumped past Jess and me, racing for the open doors, buckets in hand. One of them was barking orders, trying his best to coordinate the others into dousing the flames. They raced outside and began to fill the buckets from the stone pig head, the waterfall splashing down over them. But no matter how many buckets they passed, the fire would not be controlled, their efforts too meager to master the opposition.

It's a stone structure, I thought, squeezing Jess close to me, slithering our way to the doors. *Everything will burn up inside, but they'll get to keep their church.*

I felt a slight twist of satisfaction.

They'll always have a reminder of the day I beat them.

I pressed Jess's head down and into my shoulder, wrapping an arm protectively around her. In the chaos, no one seemed to notice us, the thick smoke obscuring their vision and the roar of the fire absorbed their attention. We worked our way down the wall towards the open doors and I kept a sharp eye on the crowd running in and out, buckets in hand.

We reached the door and I pushed us through.

We splashed down the steps through the waterfall…and that's when I heard someone yell for us.

I cast a quick look over my shoulder as we flew down the steps and into the field, the church billowing heavy lungfuls of smoke into the gloomy sky.

"Oh shit," I hissed. "Jess, RUN!"

Two Hooves had taken notice of our flight and were flying down the great stone steps, fury plastered across their smoke smudged faces. They weren't far behind.

"Nick, I can't," Jess cried, the toll on her body slowing her as she limped through the dead grass, rain pelting us.

The Hooves had reached the foot of the stairs and were now

only a couple dozen yards away. Close enough to see death in their eyes.

You can't fight them both, I thought, rain plastering my hair across my forehead, *you're too tired; they're going to kill you.*

Fatigue rippled through my muscles as I tried to help Jess along, knowing we only had seconds. My heart was pounding in my chest, my breath coming out in heavy gasps. My boots slammed into the soggy earth, kicking up clods, but Jess was falling behind.

Not now, I thought, *please not now when I've come so far.*

Jess fell, her legs giving out, and she went sprawling in the mud.

I stopped and turned as she crawled back to her feet, but the Hooves were already on us, vengeful smiles wringing their lips.

"You fucking traitor," one of them growled, drawing a long knife from his cloak. The other mirrored his action and together they advanced.

I slowly backed up, gripping Jess and pulling her behind me. I blew moisture from my lips, gasping for air, fear coiling around my throat.

"We're going to turn you inside out," the second Hoof said, twirling the knife in his hands.

This cannot be your end. You've come too far, Nick.

I planted my feet, pushing Jess back further.

The Hooves smiled, knowing they had the upper hand.

Thunder rumbled and I ground my teeth together. "You can't take her from me again."

They charged in unison, blades held high. I raised my ax and caught the first blow, deflecting it from my face. Before I could confront the second Hoof, I felt a line of fire across my ribs and I howled, squeezing my eyes shut in pain.

I was suddenly airborne as one of them tackled me, driving me face first into the ground. Darkness sparked across my vision as my head struck the soil. I felt the wind knocked out of me.

I blindly threw an elbow and felt it connect with something hard, a cry of pain following. I rolled onto my back, realizing that I had dropped my ax. A knife was whizzing towards my face and I jerked my head to the left, the blade sinking into the dirt.

A foot plowed into my side and I grunted, trying to get to my feet, trying to find my ax.

Somewhere I heard Jess screaming.

Suddenly, one of them was over me, and I took another kick, this time to the stomach. I wheezed, blinded by the rain slamming into my eyes, my arms waving wildly above me in hopes to stave off another blow.

I scrambled to my hands and knees, shaking the stars from my vision and nausea from my aching gut. Footsteps splashed to my left and suddenly a fist was plowing into the side of my face, over and over again as one of the Hooves straddled me like a horse.

I dropped to my stomach, tasting blood in my mouth and bucked him off.

More pain exploded over me as one of them grabbed my hair and slammed my face into the earth. I tasted blood and dirt on my bleeding tongue and I could hear my lungs scream as they tried to keep me alive.

Then a knife was driven deep into my shoulder.

My body rocked with blazing agony. The blade felt like a burning tooth, biting deep into my flesh.

They're killing you.

I blinked sluggishly as the knife was ripped out and a fist slammed into the open wound. I didn't have the air to howl.

I lay in the mud, panting, bleeding, the rain a relentless gale across my battered body. I could hear the two Hooves circling me, chuckling to themselves. They were savoring the kill, enjoying the sight of their broken prey.

They're going to take her back. They're going to take her away from you.

I felt my hands ball into fists, mud squishing between my fingers. Blood squirted around my teeth as I grit them, a snarl rising in my throat.

Kill them, Nick. Fucking destroy them.

Gasping, I got to my hands and knees, shoulder burning, muscles quivering with exhausted effort. I slowly raised my eyes, rain running down my face, pulling mud from my skin.

One of the Hooves had Jess on her knees, his eyes locked with mine. He was grinning. Slowly, he pressed her face into his crotch and ground her into him, laughing the whole time, his eyes never leaving mine. Jess was crying, trying to push herself away, but he wrapped his hand in her hair and ground into her harder.

Fire hotter than the deepest pits of hell burned in my chest as I got to my feet.

"Get...your fucking...hands...off her," I growled, catching my breath, ignoring the protest my body was putting up. Every part of me felt broken, but I pushed it aside, driven by the absolute hatred and cascading rage I felt.

The Hoof laughed and slapped Jess hard across the face, taking her to the ground. "I can do whatever I want with her. She's mine."

I unlocked.

Something animal inside of me emerged and I bared my teeth, screaming into the wind, charging the Hooves.

I took the first one by surprise, my speed and recovery slowing his reaction. I plowed into him and we both went hard into the mud. I didn't give him a second to resist. I sat up on him and plunged my fingers into his eyes, popping them like rotten grapes.

Then the other one was on me, the one who had slapped Jess. My shoulder screamed as he connected with it, tackling me off his friend. I rolled and splashed with him, yelling, clawing, biting, trying any way I could to make him bleed.

I ended up on top, his face hoisting a trail of bloody lines where my fingers had gouged trenches. I slammed my forehead into his nose and I heard it break, blood gushing down his face. Without pause, I shoved my hand into his mouth, completely lost in the roaring current of violence.

I ripped out his tongue.

As he gagged on his own blood, I tossed the limp meat away.

I sat up on him, watching his suffering, my words hissing between red teeth, "No one *fucking* touches her."

And then I lunged down, teeth bared, and buried them deep into his throat. I felt his windpipe burst under my jaw and my mouth filled with his blood as I ripped the flesh from his body.

I spit out the wad of skin and slowly crawled off him, his dying gurgles filling my ears with joy.

I stood shakily and walked over to the eyeless Hoof, still on his back screaming and clawing at his empty sockets. I raised my boot and caved his face in. Shards of bone clung to my feet as I pulled my boot away with a wet sucking sound, the carnage gushing over the earth and joining the rain.

And then…it was quiet.

Rain drummed the bloody earth and I slowly sank to it, my knees squishing divots into the soft soil. Exhaustion draped itself around my shoulders like an old friend, every muscle burning, my breath thin and fragile across my lips. My shoulder was a well of agony, the knife wound pulsing with heat.

I collapsed forward, darkness threatening to overtake me. My face splashed in the mud and I lay there, my chest heaving. My eyes fluttered and I fought to stay awake. I knew we needed to move, I knew we needed to get into the forest and away from the Temple...

...but goddamn it, I was *tired*.

Gentle hands pulled my face from the dirt and I was rolled onto my back. Squinting through the rain, I looked up into Jess's face and saw her eyes fill with fear. Her hand went to my shoulder and I cried out as she examined the bleeding slit.

"Nick, we need to go. We need to go right now; there's going to be more coming," she pleaded, her voice weak.

I reached up and caressed her cheek gently, "Ok...ok...just give me...a second."

I told my body to rise, but it laughed instead, my limbs like anchors sinking into the ground. I felt like stone had replaced my muscles, a useless weight pulling me under the layer of mud. We weren't that far from the Temple. Someone could have seen what happened, could have seen me kill their brothers. They'd want revenge, they'd want to take Jess away from me.

No.

Gritting my teeth, I pushed myself up, crying out as I did so. I felt like I had been run over by a truck. My ribs creaked and my shoulder sang, the combination sparking stars across my vision.

"Easy, easy," Jess whispered, helping me stand. My legs quivered and a wave of dizziness shook the world. I dragged a filthy hand across my face, pulling clinging hair away. I looked around in a daze and saw my ax a couple feet away. I pointed to it, the words caught in my throat. Jess understood and picked it up, offering it to me with a worried look.

"Clothes," I managed to croak, "take their clothes."

Jess, still naked, nodded and began to strip one of the dead Hooves. They would be loose, but it was better than freezing to death under the constant rain. I watched her pull the pants off one of the corpses and noted how mechanical her actions were, a dull lifelessness in her eyes, her mouth a white line.

That worried me.

Jess shrugged into her new garments and I shot a quick look over my shoulder at the Temple. Through the curtain of rain, I could see smoke still piling from the front doors. Red smudges ran in and out, too occupied with dousing the blaze than to bother with us.

Wincing, I used the long handle of the ax as a cane and we began to move. My thigh felt like it was one huge knot, a pulsing twist of pain. I looked towards the distant forest and tried not to dismay. It looked impossibly far away.

My plan was to use the trees as shelter and follow them all the way down to the coast where Kevin and Trent were hopefully still waiting. It was a long haul, and my body wept at the thought, but it was our only choice right now.

Just get to cover, focus on that. Don't think about how much you hurt, don't think about how impossible this all is, just get to cover. Your problems will be waiting for you there, rest assured.

Jess rolled up the sleeves of her new shirt, trying to ignore the blood stains, and slid next to me. She took my arm and put it around her shoulders, wordlessly taking some of my weight.

"Thank you," I whispered.

We silently trekked across the rolling grassland, our panting gasps a labored harmony that joined the ever-present drumbeat of rain. After a couple minutes, I stopped, catching my breath. I looked at my shoulder and saw blood still spitting from the wound. I ripped a length of my shirt off and Jess took the dirty cloth. She tied it securely around the gash and looked up into my eyes, her face unreadable.

I nodded and we continued. In the distance, we heard the roar of Pig Born and the scream of Suicidals. The red cuts in the clouds loomed over us, the long swinging ooze dancing as a wind whipped through the sky. The dead sun hung miserably at our backs, crying its black poison into the unseen ocean.

By the time we reached the tree line, I thought I was going to collapse. My leg was trembling with every step and absolute exhaustion crushed my senses every time I blinked. I knew Jess felt the same, her steps becoming more and more labored as we went. She didn't say anything, though; she just continued to help me, her support growing increasingly needed as we walked.

The trees towered overhead as we crunched into the foliage and into the gloomy interior of the woods. The relief from the rain was welcome, as was the cover of greenery. I felt slightly less exposed and allowed myself a second of elation.

And then I fell, fatigue winning over.

Darkness swallowed me up and I was gone.

Floating...floating through the nothing...I was weightless and aware but could see nothing but black, thick endless black.

I felt something on my face, a soft hand caressing my cheek. I tried to open my eyes, but my mind wasn't ready to give up the peace this place offered. There was no pain...no suffering...nothing by an endless horizon of eternal nothing.

Slowly, the world came dribbling back. It started with sound, a gentle patter of water hitting leaves, growing through the darkness. Soon after, feeling seeped back into my limbs and the familiar ache rose to a point where I couldn't ignore it any longer.

I peeled my eyes open.

"Hey," Jess cooed, looking down at me, her blue eyes filling my world.

"Hey, yourself," I said, content to lose myself in her gaze. We didn't say anything for a while, just stared at one another and I saw a sad smile begin to curl her chapped lips.

I returned the smile, emotion brimming in my chest like a hot tide rising across a lonely beach.

And then Jess started to cry. It was silent, a simple trickle of tears that welled from her eyes like reluctant rain water. I didn't say anything, just looked at her, my heart breaking, as silent sobs wracked her body. Tears dripped down her cheeks and dotted my own, her lips trembling as sorrow took her.

Ignoring my own pain, I sat up and took her in my arms, pressing her face against my chest and stroking her hair. She clung to me desperately, shivering and weeping softly. I kissed the top of her head and stared out into the woods.

"I'm so sorry..." I finally whispered, sorrow cracking my voice.

Jess remained huddled in my arms, my words bringing another wave of tender whimpers.

And in that moment...I *hated* myself.

I hated every choice I had made, every selfish act, every stupid decision that brought us to this hellish world. As I wrapped her tighter into me, I felt my own sorrow begin to bud in my chest, a deep regret filled with self-loathing and disgust.

"If…if I had been stronger…" I started, feeling something warm run down my cheek.

Jess looked up at me and shook her head, pleading, "No, Nick, please don't; this isn't your fault…"

I squeezed my eyes shut and shuddered, grief assaulting me, "Yes, it is…if I had supported you like I should have…if I had been there for you in the way you needed me to be…"

Jess sniffled and pulled away, cupping my sorrow streaked face in her hands. "I made the choice, too. I wanted to end it. It wasn't just you."

I shook my head, unable to meet her eyes, "No…no…when our baby died…shit…" I covered my face in shame, shoulders shaking as a sob tore through me.

I felt Jess rub my arm, lovingly. "You were wonderful…you are wonderful. I couldn't ask for a better man."

I gritted my teeth, the confession like acid on my tongue, "Jess, when we lost our son…"

I pulled my hands away, eyes bloodshot. "When he died, I was *relieved.*"

Silence followed and Jess's expression never changed.

I forced the words out, shame staining my teeth as they pushed past my lips. "I didn't want to give you up. I was afraid you'd love the baby more than me. I was afraid I'd lose you to him."

Jess reached out but I shook my head. "Jess, I loved our son, I truly did, but when he passed…when he passed, I felt like I got you back." I stared down at my hands, tears dripping down my face, "and when you fell into depression and started talking about suicide...shit, I couldn't imagine being left alone in the world. I killed myself because I didn't want to lose you. I didn't want to be alone."

I covered my face again, shame and disgust rattling me. "I'm a coward; I'm a fucking coward...and I'm sorry, I'm so, so sorry."

Hands took mine and gently pulled them away from my face. Jess cupped my chin and forced me to look into her eyes.

They brimmed with tears and I saw love shining through the shimmering sadness,

"Nick, I love you more than anything else in the world. Nothing, and I mean *nothing*, could ever change that."

I fell into her arms, needing to feel her, needing to be close to her. I sobbed uncontrollably, unable to help it.

Jess stroked my hair, cooing softly into my ear.

"Do you forgive me?" I whispered into her chest, sniffling.

I felt her lips brush my ear. "Of course I do, Nick."

Relief rushed through me like a warm wind and I let out a gasp as I squeezed her tighter. I felt something unraveled from around my heart and float away into the trees, leaving a gentle heat in its place.

Jess pulled me into her and whispered down to me, "You went through so much to get me out of that horrible place. The things you did, the people you killed...I could see fire in your eyes..." she lifted my face so that our eyes met. "I saw your fire for *me*. And I love you for that, Nicholas, more than I can ever express."

I smiled sadly at her. "I love you, Jessica. More than any-thing."

And then we kissed. It was gentle at first, and then the passion grew, blooming into a desperate need to feel each other, to be with each other, to taste each other. Our tongues tangled and danced together, our breath growing frantic as lust consumed us.

I guided her down, mouth exploring her neck, shoulders, arms, kissing every bruise and scrape that blemished her skin. Her fingers curled through my hair and she gasped as my hands found her breasts.

She reached for my pants, almost urgently, and I slid out of them, our need growing. Her hands groped me and I let out a sigh as I stripped her bottoms off. Her teeth bit into my shoulder and she panted hungrily as I positioned myself over her.

And then we made love, oblivious to everything around us. It was just her and me, the only two people in the entire world, locked in each other's embrace as everything else melted away.

When we were finished, collapsing off one another, I pulled Jess close to me and she rested her head on my chest. We lay like that for a while, the forest quiet around us. I stroked her hair and let the weight of everything settle back around me. We still had so far to go. And who knew what actually awaited us at the end of our journey. For a moment, I contemplated just lying there forever. It was a fleeting fantasy, one brought on by the afterglow of sex. I stared at the foliage high above, a viridescent sky that faded to darkness as I closed my eyes. I could feel Jess's breathing slow, her chest rising and falling in gentle rhythm. I touched her shoulder and discovered she had fallen asleep.

I let her, content for the moment. I could only imagine what she had gone through at the Temple. I wanted to ask her but felt that if she wanted to share, she would. I was also afraid to discover what she had endured, the weight of it sure to crush my already troubled conscious.

She forgave you...

I felt a surge of love for the woman in my arms. All this time, this burden had blazed in the back of my mind. A tremble of guilt that shuddered through me, drove me, fueled me.

And she had melted that despair with a couple of words.

You can't let her down. You have to show her now. Be the man she deserves.

I balled my hands into fists.

And find a way out of this fucking place.

Thought swirled together like color and I washed them out as exhaustion took me again. The Black Farm was quiet, a miracle in and of itself. I listened to the raindrops drip from the leaves above and blocked out all other senses. I knew it was foolish to remain where we were, but I didn't hear anything and chose to embrace the false silence. If I hadn't been so tired, caution would have won over, but my body was still in severe pain from the fight.

I craned my neck around and scanned the dark trees, but there was nothing. No Pig Born sprinting towards us, no bloodthirsty Suicidals, just the ambiance of soggy woodland. I closed my eyes, unable to resist any longer. I felt like I hadn't slept in weeks.

As the soft pull of the subconscious tugged away at my mind, a thought drifted to the surface like an air bubble.

Christ, I hope I don't wake up falling from the sky.

12

I stirred. Something moved to my right. A twig snapped and I bolted upright, searching for my ax. I picked it up and spun, now completely awake as the sound moved closer.

Jess held up her hands, her eyes wide, staring at the upraised blade. I exhaled, forcing my heart to slow. I lowered my weapon and sighed, placing a hand to my chest.

"You scared the hell out of me," I mumbled, apologetically.

She knelt down next to me, her eyes clear. "I'm sorry. I wanted to let you sleep."

I smiled up at her, the expression feeling foreign on my face. "You ok?"

She nodded, "Yeah. I was just washing some of this grime off of me. I feel like I can still taste the dirt in that basement…"

I forced myself into a sitting position, surprised at how much better I was feeling, "You have to be careful; please don't go wandering off alone…"

She looked hard into my eyes, "I know, Nick."

I averted my gaze, "I just don't want to lose you again…"

She ran a finger through my hair, "Nick…"

"Yes?"

"What are we going to do? We can't stay here forever…this place…"

I tested my wrapped shoulder and was pleased to find the burning pain had receded a little. "We're going to get out of here."

She let out a sigh, sad and hopeless, "I don't think that's an option. When I woke up here, bound to a chair, this man, Danny…he told me I had to make a choice."

"Fuck Danny," I spat.

She scooted over to me and rested her head on my shoulder, voice soft, "How are we supposed to survive here? We can't run forever. And Nick…if those monsters get me again…I don't think I can take it. They'll break me in a way I don't think I can come back from."

I rested my cheek on her head. "I won't let them do that. I have a plan. I met these two guys in a broken down town, not that far from here. They said they were building a raft. They're going to take it across the ocean, find out what lies at the end of the sea."

Jess looked up at me. "What about those…those things? I saw them, just once. The stone giants."

"The Keepers," I said, "they're called the Keepers. I know it's dangerous, mad even, but Trent, one of the guys I met, thinks we can slip past them. There's thirteen of them that roam the ocean, stalking the island. If we plan it right, it just might work."

"This is an island?" Jess whispered, almost to herself.

"Trent and Kevin think there might be a way off it, off the Black Farm. I know it sounds crazy, but it's better than waiting for something to catch us again."

Jess stared into my eyes. "Catch us again? Were you taken too, Nick? Did something happen to you?"

I shifted uncomfortably, the memories of Muck's cave swelling, "This place has taken something from all of us."

She placed her cheek back on my shoulder. "When you killed those awful men from the Temple...I..." she trailed off.

"What is it?"

Her voice became quiet, somber, "I've just never seen you like that before. It was scary, like I didn't know who you were for a second. You had this look in your eye..."

I didn't know how to respond, so I remained silent. The seconds ticked by, and finally I stood. "Come on. We should probably get moving."

Jess rose to her feet and I heard her stomach growl. She wrapped her arms around herself and we began to walk.

"Are you hungry?" I asked, crunching through the underbrush parallel to the tree line on my left.

Jess nodded and I realized that I was hungry, as well. No, not just hungry. Starving. I tried to think back on when I last had something to eat and found that I couldn't. I didn't have much time to worry about that kind of thing back at the Temple. But now that some of the dust had settled, it was just another pain that I had to ignore.

And so we walked. Jess would occasionally strip leaves from the trees and suck the water from them, finally popping the whole thing in her mouth, chewing the greenery. She offered me one and I took it wordlessly, my throat grateful for the moisture.

My leg was feeling better, the pain had receded to a dull throb. I placed the head of the ax over my shoulder and found I could manage without using it as a crutch.

Occasionally, I'd try and roll my shoulder, wincing when I extended it too far. The gouge felt sticky under the bandage and I didn't think I had the courage to check on it just yet.

Every so often, we'd hear the crash of foliage or the snapping of branches. Each time we'd duck down in unison and wait, hearts racing, for the sound to pass us by. We only saw someone once. It was a group of Suicidals, three of them. The were walking into the woods ahead of us, ragged looks on their faces, gaunt skin and empty eyes. Jess and I stopped, my fingers flexing around the ax handle.

It was two women and one man, of varying ages. They just stared at us, like they were waiting for us to speak. Instead, I brought my ax into full view and they shuffled on by, heads low, the silence bleak.

After they had gone, Jess looked over at me. "They could have come with us. They looked like they needed help."

I shook my head, watching a group of Pig Born beyond the tree line, way off in the distant fields. "There was nothing we could have done."

"But maybe they could have followed us to your friends; maybe there would be room for them on the raft?"

"They can find their own way," I said darkly.

Jess let out a sigh. "What about safety in numbers?"

Again, I shook my head. "Numbers just draws attention."

After a moment, Jess let it go, falling back into silence. I could feel her struggling. I was sure she was thinking about her time in captivity, about how she had waited for someone to help her...or for something to just kill her. She was a good woman. She wanted to protect those people.

I looked over at her, softening, "They'll be ok."

"They just looked so scared..."

I ducked under a low hanging branch. "We're all scared."

She glanced over at me, her voice neutral, "You don't seem to be."

I almost laughed. "Jess, I'm scared out of my fucking mind right now."

She walked closer and pressed her body against mine. "How did we get here, Nick...?"

I wrapped an arm around her and sighed heavily, keeping a sharp eye out for movement. "I don't know. This place, these things...none of them were supposed to exist. I thought that when we swallowed those pills, everything would fade away into serene nothingness. If I had known...if I could do it all over again...hell, life doesn't seem that bad in retrospect."

Jess stumbled over a rock and I steadied her before she spoke. "Do you really think we can get out of here?"

I was quiet for a long time and then whispered, "I don't know."

The conversation died and I let it go, embracing the steady ruffle of dead leaves and twigs beneath my boots. The woods trailed around us, an endless flow of mirrored landscape. We stayed about a dozen yards deep into the tree line, the mountain and dead sun a far off picture between the trees.

Eventually, we began to hear the sound of waves beating against the shore and I knew we were reaching the end of our trek. I didn't know how long we had walked, but it felt like days. My legs were burning and the ache in my muscles had started to jolt with every step. I could feel Jess beside me struggling as well, her breath coming out in ragged exhales.

We pressed on, the sound of water growing closer until I squinted through the trees and saw the distant outline of broken shacks.

I squeezed Jess's arm and pointed. "Look, there it is. We made it."

"Finally," she said, fatigued.

I felt a flicker of hope dart across my mind as we broke the tree line and headed for the shanty town. The twisted construction looked just as empty as the first time I had been through it, the make-shift houses standing quietly in the rolling grasslands with the long stretch of beach bordering the shambled edge.

We increased our pace, sharing a mutual feeling of encouragement that we had made it this far. The rain had let up and lazily spat from the gloomy heavens, a dampness settling back over our sweaty skin. As the houses grew closer, I looked over my shoulder and froze.

The mountain loomed on the horizon…and I saw a flash of light blink from its summit.

But it was red this time.

It sent a chill running through me and I placed a hand on the small of Jess's back, urging her on. Something about that light twisted my stomach.

We approached the first house on the edge of the town and cautiously proceeded deeper inward. A thought fluttered through my mind like a dark butterfly.

What if Trent and Kevin left already? What if they're dead?

That pit in my stomach grew, but it thankfully didn't last long.

Two people emerged from a house in front of us, their familiar faces bringing a smile to my cracked lips.

"Holy-y-y shit," Trent exclaimed, bounding down the steps and running towards me, a big grin on his face.

Kevin smiled where he stood and crossed his arms, shaking his head at us. "I can't believe it."

Trent embraced me in a hug, slapping me on the back and bringing forth a grunt of pain as my shoulder creaked.

"Goddamn it, Nick, I didn't think I'd ever see you again!" Trent said pulling away.

I chuckled, "Right back at you. Shit, but it's *good* to see you guys!"

Kevin walked toward us, still grinning. "And it looks like you found who you were looking for."

Jess clung to me, unsure. "Are these the men you were talking about?"

I nodded. "Yeah, these are the guys with the raft."

Trent looked apologetically at Jess. "I don't know if you remember us...we stumbled across you in the woods some time ago...before the Hooves came."

Kevin stood next to Trent, his eyes sad. "I'm really sorry we couldn't help you. They just came out of nowhere. We're not bad people, ya know?"

Jess looked from Kevin to Trent and then back at me. "I'm sorry, I-I don't remember much from before I was taken..."

I squeezed her hand. "It's ok, hon. Don't worry about it. What matters is that we're here now and they're going to help us. Right, guys?"

Trent held Jess's gaze for a moment longer before nodding. "Yeah, of course, chief. You two got good timing, I'll tell you that. We finished the raft a couple hours ago and we were just loading it up with a couple things. It's down by the shore."

"Finally some good news," I muttered, relieved.

Kevin looked hard at me. "Are you ok though, dude? You look pretty beat up. Both of you do actually."

I shifted my weight. "I had to do some things."

Kevin squinted at me, "How many did you kill, Nick? How did you get out of the Temple?"

Jess suddenly was shaking her head violently, "I don't want to talk about this. Please. I can't..."

Trent held his hands up. "Oh hey, no worries. It's in the past; no use dredging it back up. You two want to come down and see the raft?"

I paused. "Sure."

Trent clapped his hands. "Cool. Kevin, go grab the last of the supplies and meet us down there. No use waiting to leave now that our guests have arrived."

Kevin gave him a thumbs up and sprinted back for the shack, calling over his shoulder, "Don't leave without me!"

Trent motioned us forward and we started walking down towards the beach. I leaned into Jess's ear and whispered, "Are you ok?"

Jess's face was stone as she nodded silently.

I realized then that I would probably never know what had happened during her time beneath the Temple.

We passed by the huts and the beach opened before us. Grass and mud turned to sand and I looked out at the horizon, over the water. I could see a Keeper far off in the distance, miles from us, walking away from where we were. The sight of it stirred unease inside of me and I took in its towering form. The enormous cross jutting from its shoulders was visible, even at this distance. I could make out the glowing glyphs that lined its body, tiny slits of light shining across the black water.

Trent looked over at Jess and me. "Been watching that one for a while now. It'll start heading this way again in a couple of hours. Our window of opportunity has opened. Soon as Kevin brings our shit, we're gone."

"Right now?" Jess asked, her eyes glued to the receding titan along the skyline.

"Yeah, why wait? Something you need to do first?"

Jess shook her head and shuddered, "I've just never liked the ocean. And those...things...you said it's coming back. What if it catches us?"

Trent kicked up sand, sighing, "I've already asked myself that a million times. I'd rather risk it than stay here any longer. I have to know what's out there, I have to know if there's a way out of this damn place. Kevin feels the same way. No risk, no reward right?"

I stayed silent. My eyes soared to the edges of the horizon, a long black line of water that met the gray sky. What was out there? Could we really escape the Black Farm? And what unknown horrors awaited us if we embarked on this insane voyage?

We reached the raft, an impressive vessel considering the resources available. Trent waved his hands proudly, a smile splitting his lips.

"Not bad, right?"

It was about twelve feet long and four feet wide, a rectangle of wood strung together by tightly knotted rope. Peeking from the bottom was what looked like a brown tarp, secured to the underside. They had nailed siding along the parameter of the craft, about a foot high, a humble stack of crudely cut wood.

It reminded me of a very shallow box.

"Where did you get the supplies for all this?" I asked, hands on my hips.

Trent nodded toward the huts behind us, "Man you'd be surprised what was left behind here. They didn't build these houses with their bare hands."

"I don't get this place," I muttered.

Trent slapped a hand over my shoulder, "Don't try to. You'll drive yourself crazy. And there's already plenty out there willing to do that for you."

"Every time I think I'm familiar with the Farm, something else comes along and changes the formula," I said, walking to the raft, running my hands along the sturdy sides.

Trent snorted, "That's cause The Pig is like a child who gets bored with its toys. After a while, it discards them and creates something new to play with. Could be Pig Born or that dead sun over there, or even the rules of the Farm. You ever notice how some places have power and others don't?"

"I did notice that," I said.

Trent shrugged. "Shit like that is all over. Inconsistencies, anomalies, bent rules. It does whatever it wants because it can. There's nothing stopping it. The laws of our world don't apply here."

Jess walked over to me as Trent was talking, nervously appraising the raft. Trent turned to the ocean and made sure the Keeper was still departing. Jess put a hand on my arm.

"I don't know if I want to do this," she whispered.

I faced her. "I think we have to. Jess, we know what's here, what awaits us if we return to the forest. The Pig Born will never stop hunting us and tormenting us. And now that I royally fucked the Temple, we just gained a whole host of new people who want to kill us. Back there," I jabbed a thumb over my shoulder, "back there is hell. But this," I waved a hand at the water, "this could be something else. We have to try. I'm not spending eternity here watching you suffer, hiding in fear, just wondering how long we can last before some new horror rips us apart."

Jess hugged herself. "Those things scare me…"

I looked out at the far off Keeper. "I know, they scare me, too. But it's leaving. This could be our only chance."

I could see fear in Jess's eyes, but she bit her lip and nodded. "All right, Nick. If you think this is what's best."

Fuck if I know.

"It is," I said reassuringly, hugging her. "We can do this."

We saw Kevin stumbling toward us, carrying an armload of supplies, spilling half of them in the process. Jess squeezed my arm and turned to help him.

"Looks like he could use a hand," she said quietly.

I watched her walk up the beach, Kevin fumbling to pick up what looked like an oar, and ended up dropping a brown sack in the process, spilling tools onto the ground.

Trent silently walked to my side, crossing his arms. "I'm glad you got her back, man."

I watched Jess as she reached Kevin. "Me too."

Trent glanced sideways at me. "I know she didn't want to talk about it but…getting her out of there must have been hell, judging by the look of you both. You ok?"

A breeze rose from the ocean and ruffled my hair.

"No," I whispered.

We watched Jess help Kevin pick up the scattered items on the ground, waves lapping the shore at our backs.

Trent suddenly reached down into his boot and pulled out a knife. He passed it to me with a grim look on his face. "Look, man, if shit goes south out there…kill me."

I took the knife, eying Trent. "Your lack of confidence worries me."

Trent rolled his shoulders. "Shit, chief, you know how this place is. Just…hold on to the knife. Think of it as worst case scenario. I don't want to be swinging from a Keeper's cross for all of eternity. You know that, right? That that's what they do if they catch you. They chain you to themselves, destined to swing by the neck but never die, suffering in constant agony for as long as forever lasts."

I slid the knife into my boot, my voice grim. "Yeah…I know."

Jess and Kevin approached and dropped the items into the raft beside us. I looked over what they had brought. Two makeshift oars, a bag of tools, water gathered in glass jugs, a sack stuffed with something I guessed was food, the familiar brown bars poking out of the top.

"Just have to get the blankets," Kevin said, out of breath, "and then we're all set."

"Good," Trent said. "Let's get a move on before any more Keepers show up."

"Give me a hand, Jess?" Kevin asked. Jess nodded and the two of them returned up the beach toward the houses.

A heaviness settled in my chest as we watched them go. "Trent, there's one more thing I need to know before we go."

He looked at me cautiously. "What's that, chief?"

I pointed toward the mountain towering in the distance, "What's up there? I've seen…lights on the summit."

Trent shifted in the sand. "Yeah, I've seen them, too."

"Do you know what they are? Someone at the Temple called them the Eyes of the World. What does that mean?"

Trent looked at the mountain, his voice dropping, "They've been there for as long as I can remember. Sometimes the light is blue, other times it's red."

"But do you know what they are?" I pressed.

Trent looked hard at me, "Heaven and Hell sit at the top of that mountain."

I blinked, taken back, "W-what do you mean?"

Trent held up two fingers. "The Eyes are beings sent here by their masters. One from Heaven, one from Hell. They watch over the Farm, watch The Pig, and make sure it doesn't do anything too radical to upset the balance of their fucked up versions of the afterlife. This trinity of possibilities, these resting places for our existence after death, Heaven, Hell, the Black Farm...I think the balance is more fragile than we known. The Eyes make sure the scales don't tip one way or another. Remember, this place was created as a mutual agreement between the two extremes. It's a wild card."

I stared at the mountain, the peak poking into the sky.

Trent continued, "They don't come down here, don't mess with the system The Pig has established. Just so long it doesn't try anything crazy, like overthrow the balance or break through the planes of reality, then they'll remain on the mountain. Watching. Waiting."

"What about the lights then?" I asked.

Trent shrugged, "Not entirely sure. But I think that's how they talk to their masters. I think when we see the lights, they're sending their observations back to their realities."

"What the hell..." I muttered. "Has anyone tried going up there?"

"I don't know," Trent said, "But I wouldn't dare. Who knows what they're like? Hell, just interacting with them might break some cosmic rule and then...good luck. God only knows what they'd decide to do with you, what terrible fate they'd dish out because you dared confront them."

"Is that why no one wants to talk about them? I was warned at the Temple not to bring it up. Danny seems sensitive about the subject, too."

Trent nodded. "They're afraid of the Eyes. They represent a power higher than themselves, a threat to overthrow what they've built. If they decided they didn't like what the Temple was doing, or how Danny and The Pig conducted themselves, then they'd send word back to their masters."

"And then what?"

Trent's voice dropped low, "I don't even want to think about that. Nothing good, chief."

I watched as Jess and Kevin emerged from the cluster of houses again, carrying armfuls of blankets. "Don't you think that might be something worth pursuing? Maybe they could...shit, I don't know...don't you think they could help us?"

Trent barked a laugh. "Are you insane? Why the hell would they help us? We're trying to escape! If we actually manage to get out of here then it would upset their entire system, throw the whole triangle of power out of whack."

"Yeah, but—"

Trent poked a finger at me. "They don't give a fuck about us. Get that through your head now. In all the eons of suffering we've gone through here, not once have they offered a helping hand. They simply watch and report."

I fell into silence. I turned the new information over in my head, trying to find some angle or crack, but just ended up hopelessly frustrated. How could any of this be? Wasn't there a single person out that that gave a *damn* about us? How could the gods of our fate be so cruel? If there actually was someone in Heaven, looking down on us, that knew what we were suffering so endlessly...how could they not intervene? How could we be judged so harshly for a single action? It didn't seem fair, didn't seem just. What kind of malicious fuck was running the show up there...?

"I've seen that look before," Trent said quietly. "Don't kill yourself trying to make sense of all this. All that bullshit in Sunday School was just that...total bullshit. There ain't no all-loving God up there. Just an indecisive prick who didn't know how to settle an argument with his nemesis. And so here we are, tossed aside like yesterday's trash. Those two bastards up on the mountain? They're not here to watch us. They're here to make sure The Pig doesn't meddle in affairs it has no business meddling in. We're a forgotten people, Nick. We are totally and completely...alone."

I unclenched my jaw. "Wonderful."

Jess and Kevin drew closer. They dumped the blankets into the raft and turned to us.

"I think we're finally ready," Kevin said, breaking the grim mood. He looked out over the ocean. The Keeper was still stalking away from us, its form growing smaller and smaller on the horizon.

"Where did you get all this stuff?" Jess asked.

Trent walked to the raft and ran his hands over the rough wood, "We've had a long time to gather it all. Piece by piece, through death and rebirth we continued to gather it all. It wasn't easy, but I think we're as ready as we'll ever be."

Kevin shifted in the sand. "Now that the moment is upon is, I can't help but feel kind of nervous."

Trent gripped his shoulder. "I'd be worried if you weren't, kid." He looked up at Jess and me. "You ready?"

"One last question," I said, "What about the water? That dead sun has been dripping its black poison into it, tainting the entire ocean..."

Kevin nodded understandingly. "That was one of the first things we tested before we even started work on the raft."

"And?"

Kevin rubbed his arm. "Just don't get it in your mouth and I think we'll be ok. I tested some of it on my skin and I didn't notice any immediate effect."

"You tested it on your skin?" Jess asked incredulously.

Kevin grinned sheepishly. "Yeah, dude, first just a couple drops and then I submerged my whole arm. After a dozen or so seconds, your arm starts to tingle and go numb, like it has fallen asleep, but there's no pain."

"Couldn't that shut down your entire body though?" I asked.

"Since none of us plan on going for a swim during our voyage, I think we'll be ok," Kevin said.

"What if something destroys the raft and we fall in?" Jess asked.

Kevin sighed, "Well, then we have bigger problems."

"Are we good?" Trent asked, raising an eyebrow.

"I wouldn't go that far," Jess said, "but let's hurry up and get this over with before that stone giant comes back."

"Yes, ma'am," Trent said, smiling. "Why don't you hop in the raft with Kevin? Nick and I will shove us off."

I helped Jess over the meager railing, my foot crunching on the piece of tarp sticking out from the bottom.

What a shit show this is, I thought, *if there's anything out there that gives damn about us…please let this work.*

Jess huddled in the corner of the boat, wrapping herself in a blanket, the ocean wind kicking sand into our faces. I squinted as Kevin hopped into the craft and grabbed an oar. I realized then just how fast my heart was beating.

"Give me a hand here, Nick," Trent said, starting to push.

Together, grunting with exertion, we started to push the raft toward the waves. I gritted my teeth as we approached the impossibly black water, the reality of what we were about to do hitting hard as my boots crossed damp sand.

"Just a little bit more!" Kevin announced enthusiastically.

A wave curled and crashed, the water lapping at the front of the raft. I lowered myself further and dug my heels in, feeling the water begin to take the craft.

"Go, go, go!" Trent yelled as we splashed into the ocean, the raft now rolling in the waves. Kevin dug his oar into the black water and Jess snatched the second one, joining in the effort.

The water was up to my waist, my legs buzzing and growing sluggish, when Trent tapped me on the back.

"We're away! Get in, let's do this!"

Hauling myself over the side, I splashed into the raft, Trent following. I took Jess's oar and shoved it in the water, pulling us further from the sandy beach. The waves rocked us, the raft rising and falling dramatically, but soon we had passed through the worst of it and we leveled out. The black plane of the sea stretched out before us like a glass carpet.

"Hell yeah, chief! No stopping us now!" Trent cried, pumping a fist into the air. Kevin was laughing, the wind whipping his dark hair across his face. Jess had retreated to the comfort of her blanket, her face blank.

I shared her expression.

Now that we were inside it, the raft felt like a coffin.

13

The beach was a thin brown line behind us as our oars relentlessly churned the water. My shoulder felt like hell, but I paid it no attention. I could feel a warmth spreading underneath the bandage. Kevin kept his head on a swivel as Trent and I took the brunt of the work. Jess remained in the corner beneath her blanket, her face pale. Kevin offered her one of the brown clusters to eat and she took it thankfully, nibbling at a corner.

"What is that?" I asked, continuing to stroke.

"Just a little concoction we made," Kevin said, "it's mostly vegetation and tree sap. Doesn't taste like much, but it keeps the hunger away."

He reached into a sack and pulled out a glass jug full of water. "You want some?" I took it gratefully, passing my oar to him. I tipped the jug to my lips and swallowed a mouthful, wiping my mouth and staring out across the water.

The Keeper we had been watching was a dot in the distance now, off the right side of the raft. I looked to my left and saw two more dots, tiny smudges miles away. I pointed to them.

"You see those?"

Kevin nodded. "Yeah, I've been keeping my eye on 'em. They

don't seem to be getting any closer though. I think we're ok for now."

Even so, the sight made me uneasy.

Out of breath and looking tired, Trent offered his oar to Jess, "You mind?"

Jess shimmied out of her blanket and took it wordlessly, changing places with Trent. The rain had started again and I shivered.

Trent tossed me a blanket. "Here, stay warm; keep your muscles loose." I wrapped myself in the rough cloth and used a corner to wipe the rain from my eyes.

"How's your shoulder doing?" Kevin asked.

"I'm afraid to look," I said, recapping the water and stashing it back in the bag. "I'll be fine. If you get tired, either of you, let me know. I'm ok."

Jess dipped her oar into the water, eyes roaming to the two smudges rising from the far-off ocean, "I think they're getting closer."

Kevin shook his head. "No, trust me, I've been watching the Keepers for a long time now in preparation for this journey. They're just weaving back and forth; we're ok."

"Why would they leave such a big opening for us?" I asked.

Trent rested his head against the side of the boat. "I've learned not to question any good fortune that comes our way. I think we've earned it."

"It's almost like they want us to try and escape," Jess said quietly.

"We're off to a good start," Trent said with his eyes closed. "Let's just be grateful for that."

The sound of the ocean swelled around us and I found my mind wandering. Was there an end to this ocean? What would we find, if anything? I realized I had no clue how much water we'd have to cross as well. Could we really do this with just four people, two oars, and a meager supply of food and water? I shook the thoughts away. Thoughts like that could be dangerous. I had to stay focused and hopeful.

I almost laughed.

Time stretched and the silence grew. Soon the beach disappeared completely from sight and we were alone in the ocean. The raft held up surprisingly well, the construction impressive considering the resources. The black water seeped in just enough to soak our asses, but for the most part, it was stable and seaworthy.

I shut my eyes and let the motion of the waves lull me into a state of meditation. Occasionally, I would squint across the water, check on the Keepers, and then resume my rest. The dead sun continued to bleed its broken innards into the ocean and the inky water ingested it readily.

After some time, we switched and Trent and I were back on paddle duty. Kevin and Jess exchanged the oars for our blankets and laid down, resting while they could. Trent and I kept the conversation to a minimum, partly so we wouldn't disturb the other two and partly because we had nothing to say.

It was a grind, an ever-changing shift. Row for an hour, sleep, row for an hour, sleep. The single Keeper we had seen from the beach had disappeared, but the two off the left side of the raft remained visible. They were still far enough away that I wasn't too worried, but I wondered how long that would last.

Time stretched before us like a long, empty road.

"I can do another hour," I said to Jess when my turn was up.

"You sure?" She asked, her hair plastered to her face as a cold mist rained down on us.

I nodded, "Yeah, why don't you to back to sleep? I'm ok."

Trent motioned Kevin away as well. "Yeah, I'm good, too." Kevin shrugged and burrowed back under his blanket. Soon, the two of them were fast asleep once again.

"How you holding up?" Trent asked after a while, the raft gently rolling over the calm sea.

I glanced at him. "I'm all right. If I keep my shoulder moving it prevents it from locking up. When I started my last shift I thought I was going to pass out it was so stiff."

Trent looked at my bandage, spots of blood seeping through. "You should have said something, man. You don't look so hot."

I shook my head. "No, I'll be ok. Once I get it moving, the pain fades." I looked at Jess sleeping soundly in the corner. "Plus I think she needs to rest. I don't know what they did to her, but she's not the same."

Trent sighed, looking grim. "It's a fucked up world here, chief."

I pulled my paddle through the water. "She just sounds so…empty now. So hopeless. I can see it in her eyes; I hear it in her voice. They took that from her and God knows what else."

"That's why we're getting out," Trent said confidently. "We have to get her smiling again."

I smiled sadly. "I appreciate you saying that." After a moment, I turned to him. "Thanks for waiting. I don't know what we would have done if you had already left."

Trent grinned, "Call it good timing. Truth be told, it's nice to meet people here who aren't batshit insane and trying to kill me."

"Like Kevin?"

Trent looked at the sleeping teenager, "Kevin's a good kid. A damn good kid. I'm doing this as much for him as I am for me. He's been through a lot. He doesn't deserve this place."

I looked at Kevin, bundled in his blanket with just his face poking out. "To kill yourself so young…I remember being a teenager. Everything hits so much harder at that age."

"Mhmm," Trent agreed, "don't it ever?"

We were silent for a while and then I pointed my chin towards the horizon. "Do you think there's an end out there?"

"There has to be," Trent said, pulling his oar deeper through the water.

"How long do you think we've been going?"

Trent looked at the sky, "Well, judging by the sun and—"

"Ha ha," I said sarcastically, earning me a chuckle. "It feels like we've been rowing forever."

Trent flexed his arms, wincing. "Got that right. I'd say half a day, maybe longer." He looked over his shoulder at the dead sun. "If that fucking thing would move, maybe we'd be able to tell time easier."

"I think that's the point," I said. "There is no time. Just one long stretch of endless gloom."

"And this damn rain," Trent said, wiping it from his eyes.

"Can I ask you something?"

"Now would be the time."

I paused, readying the question on my tongue. "Why'd you kill yourself?"

Trent's face grew somber, his expression changing in a way I hadn't seen before. His eyes darkened and the corners of his mouth turned down.

"I was stupid," he said quietly, averting my gaze, "and I did a lot of stupid shit when I was alive."

"Hey if you don't want to talk about it—" I started apologetically.

"I overdosed," Trent said bluntly, "was trying to forget about my son's mama. Just kept shoving shit up my nose until finally…well…" he trailed off and I saw sorrow fill his eyes. "I left behind my little boy. He was living with me in some shit hole apartment in the projects," Trent bit his lip, voice quivering. "He was only six. Ain't no one else but me and him. Goddamn it, I pray every second that he's ok, that someone found him and is taking care of him." He wiped a tear rolling down his face, sniffling. "He deserved better than what I gave him. He deserved someone better than me."

"Hey," I said gently, "don't be so hard on yourself; I'm sure it wasn't like that."

Trent looked at me with bloodshot eyes, grief painted across them. "No, it was like that. I was a terrible father, just a selfish punk who didn't want to grow up." He wiped his face, his voice growing steady again. "If anyone deserves this hell, it's me."

I didn't know what to say and so we just rowed. Trent seemed content with the silence and so I let it grow between us. I regretted bringing it up.

Everyone who entered the Black Farm carried hell with them.

Eventually, Jess stirred and rubbed the sleep from her eyes. I watched her and saw the dread settle back across her features as she realized where she was. She sat up and pushed the blankets away.

"How long have I been out?" She asked groggily.

I shrugged, "I'm not sure. A while, now. How're you feeling?"

"You should have woken me up," she said, toeing Kevin from his covers.

Kevin yawned and pulled himself out from his nest. "Did we make it out yet?"

Trent tossed him his oar, "Not yet, chief. But your shift starts now."

Jess crawled over to me, unsteady on the rolling craft, and touched my shoulder, "I need to change your bandage."

Her eyes were ringed with darkness and bags drooped from them. Her blond hair was tussled and stuck up in the back.

"I can keep going for a little while longer," I said, offering her a smile.

Jess shook her head, "You look dead, Nick. Let me re-wrap your shoulder and then I'll take over. You and Trent should get some sleep."

I gratefully allowed her to peel away my filthy, bloodstained bandage, wincing as she touched the wound. It stunk and a nasty, vile slime coated the partially scabbed hole. I turned away as she gently poured water over it and then wiped away the excess filth. As she dug in a bag for something to wrap my shoulder with, I turned away and looked out over the ocean.

The two Keepers still roamed in the far distance, their enormous cross-shaped heads nothing more than smudges in the gloom. I looked to my right and the empty expanse of endless water filled my vision. Where had the other one gone? Were they following a pattern or patrol route? What drove them?

I shivered as a thought snaked its way like ice through my veins. What if it was attacking Suicidals? What if some unlucky bastard had tried to make their way across the ocean, just like us? Could that be why it had disappeared?

Jess had torn the corner off a blanket and was finishing binding my shoulder again when I handed her my oar.

"I think you're right," I said suddenly exhausted. "I need some sleep. Thank you."

Jess took my oar and offered a weak smile. "Sleep then. I hope we have good news when you wake up."

I kissed her on the cheek and then crawled into the corner. Trent was already three blankets deep with his eyes closed. I covered myself, the fabric still warm from Jess's touch, and sighed heavily. I focused on the subtle rocking of the raft, closing my eyes and allowing my mind to decompress.

Sleep came easily, but it was filled with more than just empty darkness.

I dreamed I was back in Muck's cave, chained to the floor. Someone was screaming behind me and I tried to turn around, dirt scraping my cheek, but I couldn't. My neck was wrapped in a leash that connected to a spike driven deep into the floor. Someone screamed again. A woman.

It was Jess. She was screaming my name and I could hear Muck grunting and breathing heavily. I howled, thrashing about, desperate to free myself and help her, but the harder I struggled, the deeper the spike sank, driving my face into the dirt.

Something behind me cracked, sounding like bone, and Jess lost it. Her cries split my skull and I felt tears roll down my cheeks as I fought against my restraints. The spike holding me sank deeper and then disappeared completely underground, and without warning, my head went with it. Dirt and rock pressed in around me, filling my mouth and nose with grit. I spat and choked in the darkness as I was pulled further down, my shoulders joining me in the black.

I tried calling for help, tried screaming for Jess, but every time I moved, I slid deeper into the earth.

I could feel myself suffocating, the coarse soil pouring down my throat and cramming up my nose. I coughed, but only inhaled more of it. I felt myself dying.

And then something rocketed towards me from deep, deep down. I could feel the ground shake around me, a rumble buzzing in my head. Whatever was coming was absolutely enormous.

Fear seared my chest and my heart raced, a desperate drum. My eyes burned and my tongue filled with dry filth.

It was getting closer, burrowing right toward my face at an alarming speed, my world rocking. Right before it reached me, I heard something so earsplitting that it jolted me awake.

It was the scream of a pig.

A hand slid over my mouth, startling me from my troubled dreams. I jumped up, but was hurriedly pushed back down, a face looming over me in the darkness. Cold sweat soaked my clothes as I tried to recover from the nightmare. I blinked, trying not to panic, as reality pushed aside the hell in my head.

"Shhhh," Jess urged, hovering over me, a hand still locked over my lips. Her face was inches from mine and her eyes were wide and terrified.

And that's when I realized something.

The sky was pitch black.

Dread seeped into my stomach as I stared past Jess and up into the empty, ebony expanse.

What the hell...?

Slowly, Jess peeled her hand away and put her lips to my ear.

"Be quiet; don't make a sound. There's something you need to see."

Dazed, I sat up, placing a hand on my chest. Kevin had his back to me, bent over the side of the raft, staring into the water. I looked and saw Trent awake and doing the same. He turned to face me, and in the darkness, I saw terror spark in his eyes.

"What is it?" I whispered.

Kevin pointed into the water, his voice shaking, barely a whisper, "Look."

The feeling of dread wrapped itself around my body and began to squeeze as I crawled to his side and peered over the railing.

At first, I saw nothing…

…and then the depths flared, an eerie blue color far, far below at the bottom of the sea.

"W-what is that—" I started and then paused as the color faded and ignited once again.

It was a Keeper, laying along the length of the ocean floor, its immense size stretching out below us like a downed sky-scraper. The glyphs on its bizarre, rocky body pulsed in rhythm, the alien markings lighting the colossal shape.

We were directly over its head, the glow from the glyphs lining its arms casting murky shadows that revealed the mammoth cross that rose from its unmoving shoulders. I could see hundreds of long chains floating in place, reaching out toward us from the great metal arms of the cross.

But at the end of the chains…were people, countless Suicidals all staring up at us from their eternal hell. Their eyes glowed with every pulse of the Keeper's body, every head upturned to watch us as we passed.

"Jesus...*Christ*..." Kevin croaked, unable to pull himself away, horror cracking his voice.

Trent raised a trembling finger to his lips, his voice barely audible. "Quiet...we need to be so, so quiet."

The raft drifted forward, crawling at a snail's pace along the entirety of the behemoth. My knuckles were white as they gripped the railing, my heart slamming into my chest. Everyone was completely still, frozen in place by fear.

"Is it dead?" Kevin hissed.

Jess put a finger to her lips. "I think it's sleeping. Look at the way those markings are lighting up. It's almost as if it's breathing through them."

"Keep it down!" Trent hissed, his eyes as big as baseballs. "I don't care what it's doing if it sees us we're all fucked!"

I looked out into the open darkness, craning my neck to stare up at the starless sky.

I leaned into Jess's ear. "What happened? Why is it so dark? Where are we?"

"I don't know," she said quietly. "Everything suddenly changed. We tried rowing back a little bit before we woke you, but I think we got turned around."

Kevin gently sat back in the raft, wrapping his arms around himself. "We're dead, we're all dead..."

Trent slid next to him, placing his arm around the kid. "Don't freak out, chief. Just stay quiet and we'll make it through this."

I squinted into the water, searching along the entirety of the Keeper. Its size astounded and terrified me. The chains swayed from the depths, the eyes of damned locking with mine, unblinking and pale in the blue light.

"We've stopped moving," I muttered, voice low.

Kevin curled into himself, panic growing. Trent shushed him and came to my side, looking at Jess. "Can you help him? Please? He's on the brink of losing it and if he gets any worse, it's bad news for all of us."

Jess nodded silently and crawled over to Kevin, bringing a blanket with her. Every creak of wood sounded like a gunshot and I winced as she settled next to him, whispering soothingly into his ear.

Trent gripped my shoulder. "If we don't get the hell out of here, then this could be the end of the road."

I picked up a discarded oar and handed it to him. "Then let's move...*quietly.*"

He took the oar and licked his lips nervously. "Nick, what the hell do you think happened? Why is it so dark out?"

"I have no idea," I whispered, gently picking up the second oar, "but something's changed. Something is different now. Which could either be very good or very, very bad. Let's just focus on moving away from the Keeper and worry about the rest later."

Trent bobbed his head nervously in agreement and slid on his belly to the opposite side of the raft. Together, we ever-so-quietly dipped our oars into the black water and rowed past the Keeper.

It was agonizing and I held my breath with every stroke. I expected the stone giant to come surging from the depths at any second...but it didn't. My oar was a ghost, sliding into the waiting water, the phantom strokes generating silent ripples as we floated directly over the cross-beam below and then finally past the tip of the head.

I looked over at Trent and nodded my head encouragingly. Jess was laying next to Kevin with her arm around him, calming him with soft assurances. Kevin had his eyes closed and was shaking beneath the blanket, fear rocking him like a tornado.

I fought against my own crippling terror as we put distance between us and the slumbering monster. The inky sky was infectious, the darkness clawing around us and pressing in. As the blue light of the Keeper disappeared, I began to feel claustrophobic. I could hear Trent breathing across the raft and heard Kevin mumbling next to me, but they were just spaces in the black.

I don't know how long we rowed into the eternal emptiness. If I hadn't heard the water lapping around us, I would have thought we had drifted into endless space, devoid of stars or life.

Eventually, Kevin settled and his whimpers diminished into the night. Jess crept to my side and wrapped her arms around my waist from behind, her head resting on my back.

"He's asleep," she whispered.

Continuing to row, I sighed, "Good. Thank you. If he had started screaming…"

"I know," Jess said, her cheek pressed against my shoulder blade. "Nick…where do you think we are?"

"Somewhere we're not supposed to be," I said softly. "But I think the immediate danger is past. I can't even see the light anymore."

"You've been going at it for a while now, you want me to take over?" Jess offered.

"No, I'm ok," I said gently. "Just…stay with me for a little while."

Jess tightened her grip around my waist and we continued our voyage into the nothing. I scanned the horizon, searching for something, anything to give us some kind of clue where we were, but the coal black night offered no answer.

After a while, I began to feel increasingly uneasy. Trent remained silent, just a shadowy figure across from me. My shoulder was burning, but I refused to acknowledge the pain. I had bigger issues to deal with right now. What if *this* was the end of the Black Farm? What if we had reached the final plane and were doomed to float in the empty waters until we died? What if we didn't die? Would we be damned to suffer this eternal darkness as punishment for our attempted escape? I shivered at the horrifying thought, feeling the walls of claustrophobia press in closer.

"Someone say something," Trent called quietly. "I can't fucking stand this. I feel like I'm trapped with my eyes closed."

I was about to respond when something caused us all to freeze, my heart crawling up into my throat.

It was a sound, drifting across the rolling waters from the infinite night.

Drums.

Drums from the darkness, a deep ominous note that echoed into the empty ocean air.

Boom...boom...boom...

After a few moments, it died, leaving us in petrified silence.

"What...the fuck...was that?" Kevin asked, sitting up, now completely awake.

None of us moved and I felt Jess's grip tighten around my waist. After a moment, it began again, off to right side of the raft, still distant.

Boom...boom...boom...

"Nick?" Trent croaked worriedly.

"I...I don't know..." I said softly, listening to the drums fade again.

"Guys, we need to move," Kevin said, shoving blankets away, that edge of panic back in his voice.

"It sounds far away," Jess whispered.

I dug my oar into the water, faster now. "Trent, let's go. I don't want to find out what that is. I doubt it's going to happy we're here though."

Boom...boom...boom...

"Fuck me," Trent cried, voice shaking.

Not knowing what else we could do, we continued on. An urgency spurred us to row faster, the drums sounding off to our right and then fading, only to start again a few moments later.

A bead of sweat ran down my face as I pushed myself to dig deeper, go faster. I felt like the darkness we found ourselves in signaled something, it had to, good or bad. I wanted to find out what before whatever was out there found us.

Claustrophobic minutes bled together and formed a scared stretch of time, the four of us pale faced and tense. The water splashed around our oars, the noise filled only by the steady beat of the drums. After a little while, I realized that the sound was fading.

The intervals became more and more distant, the dull beat trailing behind the black horizon behind us. I slowly allowed myself a breath and slowed my frantic pace, my shoulder blazing. Jess sensed my pain and took my paddle without asking. I let her and shuffled to sit against the railing in front of her. I wiped sweat from my face and heard Trent and Kevin exchange duties across from me.

"Jesus Christ," Trent breathed, slumping back against the railing. "I wasn't sure there for a second."

"We're not out of it yet," Jess said quietly. "I can still hear it."

"So can I," Kevin agreed, "but it's so far away now. I think we passed by undetected. What the hell was that?"

"That's not something I want to think about," Trent said, fatigue filling his voice.

We fell into silence for a while, the darkness pressing in around us. I could almost feel it, the black was so thick, almost like we were passing through an inky cloud. I tenderly placed a hand on my shoulder and winced as I felt it bleeding through the bandage.

As time extended before us in the grim stillness, I began to feel sleepy. I rubbed my eyes and begged energy into my body. I didn't want to fall asleep, not now when I might need to take action at any moment.

And what the hell would you do exactly?

I sighed.

You're stranded in the middle of an ocean, surrounded by eternal night and huge stone monsters. Not to mention whatever is playing that drum.

"You asleep, Nick?" Trent asked softly, interrupting the steady pattern of the oars.

"Yes," I answered, "fast asleep and dreaming about the sun."

Trent snorted and I heard him uncap a water jug.

"Guys…" Kevin said suddenly, "hey, guys, do you see that?"

I felt my heart leap in my chest as I spun my head around. "What? See what!?"

"I see it," Jess said softly next to me. Her voice was tinged with…excitement.

"Look!" Kevin said, voice cracking with joy. "Look in front of us! Up in the sky! Don't you see it?"

I cocked my head and squinted in the night, staring out over the water.

I felt my breath seize in my throat and my eyes widened. Holy…shit.

It was a sliver of golden light. Its long rays reached down from coal-smoke clouds and illuminated a patch of ocean a couple miles ahead of us like a spotlight.

"No…way…" Trent whispered in awe.

"What is it?!" Kevin cried. I could tell he was smiling.

I stared at the light, the strange, beautiful rays spilling out from oppressive clouds like a trickle of spring water through a congregation of rocks.

It was the most beautiful thing I had ever seen. And it was close.

BOOM….BOOM…BOOM…

We all jumped at the explosion of noise, directly to our left. The beat of the drum sounded like a cannon blast and I winced, my heart skipping a beat.

"Oh no…no.." Kevin whimpered and I heard him drop his oar into the boat.

"Jesus Christ, that was close!" Trent yelled, scrambling to recover. He grabbed Kevin's oar, desperation and hope in his voice, "Let's move! Head for the light! QUICK!"

I turned and grabbed the oar out of Jess's hands and plunged it into the water, pulling us along as fast as we could manage.

BOOM…BOOM…BOOM…

I shuddered at the blasts, scanning the darkness off my side of the raft. It sounded like it was right there, right next to us.

Still rowing with a fury, I noticed something rising out of the water, the far off light painting the faintest image on the ocean.

"Are you seeing this?" I gasped to Jess, nodding at the sudden shape rising out of the water.

"Keep going, Nick, please…I see it," Jess answered, fear back in her voice.

I gritted my teeth and pulled us past the shape, eyes nervously roaming its form. It was a huge rock rising out of the water, like a stalagmite. It rose dozens of feet into the air, a single spire emerging from the still surface.

And impaled on the slick stone was the impossibly long body of a human-shaped creature. It was naked, its skin almost glowing it was so white. Its long, bony legs squirmed and kicked against the stalagmite like it was in agony. Its head was arched back slightly, huge square teeth clinking against the sharp tip of the stone it was impaled upon. The spire protruded from its gaping mouth like the end of a spear, a constant stream of thick yellow fluid running down its massive body. Its face expanded out, a long pig snout growing below human eyes.

Strapped to its body was a massive drum, the crude instrument driven into its flesh with nails the size of baseball bats. Despite the creature's obvious pain, it raised its arms and pounded on it with a huge piece of waterlogged wood.

BOOM…BOOM…BOOM…

I turned away from the hideous thing, fear melting over my body like cold snow. *Keep going; just keep going.* I focused on the light in the sky, the golden rays offering a hope I didn't dare believe in.

Kevin saw the mutilation rising out of the water and began to scream, fear brutally taking him at the sight of it. Jess crawled to him and held him in her arms, trying her best to quiet his cries. I could hear Trent mumbling to himself, frantic, his strokes fast and hard.

We shot across the water, the yellow light growing closer across the distant sky. We passed the impaled monster but were rattled again as it smashed on its drum.

It's sending out a warning, I thought suddenly.

Trent seemed to be thinking the same thing as he cried out across to me, "Faster, Nick, faster! The light is the answer! If we can make it, we can get out of here! I just know it! DIG DEEP! MOVE!"

Panting, I responded with vigor, a deep dread spreading across my chest as the drum continued to thrash behind us.

And then I heard another one, ahead of us on Trent's side of the raft. I leaned into the darkness and after a moment I spotted another spire rising from the unmoving black, a sprouting formation jutting from the water that held a creature identical to the last. As we steered away from it, towards the light, I shuddered. Its paralyzed body was oozing yellow from its mouth and coating its pale skin.

BOOMBOOMBOOMBOOM!

The drums were constant now, a neverending jolt of deafening noise. I leaned into my oar, gasping, my back slick with sweat. The golden rays were getting closer, the color like long fingers goading us towards them.

That had to be a way out. It just had to be.

"Nick…"

I ignored Jess, focusing every ounce of my attention on rowing faster and continuing to breathe.

"Nick!" She cried again, "Nick, look!"

I heard the terror in her voice and I took a second to throw a glance over my shoulder at her. My eyes went wide and I felt my heart slam to a stop. My oar slid uselessly between my fingers onto the deck.

"Nick…do you see them?" I heard Jess plead, voice shaking.

My eyes soared past her toward the horizon at our backs.

I counted nine Keepers.

And they were hauling ass towards us. The glowing glyphs lining their bodies shot out across the darkness, pulsing with alarming urgency. They blinked in the empty expanse between us like larger than life fireflies, rocketing toward our meager raft at a speed I couldn't comprehend.

Kevin huddled into himself, eyes wide, mouth forming words that dribbled across his lips in silence. He had picked up my ax from the bottom of the raft and clutched it to his chest, terrified.

"Oh my god…" Trent hissed as he saw the approaching horrors.

"It's over, it's over, it's over," Kevin mumbled, tears rolling down his cheeks. "We should never have come out here…we knew we weren't supposed to…"

Jess squeezed my arm, her face pale. I looked into her eyes and wished I had words of comfort to offer.

"Row!" Trent suddenly yelled, "We have to try! We're so CLOSE!" In frantic desperation, he began to churn the water at a furious pace.

My heart sunk into my chest as the figures on the horizon grew, a rolling mass of lumbering power and stone. Even from this distance, I could hear the screams of the damned as they swung on their chains, dangling for eternity from the enormous crosses.

And we were about to join them.

"NICK!"

Trent's pleading shriek snapped me out of my daze and I quickly grabbed my oar and plunged it into the water. I grit my teeth and rowed as hard and as fast as I could, feeling the growing threat at my back. Jess was at my side, watching the Keepers, her face blank and ghostly. We let Kevin cry.

The beam of golden light grew closer as we shot the raft through the black ocean; Trent and I put every ounce of strength we had into our efforts. Water sprayed into my face and sweat rolled down my neck. My shoulder screamed and my muscles threatened to cramp, but I pushed through it all, the sound of our pursuers growing louder at my back.

I could hear a faint rush of water as the giants approached, their massive legs cutting through the ocean like it was nothing. And it was getting louder...and louder...

I shot a quick look over my shoulder and almost stopped paddling, my heart dropping into my stomach. The Keepers rose from the darkness, close, way too close. The illumination from their bodies lit the sky in blue color and I stared up at a sky of dark crosses.

"Don't stop Nick! ROW!" Trent urged, panting. But even I could hear the hopelessness in his voice.

We weren't going to make it.

Wordlessly, Jess wrapped me into a hug and buried her face in my chest. I let go of my oar and pressed her into me, my heart drumming against her ear. Trent was screaming for me to not give up, but his voice was lost in the roar of water, the Keepers only a couple hundred yards away now. I looked at the golden light in the sky and squeezed my eyes shut. We had almost made it...we were so fucking close...

A blast of wind shook us as the Keepers towered closer, the roar of their approach deafening the world. The raft was bathed in blue light and I knew we only had seconds before they were upon us.

Trent was lost in himself, screaming madness and continuing to row, unwilling to acknowledge that this was the end for us. Kevin had pulled a blanket over his head, cuddling next to my ax as if that would somehow protect him.

I pulled Jess away and cupped her face in my hands, staring lovingly into her eyes. "I love you," I whispered into the torrent around us.

Jess smiled sadly. "This is it. This is where our journey ends. We're going to swing from those monsters forever."

A tear rolled down my face as the Keepers reached us. "I've gone through the darkest hells to find you. I can find you again." I leaned in and kissed her fiercely. "I fucking love you, Jess."

And then I pulled Trent's knife out of my boot and stabbed her in the head.

I screamed as I did it, blood gushing over the handle and down my arm. Jess's eyes went wide for a split second…and then she was gone. Her body slumped over into me and I pulled my hands away shaking, screaming.

I turned my bloodshot eyes to the monsters looming over us, tears blurring my vision, agony and self-hatred coursing through me in overwhelming currents. The Keepers were lined shoulder to shoulder in a semi-circle, their titanic bodies like mountains rising from the depths.

And then they began to fall on us, a great creaking wave of stone and water and wind.

Seconds before they hit the raft, I pulled the knife from Jess's head…

….and plunged it into my heart.

I felt an explosion of force throw me from the raft as I gasped, splinters and wood raining down around me. I soared through the air, gobbled up into the dark sky like a dying star. And for the third time...I died.

14

I begged not to wake up. I knew what awaited me on the other side of the calm nothingness I found myself floating in. I willed the seconds of still silence to stretch on forever, a soothing ocean of numb euphoria.

But that wasn't what the Black Farm demanded of me.

I swam through the currents of emptiness and felt a riptide pulling me back to reality. A slow dawn of swirling sensations tickled my mind and I felt the rain on my face. I smelled the wet dirt beneath me. I felt the mud squishing my face.

Get up.

Gritting my teeth, I pulled my eyes open. Dull gray pushed aside the darkness and a world of gloom rushed in around me. I groaned and blinked, trying to get my bearings.

What…had happened? Where was I?

I coughed and scrubbed rain and muck from my face. The raft…the Keepers…

…Jess.

I was suddenly shocked into alertness as the memories came rocketing back. I scrambled to my hands and knees, eyes tearing across the rolling grassland around me. The mountain towered before me, an immense symbol of the impossibility I had tried to overcome.

Escape the Black Farm...

"JESS!" I screamed into the wind, eyes watering. Where was she? Where had she been reborn?

I cupped my hands to my mouth, heart racing, "JESSSSS!"

The rain stung my face like a swarm of bees, a gale pushing the curtains of moisture into me almost as if I was being punished for my actions.

Jesus Christ, where was Jess? What had happened to Trent and Kevin?

I found myself gasping into the storm, disoriented and scared.

Take a breath, Nick. Figure out exactly where you are first and then formulate a course of action. Don't panic. You've done this before, you can do it again.

I shivered and wrapped my arms around myself. I looked around where I had fallen from the sky, hoping to see my ax.

"Shit," I hissed, teeth chattering. I felt naked without it in my hands.

Squinting, I looked around again, searching for landmarks. I almost jumped as the Needle Fields sprang into view, alarmingly close. I swallowed hard, the acres before me filled with endless rows of sharp spires, littered with bodies. So many Suicidals...so many dead...

Muck's cave is close. You need to get out of here. Don't let him take you again. You're alone, exposed, and without a weapon. You're an easy target right now.

I balled my hands into fists, standing. I wrapped my arms around myself as the cold wind whipped and pulled at my shirt, raking my hair across my face. What the hell was I supposed to do now? Where was I supposed to go? I didn't have a plan, didn't have any clue where Jess was, and had no idea where to go even if I found her.

I felt terror and despair slowly drip into my stomach, churning like a poisonous mill. I was back to square one.

"Fuck, fuck, fuck, FUCK!" I screamed, trembling under the shadow of the mountain. I had put so much faith in our plan, in the raft and the ocean. I thought for sure…maybe…

I shook my head angrily, trying to replace my fear with rage.

I heard the howl of Pig Born in the distance, in the direction of the unseen ocean. I had to move.

"You are so fucked," I whispered, rain streaking down my face.

As I raised my eyes, something on the mountain flashed, high up on the summit. It was a red light, followed quickly by a blue one. They blinked once, twice…and then vanished.

I counted the seconds in my head, never breaking eye contact with the mountain. The gray sky pressed down on me and I felt something click in my head. It wasn't much, but it was something to latch onto. A *drive*.

"I think it's time someone met the Eyes of the World," I muttered. My options were running out and I was finding fewer and fewer places to turn. I knew Jess was out there somewhere, and it absolutely killed me to think of her in solitude again. But I needed a plan. I needed something to offer her if—when—I found her. I had saved her from an eternal chain on the Keeper's cross, but she wasn't safe by any stretch.

You saved her by killing her…

"Please know that I am going to find you again," I whispered. "Just stay safe until I can."

Naked of belongings, I started to trudge toward the mountain. The Needle Fields on my left stretched before me like the border of some horrific country, a world filled with pain and endless torment. I tried to avert my eyes as best I could from the rising spires. It wasn't easy.

My boots splashed through the mud and I looked in the distance for the Temple, still trying to cement my sense of direction. No part of me wanted to run into the Hooves, not now, not ever again. The rolling grassland wrapped around the base of mountain and I knew that on the opposite side sat the broken remains of whatever was left of the Temple.

The mountain rose ahead of me as I walked, my sense of time washed away in the rain. The closer I walked, the more my resolve grew. I had to reach the summit and get some answers. Part of me wondered if I was just torturing myself with false hope. I hadn't stopped looking for answers since I had arrived. The forest, the temple, the ocean, and now the mountain. What was I going to do when my options ran out?

You'll make your own options, then.

I wiped rain from my face as I drew closer to the mountain, a thin line of trees lining the foot of the great summit. I trained my eyes upward and saw that a thick forest crawled up the slope until about halfway up where the forest gave way to bald rock.

I pressed on, my mind numbing in the gray and constant rain. I didn't want to think about anything and so I didn't, the crunch of grass beneath my feet marking my weary steps.

Eventually, I found myself standing at the tree line, the Black Farm at my back, the mountain staring down at me with snow-capped eyes. It looked impossibly imposing.

Right before I stepped into the woods, I saw something in my peripheral, a figure emerging from the Needle Fields.

I immediately went on alert, spinning, readying myself for confrontation. Being this close to the Fields, my first thought was that it was Muck. But what I saw made me pause, fear melting into worried caution.

It was a man dressed in filthy overalls. His stomach stretched the fabric and his double chins were littered with stubble and dirt. His greasy hair was held back in a ponytail and his eyes were dangerously dark.

And in his arms, he held a sawed-off shotgun.

I didn't move as he approached, his gun trained at my chest. As he got closer, my suspicions were confirmed. This was a Suicidal, not a Pig Born. I held his eyes as he stopped a dozen feet from where I stood.

"Who're you?" he asked, his gruff voice cutting through a Southern accent.

I blinked, a slow recognition dawning. "I know you...I've seen you somewhere before..."

The man dragged his tongue across his gums. "Reckon you have, partner. I been here a spell. You didn't answer my question. Who in the hell are you?"

I let my shoulders drop, trying to appear at ease. "Name's Nick."

"Nick..." he drawled. "Nick, Nick, Nick....nope I don't know a Nick. Whachoo doing all the way out here?"

A light when off in my head. "The kid! You killed the kid! The little Pig Born kid in the plastic devil mask!"

The man snorted. "Yup, plugged him real good. Little shit was always fuckin' with me. He got what he had comin' to him."

"Yeah, he didn't seem to be a big fan of yours. He told me your name..." I said, snapping my fingers. "It was uh...shit...Pudge?"

The man nodded and kept his gun trained at my chest as he continued,."Yup, that's me. So whachoo doing out here? You's a long way from anything good, Nick."

I pointed at the mountain above us. "Going to have a word with the lights."

Pudge squinted toward the summit. "You going to see the Eyes? Why in the hell would you want to do that?"

I nodded. "I have a few questions I need to ask them."

Pudge snorted. "That's just about the most plum-stupid idea I've ever heard. No ones goes up the mountain. You lookin' for trouble or just a painful death?"

"I'm going to get some answers," I repeated, voice hardening.

The man, Pudge, squinted at me. "Can't tell if you're slow or just an ignorant. Either way, best of luck to you."

"Do you wanna come?" I offered, surprising myself.

Pudge looked at me hard and then chuckled. "Go see the Eyes? Shee-it, now why would I want to do that? Plenty of Pig Born down here to hunt. Don't need to go sticking my nose where it shouldn't sniff."

"Aren't you curious though?" I pressed. "Aren't you tired of this shit? Who knows what's up there, but maybe it's something better."

Pudge giggled, an odd sound to come from such an ugly man. "Sure, I'm curious. Been seein' those damn lights blinking down at us for ages. But I like it down here just fine. Poppin' the Pig Born is easy round these parts." He wiggled his fingers. "I like the way their guts squish up in my hands."

I cocked my head. "Probably some good guts up on the mountain for you to...squish. You have that gun; who's going to mess with you? So come on, let's go see what they are. What's the worst that could happen? We die?" I snorted. "I don't know about you, but I've already done that a couple times."

Pudge clicked his front teeth together, like he was cold. "Hmm…good guts you say? Mm, I reckon the Eyes have some mighty fine guts to squish around in. They probably feel different too, seein' as how they're supposed to be different than everything else down here. Shee-it partner, you do make a tough case. I'd be lyin' if I said I hadn't considered it a time or two. Never met a soul dumb enough to climb the mountain though." He scratched his chin, turning over the idea. "And I am gettin' kind of bored hunting these Pig Born down here…"

I spread my arms. "Train's leaving."

Pudge nodded slowly. "Aw shoot, why not? I ain't got plans today anyway."

I pointed to his gun. "That's fantastic. Now, can you please point that somewhere else?"

Pudge looked down at it and his eyes lit up like he was seeing it for the first time, "Oh would you look at that! All right, now that that's fixed, why don't you lead the way, Nick?"

So together, we entered the forest at the foot of the mountain and began the long ascent. Pudge stayed behind me, which made me nervous. Something about the man set me on edge, but I knew he could be useful. That gun of his certainly would.

And more importantly…I *wanted* it.

It was strange to have such a sudden companion; my invitation was impulsive and rash. Even though he was a Suicidal, I knew nothing about him other than he apparently hunted Pig Born. I supposed that would have to be good enough for now.

The trees pressed in around as we walked, the plane before us rising upward slightly, my boots crunching across dead leaves and underbrush. Pudge huffed and puffed at my back, muttering to himself and giggling. I didn't like that. Clearly, something wasn't right with my new traveling buddy.

He's got a gun, he's not Pig Born, that's all that matters right now.

After a while, I looked over my shoulder. "How'd you get that?"

Pudge looked up at me from a couple feet down the slope, his face streaked with greasy sweat. "My shotty?"

"Yeah," I said, pushing a branch out of my way. "That's the only gun I've seen on the Black Farm. How'd you get it?"

Pudge wiped his face, panting as we continued. "I made it, right here on the Farm."

I stepped over a rock, cocking an eyebrow. "You made it? Like, from scratch?"

Pudge grinned proudly. "Shore did. Back when I was alive, I use to made guns for fun. Smithed 'em, so to speak."

"Let me get this straight," I said, "you not only found and collected the materials you needed, but you built a forge too? On the Black Farm?"

Pudge snorted. "Probably seems impossible to a fancy talking city boy like you, but us down-to-earth folk aren't afraid of putting in a little hard work. And that's exactly what I did. I never claimed it was an easy undertaking, but by God, I sure did set my mind to it. And Nick, once I set my mind to something, there ain't nothing going to stop me."

"Clearly," I said. "I gotta say, I'm impressed. Did you make the bullets, too?"

"Wouldn't be much of a shotgun without a couple shells, now would it?" Pudge asked. He suddenly stopped and I turned.

"You sure are asking a lot of questions bout my gun..." he said, eyes narrowed.

I shrugged. "Like I said, it's just the first one I've seen on the Farm."

Pudge stared at me a moment longer and then relaxed, pressing forward. "You'll have to forgive my suspicious nature, a lotta scum has tried to take my weapon from me. Ain't no one takes Pudge's weapon, I'll tell you that much."

I raised my hands over my head. "Hey, no worries, big guy. I wouldn't dare touch it. Never been a gun man myself."

Until I rip it from your filthy hands.

We fell into silence, reserving our energy for the long climb. As we continued into the forest, I noticed that the woodland floor was slowly growing steeper and steeper, the endless trees growing thicker and closer. I was worried that Pudge would slow me down, but he was like an unstoppable locomotive. His face had turned beet red and dripped with sweat, steam practically pouring from his ears, but he kept pace with me without a problem.

As our surroundings became more and more gloomy, I was grateful for our uneasy alliance. If we were ambushed, I didn't know if I would have the strength to fight back against our attackers. My legs were slowly becoming slabs of cramped muscle the further we climbed, my breath ragged and labored. I wanted to pause and catch my breath but forced myself through it. Not yet.

Just keep walking.

After a while, Pudge ran a grubby hand across his face and muttered, "Not a whole lot of Pig Born up on these slopes, huh?"

"Probably scared of the Eyes," I said between breaths.

Pudge turned this over in his mind and then snorted, "Reckon so."

Time bled out before us like blood from a gut wound, and I felt my energy leaving with it. We had climbed for what felt like hours and I knew we needed to stop soon. Exhaustion was crashing over me in big angry waves and my knees had begun to tremble with every step. The trees around us were shorter now and I could feel the rain spitting down on us again. The underbrush had grown thin and had gradually been overtaken by pine needles and naked rock.

We were getting there.

Finally, after what felt like an eternity, I spotted the end of the forest ahead of us. Past that lay a bald expanse of soaring rock cliffs. They burst away from the greenery, steep inclines reaching all the way up to the snow-capped summit. I held up a hand to Pudge.

"Let's rest. We've been going at it for hours now; let's take a breather. I'm tired, and you must be too, huh?"

Pudge plopped himself down on the ground, gasping, "Shee-it, I never thought you'd stop. Take as much time as you need, I'll just be sitting here collecting my lungs again."

"You could have said something," I said, sitting down across from him, panting, chest heaving.

"This is your shit show," Pudge shrugged, stretching out on his back and folding his hands over his chest. "Think I might close my eyes for a spell if it's all the same to you. Can't recall the last time I had myself a snooze."

"Knock yourself out," I said, scooting over to a rock. I sat against it, resting my head against its hard surface.

I closed my eyes and exhaled heavily. Sleep…that sounded good. Just for a couple minutes. Then we'd get moving again.

Right as I swam into the shallow waters of my subconscious, I heard a wet meaty sound. It jolted me awake, my eyes snapping open in a hurry.

Pudge was viciously masturbating, soft groans escaping his lips.

"Jesus! SHIT, man, what in the hell are you doing?!" I yelled, disgusted.

Pudge opened one eye and looked at me, never slowing. "Oh yeah, sorry, Nick. I can't fall asleep without a good wank. You understand, right? Won't be but a minute. Got a good nut coming up the pipeline."

I turned away, grimacing, right as the fat man ejaculated. I heard him release a sigh of pleasure and wipe his hand off in the pine needles. I dared to look back and saw him buttoning himself back up and placing his shotgun on his chest. He folded his hands over it and smiled.

"Night, Nick."

I remained silent, resting my head back on the rock. My stomach churned.

Fucking animal...

Now that I had been rudely awoken, I found sleep elusive. I shut my eyes and let my mind drift, forcing my body to relax. After a while, I heard gentle snores come from the mound of a man on the ground in front of me.

Just take his gun and go, my mind whispered. I considered it as I paced along the shores of sleep. If I could manage to slip it from his grasp, I could probably get away and rid myself of Pudge's offensive presence. I didn't need him, just his weapon. I missed my ax.

Before I could make up my mind, I was suddenly pulled

back into exhaustion and I was soon floating through the choppy waters of sleep.

I rubbed my eyes, groaning. How long had I been out? I pulled my hands away and opened my eyes. I froze, heart screeching to a halt in my chest.

Pudge was standing over me, the twin barrels of his shotgun inches from my face. I looked up at him, confusion and fear an avalanche in my throat, rushing down into my stomach and chilling me with icy uncertainty.

"Pudge?" I croaked.

The big man's face was a slab of unreadable emotion. He didn't move, his gun never wavering from my face, the barrel practically touching my nose. After another second, he finally let out a haughty laugh and lowered the weapon.

"Oh man, you shoulda seen the look on your face," he brayed, wiping a tear from his eye, "I was seeing how long it'd take you to wake up like that."

I closed my eyes, gritting my teeth, my fear burned up in a blaze of anger. I stood up and faced him, jabbing a finger into his chest, voice like iron.

"You do that again and I'll fucking bury you on this mountain. That's not fucking funny."

Pudge waved a hand at me, unaffected by my threat. "Oh lighten up, ya big baby. Just having some fun."

I forced myself to calm my trembling nerves, unclenched my fists, breath hissing between my teeth. "Well, from now on, let's keep the comedy to a minimum, yeah?"

Pudge chuckled, his belly rolling. "Aw come on, you got no sense of humor. This must be one of them cultural differences I always hear about."

"Do that again and you'll see just how uncultured I can be," I growled, finally relaxing. "Now, why the hell were you trying to wake me up?"

Pudge pointed a stubby finger up the mountain. "Saw them lights flashing again. Figured we should be on the move."

I looked at the summit. "Good to know they haven't gone anywhere. All right, let's go. And keep that thing pointed at the fucking ground unless something is trying to kill us, ok?"

We emerged from the trees into the wide open space before us, naked rock and soaring cliffs stretching toward the peak of the mountain. Pudge and I exchanged a look and then started walking. The rain was bitter cold now and I noticed a drop in temperature. No longer beneath the cover of the forest, the icy wind bit into us with frostbitten jaws.

My boots scraped over the cold stones, a stumbling shuffle that seemed to never end. Pudge almost split his head open a couple times, but always caught himself at the last second. He'd giggle and adjust himself, pulling the straps of his overalls back up his shoulders and then we'd continue.

I dared not look up as we walked. I didn't want to see how much further we had to go. After an hour I could already feel my legs begin to tire. The cold didn't help, my teeth chattering with every blast of air, my arms wrapped tightly around myself. Pudge seemed unaffected by the weather, but I heard him sucking air behind me.

After some time, I stopped and gulped down a couple mouthfuls of oxygen. My chest heaved as I looked behind us and saw the treeline was just a sliver of green below a sloping field of gray rock. We were progressing, but as I looked ahead I saw that we still had a ways to go, the angle of our ascent sharply rising.

Pudge sat down next to me, staring at his feet and gasped thick, wet lungfuls of air. He mopped sweat off his greasy face and shook his head, a giggle escaping his lips.

"Going to need a second before we take those cliffs," he said, rolling his head back to look at me.

I stared down at him. "We're doing ok so far. This wind is killing me, but if I keep moving it's manageable."

Pudge slapped his bulging belly. "You need to put away a couple pork rinds and build up a tolerance!"

I rubbed warmth into my arms. "Don't talk to me about pork." I looked ahead of us, stomping my feet, trying to keep my blood flowing. "I'm going to scout ahead while you catch your breath. I have to keep moving or I'm going to freeze. I'll be back in a little bit, ok?"

Pudge waved his fingers at me. "All right, go on then. You ain't no use to no one if you turn into a popsicle."

"Can I have the gun in case I run into any Pig Born?" I asked casually.

Pudge's eyes narrowed. "We ain't seen a Pig Born for miles. I reckon you'll be ok without it."

I shrugged, acting like it wasn't a big deal. "No harm in asking." Without waiting for a response, I turned and began to climb.

The cliffs began to jut from the mountain at increasingly dangerous angles and I was soon heaving myself up, hand over fist. I could feel my fingers numbing against the stone, the rough surfaces feeling like pure ice.

My hair whipped into my face and I blinked it away, getting lost in the steady rhythm of my climb. After a little bit, I spotted a flat outlook a couple dozen feet above me and shimmed over to it. Grunting, I pulled myself up and rolled onto my back, panting.

What are you doing, Nick?

I shut my eyes against the freezing gale, the wind howling across the rocks.

Why do you continue? You don't have any idea what's up here. Jess is gone. Do you remember what you had to do last time you got her back? Do you really think you can do that again?

I knew it was just the exhaustion talking, but I couldn't stop the doubt.

Just lay here and die. Let the Farm spit you out somewhere else and go hide in the woods with the rest of the Suicidals. This madness needs to stop. You can't escape this place. This is it for you.

Gritting my teeth, I climbed to my feet. I clutched myself and stared out over the hellish world. From this height, I could see all the way to the forest that separated the two sides of the island. I thought I could see something on the horizon past it, maybe the Barn, but I couldn't be sure. I looked down across the left slope and grunted. The Temple of the Pig was a tiny smoldering structure nestled at the base of the mountain, a gray square of billowing smoke. I raised my thumb and shut one eye, smudging its existence from view.

I looked at the far-off ocean and saw the dead sun hanging like a sphere of rot between the gray clouds. The red gashes in the sky hung like tinsel from a forgotten Christmas tree and I watched as Suicidals bled through the long ooze and dripped to the soggy earth below.

I continued to take in the dismal sights and spotted a trio of Keepers lumbering along the coast, their enormous crosses like grave markers in the sky.

Trent...Kevin...

I knew deep down that they were probably swinging from one of those monstrous creations.

Shaking the view from my eyes, I looked back down the way I had come. I really didn't want to go back down, but knew Pudge probably wouldn't come unless I went and retrieved him. The idea was alluring, but I needed him. I needed his gun. Just because we hadn't run into any Pig Born didn't mean we wouldn't. And who knew what awaited us at the summit.

Exhaling, I slowly began to make my way back down toward my dim witted companion. I almost fell as I descended, but breathlessly caught myself a split second before I tumbled down the length of the mountain. Heart hammering in my chest, wind beating against my face, I made my way back to Pudge.

As he came into view, I saw he was still sitting exactly where I had left him.

But something was wrong. He was clutching his shotgun to his chest, his knuckles white against the barrel. I climbed the last few feet, brushed my cracked hands against my pants, and stood silently next to the big man. His eyes were wide and his face was ghostly pale.

"Pudge?"

He didn't move, just continued to stare off into the distance.

I nudged him with the toe of my boot. "Hey, what's going on?"

He jumped at my touch and shivered violently. Slowly, he raised his hand and pointed toward the rocks.

His voice was a trembling whisper, "I seen 'em…"

I looked at where he was pointing. "What have you seen?"

He gripped his shotgun tighter. "The Eyes…they were watching me."

I felt something cold sink into my stomach and I scanned the array of jutting mountain sprawling out in front us. I didn't see anything, the wind whistling around us. It almost sounded human.

Fear began to grip my throat and I licked my chapped lips, "What do you mean? How do you know it was the Eyes?"

Pudge looked up at me, terror written across his face. "It was them. I know it was. I was just sitting here, thinkin', and suddenly I...I saw two...figures...walking over that way," he said pointing again. "I didn't move, the sight of 'em scared the ever-living shit right out of me. I felt like I was paralyzed. After a second, one of them looked at me...just...just looked right at me..." he swallowed hard. "Think I pissed myself."

I realized my heart was racing. "What'd they look like? Where'd they go?"

Pudge squeezed his eyes shut. "After a couple seconds, they started laughing...just...looked at me and laughed. And then they were gone...back up the mountain."

I tore the landscape open with my eyes, gutting every nook and cranny. "Pudge, we need to keep moving. We have to catch up to them."

Pudge's eyes were as big as twin moons as he shook his head. "Hell no, I ain't takin' another step up this damned mountain. I ain't never been so terrified in my life," he shuddered, his voice dropping. "We ain't supposed to be here. We shoulda never come."

"Pudge," I said, voice hardening despite my creeping fear, "don't you wimp out on me now. We're getting close; we can't give up now. Don't you want to confront them? Don't you want to get some goddamn answers?"

Pudge exhaled loudly out his nose. "No, sir. I'm done with

this hunt. If you want to die alone up here, then keep truckin'. But I ain't takin' another step. I'm through, you hear me?"

Do not let him leave with that gun.

I slowly squat down next to him, my hand reaching discreetly behind my back. I picked up a rock as I addressed Pudge.

"Don't do this," I hissed, my fear giving way to anger. "Don't abandon me completely defenseless up here."

Pudge shook his head, "I'm sorry, but I'm going back down. This hunt ain't worth it."

I squeezed the rock hidden behind my back. "Well...if your mind is set, then I guess I can't talk you out of it. But I'm going to need that gun."

Pudge shook his head, still sitting, and pulled it into his chest. "I ain't givin' you my gun so stop askin'. I'm sorry."

I leaned forward and brought my lips to his ear. "Don't make me fucking do this."

Pudge turned to look at me, shock sparking across his eyes as I raised the rock over my head.

He only had a second to scream before I brought it down into his face, crushing his nose in a single blow. Pudge fell onto his back, blood pouring down his face and into his mouth as I stood over him. I planted a boot into his massive gut, forcing the air from his lungs. Pudge wheezed, trying to recover, fumbling with the shotgun.

I kicked him in the balls as hard as I could, reaching down as he gasped, and snatched the gun from his grip.

"Sorry it had to be like this," I said, dropping the rock and pointing the twin barrels at his face. "But I need this. Now get your fat ass back down the mountain and don't look back."

Pudge, eyes bulging, curled into the feeble position, still had the breath to snarl, his voice pained but full of fury. "Oh...you fucked up now...Nick. No one...takes my gun from me."

"Don't be stupid," I growled. "You'll be fine. Go make another one."

"Fuck you, you back stabbin' traitor," he spat, glaring knives at me.

"You're not going to let this go, are you?" I asked, towering over him.

Pudge's face twisted into a sneer. "Would you?"

I pulled the hammers back. "Probably not."

I blew his head off, the report deafening. The blast echoed off the mountain side as gore erupted from Pudge's face, the buckshot annihilating his head and spitting bloody chunks onto my clothes.

I lowered the smoking gun, face grim. I stood there for a moment, watching as Pudge's blood emptied from the gaping ruin that had been his face. Tiny red waterfalls dripped down the rocks and painting the gray with the color of death.

I fumbled with the gun and found the release. I popped it open and discarded the shells, tossing them aside like empty candy wrappers. I knelt down and searched Pudge's overalls for more ammo. I found six more shells in his pocket and stuffed four of them into my own. I reloaded the gun and snapped it closed. I looked down at the corpse.

He didn't deserve that...

"The fuck do I care...?" I muttered and turned to leave.

It was time to finish this climb.

15

The mountain was beating me. Snow swirled and blew across my blue lips as I tried to stop the constant chatter of my teeth. I had lost feeling in my fingers hours ago and the nasty color they were turning worried me. I couldn't even remember what warmth felt like.

I forced myself to take another step up the mountain, the rocky terrain buried beneath a foot of snow. Each step was a risk and a prayer as I begged my boot to find solid ground beneath the layer of white. I reached above me and gripped the next ledge. Arms quivering, I hoisted myself up. The shotgun stuffed down the back of my shirt felt like a long cold tongue against my skin. Breath billowing from frozen lips as I pulled myself the rest of the way up and knelt for a moment. I dared myself to look up and saw the peak of the mountain before me. It was impossible to tell how much more I had to go, the sheet of snow distorting my sense of distance.

But I was getting closer.

You're going to freeze to death first, my mind whispered, a cold voice in the back of my head. *You need to get out of the storm.*

I trudged forward wearily as snowflakes struck my face like

shards of glass. The wind roared and threatened to knock me over as I plowed through snow which was now up to my knees. My feet were like chunks of ice, my boots anchors dragging me to the earth.

"Do…not…stop…" I growled, exhaustion clinging to every muscle in my body like a parasite.

The summit had been silent as it loomed closer. I begged for some sign that my trek would not be in vain—a spark of light, a glimmer of color—if only to affirm my conviction. Where the hell were the Eyes? What had Pudge seen down there? They had to know I was coming.

I tripped suddenly, collapsing into the snow. A new layer of cold swallowed my body as I sank into it, struggling to find a handhold. My fingers met freezing rock and I tried to push myself up. A cramp exploded up my calf and I cried out, rolling onto my back, clutching the contracting muscle. Gritting my teeth, I desperately rubbed my leg, begging the pain to leave.

My breath blew thick clouds as I gasped, the agonizing sensation slowly leaving. I gently lowered my leg, afraid it'd suddenly seize again. The pain remained a phantom in my calf as I stretched it. I plopped my head back to stare up at the gray skies. I scooped up a handful of snow and shoveled it into my mouth. I sucked it and drank the cold water gratefully, the shotgun digging into my back. I needed to get up.

Just give yourself a second…

No! No, I needed to move. I was going to die if didn't get up.

The thought of getting up almost made me weep. Now that I was on my back, I found my eyes begging to close. I wrapped my arms around myself, shivering violently, and slowly counted to ten. When I reached ten, I almost laughed. Was I supposed to get up now?

Darkness danced across the sky and I blinked lazily, fatigue seeping deep into my bones. The darkness took shape and I began to see it twist in on itself like whirlpools. The circular black grew eyes and they stared down at my freezing body. They slowly flew closer and closer, their large eyes never blinking.

You're hallucinating...

"I'm not ready yet," I whispered. "I'm not done..."

The dark forms pressed in overhead and slowly filled my vision, pressing deep into the corners of my eyes.

"Please," I croaked, my consciousness leaving.

As the black swarmed tighter, I fought to open my eyes one last time.

And I saw I wasn't alone anymore. Standing over me were two tall, obscured figures.

One of them glowed blue, the other red.

I struggled to focus on their faces but was rushed by inky black and felt myself fall down a deep well of darkness, my body and mind giving in to exhaustion.

Warmth. That was the first thing I noticed. I tried to open my eyes but found I wasn't quite ready for that. I let the world slowly seep back, one sensation at a time. Sound bled through the stillness and I heard voices. They were conversing. I tried to latch onto the words, but the sounds tumbled into one another. I smelled wood burning and my nose tingled pleasantly.

I tested my limbs and found them stubbornly unable to move. Something was digging into my wrists and I realized I was sitting upright, my hands tied behind my back.

The voices grew louder and I tried again to open my eyes.

Before the color could take form, something slammed into

my face, hard. I rocked backward, consciousness jolting me into forced alertness. Warmth trickled from my lips and I gasped, mouth burning from the blow.

"Wake the fuck up."

I raised my head, panting, and everything shifted and then aligned. A man in his forties stood before me, hands clenched at his sides. He was wearing a black suit that matched the color of his eyes. Blond hair spilled across his shoulders like golden corn silk.

I licked blood from my lips and realized I was in the middle of a cabin. A pile of logs burned brightly in a fireplace to my right, the light dancing across the polished wooden walls. A table sat behind the man who had struck me, and I spotted another person comfortably reclined with his feet propped up on the tabletop.

The second man wore a gray suit and his age matched the first man. His slicked back hair was blond as well, but he had it tied neatly in a ponytail. His blue eyes sparkled as they met mine, a smile revealing perfect teeth.

"Hello there," he greeted, his smile frozen in place. "Now that you're awake, there's no need for any more violence."

The first man didn't move, his eyes boring down into my own. "I'll be the judge of that."

Gray Suit rolled his eyes. "Oh come on, he's tied to a chair. We took his gun. Can you just relax so we can hear his story?"

Black Suit looked at me for another second and then went and stood next to the fireplace, crossing his arms. Gray Suit nodded approvingly.

It was then that I noticed something about both of them. The man in the gray suit had tendrils of red wafting from his shoulders like gentle smoke. I turned to Black Suit and saw blue emanating from him in the same manner.

"W-who are you?" I asked, finding my voice.

"You know who we are," Black Suit growled.

Gray Suit raised his hands. "Just let the man clear his head, will you?"

I paused and collected myself, eyes roaming about the spacious cabin. The windows revealed a snow torn sky and I started putting pieces together.

"Holy shit," I breathed, "you two...are the Eyes of the World."

Gray Suit chuckled. "In the flesh."

"Don't know why that's so surprising," Black Suit snarled. "Seems like you were looking for us along with that fat redneck. Whatever happened to him by the way?"

I cleared my throat, testing my bindings. "I shot him."

"How come?" Gray Suit asked.

"Wanted his gun."

Black Suit shifted by the fireplace. "And what were you planning on doing with it?"

I tested my split lip with my tongue before answering, the fog of my fatigue slowly fading. "I was planning on killing anything that got in my way." I looked at Black Suit. "Or fucking punched me in the face."

Gray Suit laughed, leaning back in his chair. "Seems like this one has some grit, Ansom."

I twisted my tied wrists. "Is that your name? Ansom?"

Black Suit just stared at me, blue ribbons streaming from his body.

Gray Suit nodded, "Yup, that's Ansom. My name is Tolin." He suddenly leaned forward, "But who on God's green earth are you?"

Black Suit, Ansom, uncrossed his arms, annoyed. "Why are we wasting our time? We know who he is. Why don't we just—"

"Because I want to hear it from him," Tolin spat, suddenly hostile. Red flared around him and I felt something pulse through the air like electricity.

Ansom sighed and took a seat at the table. "Have it your way."

Tolin smiled, his composure returning. "Thank you. Now...back to the question. Your name?"

My boots scraped against the chair. "Nick. Where's my gun?"

Wordlessly, Ansom pointed to the fireplace. I turned and spotted the sawed-off sitting on the mantle.

"Why am I here?" I asked.

Tolin shrugged casually. "We found you in the snow, decided to bring you back with us. We don't get a lot of visitors, as you can imagine. Call it curiosity. Be honest: what did you expect to find up here?"

"I want some answers," I stated, the fire popping beside me, "and I wanted to see what kind of beings were up here, watching the hell we Suicidals were going through. I have to say, I was expecting something else."

As Ansom continued to glare at me, Tolin nodded sadly. "Ah yes, sorry to disappoint you. I'm afraid we've been cursed with the same biology as you humans. We were told it would 'keep us humble' in our new positions of power."

"Keep us humble," Ansom said, his mouth turned down at the corners. "There's no glory in what we do. We sit up here observing you pathetic creatures and try to keep warm. There's no honor or status in that. The more I watch you Suicidals the more I grow to hate you. You have no idea the gift you were given at birth. A lifetime of free will and choice...and what do you do with it? You throw it away because things get a little blue." He spat on the floor. "Disgusting."

Tolin waved a hand at Ansom, "Yes, yes, it's a little irritating, but someone has to do it. Speaking of which, shouldn't you go report our guest to your master? I'm sure he'll be interested."

I was growing increasingly uncomfortable, the weight of my situation numbing the flare of confusion and anger I had first felt.

"Who are your masters?" I asked cautiously, "What are you two exactly?"

Ansom stood up, pushing his chair back. "We're descendants of the afterlife. We were chosen by our Lords to keep an eye on The Pig and ensure it doesn't get too power-hungry."

"To put it simply," Tolin added, "I'm from Hell. And dear sweet Ansom here is from Heaven, if you can believe that. Two opposites forced to live together in this wonderful shack and watch the meddling of a being far inferior to our masters."

"The Pig is like a child in a sandbox," Ansom said, disgusted, "forming and shaping its world however it wants. We just make sure none of that sand spills out beyond the walls of its reality."

I leaned forward as much as I could. "How can your masters be content to cast us aside like this? We're all but forgotten here, damned to suffer for eternity because of one mistake."

Tolin laughed, red flaring around his shoulders. "Trust me, Hell would love to have you. But my master abides by the rules agreed upon eons ago. Who am I to say otherwise?" He stared directly at me then. "And why should I give a shit about you people?"

I tore my eyes away from him and looked at Ansom who was walking to the door. "And what about you, huh? If you're from

Heaven, doesn't that make you some kind of angel? How can you or your all-loving God stand to watch us suffer like this?"

Ansom paused, one hand on the door knob. "I'm no angel. I was stripped of that when I got assigned here. Like Tolin said, we are flesh and blood just like you. And as for God?" He looked over his shoulder at me, "he weeps for you."

"Then why doesn't he DO SOMETHING!?" I yelled, suddenly angry, "if he loves us so GODDAMN much, then how can he abandon us!?"

Ansom opened the door, snow howling through the crack. "It was you who abandoned him." Without waiting for my response, he went outside and slammed the door closed behind him. I stared after him, shaking.

"He's so dramatic," Tolin said rolling his eyes. "He's always been like that: dramatic and formal."

I turned to him, eyes pleading. "Help us…please. Your master must hold great power. Get me out of this place. Get us *all* out of this place. Destroy the Farm; wipe it out of existence."

Tolin shook his head. "My master has no desire to eliminate the Black Farm. After all, The Pig still drives traffic our way, depending on the state of the person it devours. It's not as much as we'd like, but it's something."

I rattled in my bindings, voice rising. "Then go ask God! I don't care where you're from; you seem like a decent person! Show him how much pain and agony we're in! Show him how we suffer needlessly because of *one action!*"

Tolin sighed, leaning back in his chair again. "Oh stop it. You know nothing about the ways of our worlds. And besides, it's impossible for me to even glimpse at Heaven."

"Why!?" I asked, frustrated.

"Because even though I am composed of skin and bone,

these materials were crafted from the darkest evils. I am a vessel of sin and inequity. Just seeing Heaven would corrupt and destroy the very fiber of my being. Heaven is holiness and unending purity. It's physically and spiritually impossible for me to get near the place."

I paused, digesting this new information. My mind felt heavy and overloaded, a corrupted circuit board of disconnected wires and logic. Tolin watched me process everything, and as he did, something began to rise from the mess of confusion and chaos.

I nodded my head towards the door. "And what about Ansom? Is he the same?"

"Sure is. He's my complete opposite. Born of the heavens and filled with the light of the Lord. He is a vessel of complete purity, untainted in any way by the evils of Hell." Tolin smirked. "It's a real shame, though...I can't even touch him. Sometimes I wish I could. If I had a drop of goodness in me...well...that'd be a different story."

"What do you mean you can't touch him?" I asked.

Tolin rolled his head back, sighing. "We would destroy one another. We are human vessels at the complete opposite ends of judgment. Touching him would destroy me and vice versa. He cannot enter my world, and I cannot enter his. Think of it like this: I am ice and he is fire. If we were to touch, then we would cease to be what we are. We would extinguish our own existences."

He suddenly grabbed his own arm, squeezing the flesh. "This? This right here? It is composed of raw sin. Do you get that? Are you starting to understand?"

I just stared at him, pieces slowly unlocking in my mind, one turn of the key at a time. And then I began to assemble something, questions evolving into answers. Answers I could use.

Suddenly, from the windows, I saw blue light flair and fill the sky, a burst of color that spilled into the cabin. After a moment, the cobalt glow faded back to dull gray.

"Bombs away," Tolin muttered.

"Why are you telling me all this?" I asked after a moment.

Tolin stretched his arms, groaning. "Because I get so bored up here. Do you know how long Ansom and I have been stuck on this mountain? It's nice to converse with a new face. But enough about me. Let's hear about you, yeah? I've been a real gentleman and answered your questions. So what now, huh? What was your plan after reaching the summit of this majestic mountain?"

I slumped in my chair. "I don't know…I thought…I thought maybe I would learn something that could help me."

"Help you do what exactly?"

I looked up. "I want to get the hell off the Farm."

Tolin folded his hands across his chest, eying me over them. "Mmm, yes, you have been trying quite desperately to escape haven't you? But there's something else driving you, too. Perhaps…another person? Someone you care deeply about?"

"My girlfriend…Jess," I said quietly. "She came here with me."

"Ahhhh," Tolin smiled, "a woman. Of course, it was a woman. Who else could ignite such fierce will in a man's heart? Love is a powerful thing, is it not? It can build us up and tear us down with the force of a thousand suns. It is an elusive idea and a fantasy that so many strive their whole lives to feel…while others are left devastated by the ruin it can leave in its wake.

Love is both good and evil. It is the antidote and the poison of your entire species. And you know what's funny about it?"

I stared at him, unblinking.

Tolin rubbed his fingers together. "You can't feel love. You can't see it, you can't taste it…you can't hold it in your hands. You can't buy it and you can't sell it. Love is an idea that has to grow in the individual's mind, fertilized and cared for with great tenderness." Tolin spread his arms. "For a race obsessed with material objects, isn't it funny that the most desired possession of the human heart…is love?"

Silence filled the room as Tolin's words sank deep into my chest. I cleared my throat to speak, but before I could, Ansom pushed his way back into the cabin, snow roaring around him. He shut the door at his back and shook snow out of his golden hair.

"All set?" Tolin asked.

Ansom stomped his boots, shivering, "Report sent." He walked around me and stood by the fire, rubbing his hands. "What about him? Did he fess up to what he's been doing?"

"More or less," Tolin said. "Nothing we didn't already know. He hasn't mentioned his little voyage yet, but I'd be pretty embarrassed about that, too."

"Wait a second," I said, wrestling against the rope, "you knew about me?"

Ansom snorted, "Of course we did. We've been watching you ever since you came here. Not as closely as we should have been, but we've seen the trouble you've stirred up. Burning down the Temple, braving the ocean, trying to slip past the Keepers. You've been relentless."

"So what's all this back and forth bullshit?" I asked.

Ansom turned his back to me, hands warming over the fire. "Don't ask me. It wasn't my idea to bring you here."

Tolin rolled his eye., "Oh, must everything be so serious all the time? Do we really need answers for everything? Why can't you just go with the flow and live in the moment? You people are so set in your ways: always making plans, setting up schedules weeks in advance, your entire lives one big boring predestined blur or normality. Just…just go with things; allow yourself to get lost in the rush!"

Ansom looked over his shoulder at his companion. "Are you trying to tell me you don't know what we're going to do with him?"

Tolin chuckled, "Not a fucking clue."

"Oh brother," Ansom groaned, "he's not even supposed to be here. We are dangerously close to breaking code."

"There we go again," Tolin muttered.

I started to hear a clock tick in the back of my mind. I knew that this conversation was drawing to a close and I didn't want to find out what fate awaited me on the other side of it. My eyes quickly scanned the room, sucking in the location of every object. The fragmented ideas that I had unearthed earlier began to take form and cement, a desperate, insane plan blooming across my scattered mind.

"Why don't you just get permission to send him to Hell?" Ansom was saying. "I don't want him here and it's not like we can release him back to the Farm."

"Why not?" Tolin asked, "Who cares?"

"He's been exposed to too much," Ansom continued, "all thanks to you and those loose lips of yours."

Nick, this is madness, my mind cautioned, *what you're think-*

ing is crazy. I know your options are limited, but what you're planning is an impossible stretch.

I tested my wrists once again, sliding my boots along the floor. My legs weren't tied to the chair so I knew I could stand. I glanced at Ansom, his back still to me, and then to the shotgun on the mantle.

You don't even know if it'll work. You're not thinking this through.

I didn't have time to think. I silently tested the chair I was bound to, the flimsy wood creaking as I shifted my weight. I glanced at Tolin and then at Ansom's back. My heart began to race as I took a deep breath. It was now or never.

Ansom was mid-sentence when I made my move. I bolted upright, still strapped to the chair, and plowed into him as hard as I could. He cried out in shocked surprise and then screamed as he fell into the fire. Without pausing, I swung myself around and smashed the chair against the brick fireplace, sending splinters flying.

As the chair and rope fell away from me, Tolin stood, mouth open, eyes wide, one hand outstretched towards Ansom who was desperately trying to pull himself from the blaze. Like lightning, I wriggled the rope from my hands and snatched the shotgun from the mantle.

I spun and around toward Tolin and saw that the red ribbons flowing off his shoulders were growing in color and frequency like he was readying some power, some cry for help from his master.

I whipped the shotgun around and pointed it at his face. "Not a fucking word! Sit down! SIT THE FUCK DOWN!"

Still dazed by my aggression, Tolin slumped into his chair, his face going white. Ansom was at my feet clawing, still screaming as tongues of flame licked at his clothes and hair. I looked down at him and then flipped my shotgun around.

I swung it as hard as I could, like a baseball bat, and smashed the butt into the side of his face. Ansom didn't even cry out as he collapsed, body going limp.

"No! Stop it!" Tolin yelled, half standing, the red ribbons glowing hot.

I shoved the gun in his face, a vein pulsing in my neck. "I TOLD YOU NOT TO FUCKING TALK GODDAMN IT!"

Adrenaline coursing through my veins, my body fueled with roaring anger and I kicked the table into his chest. He fell backward in his chair, grunting as the wind was knocked out of him. I leaped over the table and fell onto him, snarling, "Good thing you've been cursed with a human body or you wouldn't feel this at all."

I grabbed him by the shirt and crunched my forehead into his nose, headbutting him hard. Blood exploded across his face and his eyes rolled from the blow.

I gripped his throat, fingers tightening. "If this red shit is how you communicate with your master, then I don't want to see it. Do you understand? If you raise the alarm, I will cut Ansom's fucking head off and dribble his blood onto your face, one drop at a time. GOT THAT?!" I screamed shaking him. Tolin mumbled something under a waterfall of blood and I noticed that the smokey ribbons were far less bright now.

I leaned in close, voice hissing between my teeth, "Does that mean you're complying? Or is it the pain that's doing that? Hmm? Which is it?"

I punched him in the face, knuckles plowing into his mouth, and I saw the red glow fade even more.

"Ahhhh," I said satisfied, shaking my stinging fist, "seems

like when I beat the ever-living shit out of you, your abilities diminish." I stood up over him, "I'm not going to pretend to know how you function or what exactly you're capable of, but I do know that you bleed and that's good enough for now."

I grabbed him by the hair and pulled him upright, back into his chair. I scooted him tight against the table, whispering into his ear.

"I'm going to need you to pay attention in a little bit. But while I get things set up, why don't you take a little nap, yeah?" I slammed his face into the tabletop and his body went limp. I released him and went over to Ansom, smacking the lingering flames from his suit. When they were extinguished, I surveyed the two men.

"Let's do this," I muttered darkly.

16

I sat across from Tolin, drumming my fingers on the table as he stirred. It had been at least twenty minutes since I knocked him out. The hatchet I had found out back by the wood pile was planted in front of me, the blade biting deep into the wood. I looked over it at my prisoner. Tolin groaned and his eyes fluttered open. I could see pain start to creep into his consciousness and I grinned. I had used the rope to bind him to his chair and then driven a broken chair leg through his hands, pinning them together behind his back.

Tolin looked at me and I saw everything flood back. His eyes went wide as he saw Ansom stretched out on the table between us, still unconscious.

"W-what the hell is this!?" he cried. He winced as he tried to get up, the wood skewering his hands and cutting deep.

I ran a finger down the length of the hatchet. "I'm getting out of here, one way or another. And you're going to watch me do it."

Tolin blinked, his face streaked with blood. "What are you talking about? Are you insane? You can't escape the Black Farm! How many times do you have to fail for you to understand that!?"

I stared death at him. "That's what everyone keeps telling me…and you're mostly right. After everything I've been through, after everything I've seen…I've come to realize that there's only one way out of here." I gripped the hatchet. "And that would be The Pig."

Tolin struggled in his chair, blood running down the legs and onto the floor. "What the hell does that have to do with us?"

I jerked the hatchet free and tapped Ansom's unconscious body with it. "From what you told me, Ansom was given this human body. It was molded and created out of God's holiness. He is a walking incarnation of purity."

"So WHAT!?" Tolin shrieked. The red ribbons wafting from his body flared slightly but remained dim, almost invisible. I would have to keep an eye on that.

"So," I said, standing, "nothing so pure could enter Hell. You said so yourself. You told me that neither of you can come in contact with one another. You said that you can't even look at Heaven because it would destroy the very fabric of your being. I'm going to assume the same applies to Ansom here."

Tolin bared his teeth at me, blood dribbling down his chin. "What the fuck are you going on about? What do you plan to do?"

I went and stood at the end of the table, hatchet in hand, and tapped on Ansom's head. "Well, I know that The Pig either sends souls to Hell or back to Earth for a second chance. I've done some pretty bad things here, so I'm a little worried about where he'd send me."

"You're damn right he'd send you to Hell," Tolin snarled.

I smiled grimly. "That's why I'm going to eat Ansom."

Tolin's eyes grew wide, his face paling. "W-what the fuck are you saying?"

I hefted the hatchet. "Well, if I consume the purity of God, how could The Pig possibly damn me to Hell?"

"I-I...well—" Tolin stuttered, shaking his head, "t-that's madness! You've lost your fucking mind!"

I nodded. "I know. But it just might work." I leaned over Ansom and gripped Tolin's face, my eyes growing dark. "And you're going to sit there and fucking watch me cannibalize your friend. You're going to watch me rip him apart just like you watched the Suicidals get ripped apart for all these years. And if you so much as blink or try to call for help, I will show you the extent of pain the human body can endure," my voice dripped with hatred, "and then I'll show you what lies past that. Do you understand me?"

Tolin jerked his head away from my grasp, breathing heavily. I saw him fighting with himself, anger and fear mixing in his mind like acid. I knew I was playing a dangerous game with him, the mystery of his powers still hidden from my understanding. But he hadn't done anything yet. Maybe he couldn't.

After a second, Tolin looked up at me, eyes burning. "You don't know what you're fucking with. The careful balance we represent here is teetering on a knife's edge and you are seriously testing that. If you go through with this and kill Ansom...I can't promise the armies of Heaven won't swarm us. These waters you're testing have never undergone such contamination. You could undo everything."

I took my place by Ansom again, his head hanging off the lip of the table.

I raised the hatchet. "Well, let's find out then." I brought the blade down into Ansom's neck. Blood spewed from the wound and onto my face. I closed my eyes, licking it from my lips. Tolin began to squirm, horrified, but I ignored him, wrenching the blade free and bringing it down again.

Two more chops and Ansom's head dropped to the floor. Blood gushed from the stump and I cupped my hands underneath the flow. I watched as my palms filled and then I raised them to my lips and drank deeply.

The blood hit my gag reflex hard, but I managed to get it all down, sucking on my fingers and sighing. I looked at Tolin and saw the smokey red around him gaining intensity.

"Don't even think about calling for help," I growled. I reached out and wiped a bloody finger across his forehead. The reaction was immediate. Tolin buckled under my touch, howling as his skin sizzled like acid. I stood watching him scream, bucking and thrashing in his chair until the seizure passed.

He fell into a whimper and I placed my hands on the table. "If I see you flaring up again, I won't be so gentle next time."

Tolin's voice rattled in his throat. "I'm going to send the entirety of Hell after you, you deprived motherfucker."

I hefted the hatchet. "Funny thing about the human body—something you might not completely understand yet—but we die. Our bodies rot and bleed and shit. And seeing as how your master stuffed you inside one to keep your ego in check, I'd watch your mouth. Because if I bury this blade in your face, then that's it for you. You're done."

"You don't know anything about me," Tolin growled, chest heaving.

I spread my arms. "I know that the entire Farm is terrified of you. The Eyes of the World! The Gods on the Mountain! Oh, they are just shaking in their boots down there. I'm always being told, 'We mustn't talk about the Eyes, don't mention the

16

Eyes'...and look at you. A pair of pathetic egomaniacs who think they're special because their masters trusted them enough to spy on The Pig."

"They should fear us," Tolin spat. "They should all fear us. We have the ability to bring wrath upon this place like no one has ever seen before."

I pointed a finger at him. "No, you don't have the power to do that. Your masters do. Not you. You're just a couple of messenger boys, hiding up here, glowing, pulsing your reports back to your enslavers. No, Tolin...you're fucking *nothing*."

I could hear Tolin's jaw pop and his eyes flared. I picked up the shotgun leaning against the table leg and casually pointed it at him.

"I know what happens when I die. Do you?"

Tolin ground his teeth together, but I saw some of the fire fade from his face, the red glow dimming.

"Great," I said, placing the shotgun back down and gripping the hatchet. "Well, I guess it's time to eat then."

"Don't do this," Tolin whispered.

I tore open Ansom's shirt and looked at Tolin in his chair. "Do you think I *want* to do this? Do you think this is where I idealized myself at the end of this shitty, brutal road? Do you know what I've gone through? What I've felt? What I've seen? Hmm?"

Tolin held my gaze but kept his mouth shut.

I turned back to the corpse on the table and took a deep breath. I dug the tip of my hatchet into Ansom's chest and sliced upwards, carving out a square of flesh. My fingers slicked with blood as I reached down and pulled meat from the bone, holding it up for Tolin to see.

"Down the hatch," I muttered. I opened my mouth, squeezing my eyes shut, and dropped the dripping flesh into my mouth. It squished around my teeth as I chewed, warmth running down my throat. I felt vomit surge in my gut but managed to keep it at bay. Grimacing, I finished chewing and swallowed hard.

Gasping, I opened my eyes. I waited, trying to detect if I would feel any changes, either physical or mental. When nothing happened, I started carving into the body once again.

"Not sure what I was expecting," I mused, digging deep for a chunk of muscle.

"Why are you making me watch this?" Tolin asked softly, his eyes lowered.

I pulled free a long string of sinewy red. "I already told you why. It's not easy, is it? Watching the violence and horror up close." I tilted my head back and lowered the meat into my mouth like gory spaghetti. I chewed slowly, focusing on breathing so I wouldn't gag. I had considered cooking Ansom but chose not to. I didn't know if the fire would burn away the purity of his body. Honestly, I didn't know if any of this would work. As I licked my lips, I suddenly had the urge to laugh.

"You're a monster," Tolin said, watching me wipe my mouth.

I sliced into Ansom's stomach and began pulling out the gooey bits. Blood dripped from my hands and splattered onto the table top. Tolin winced away, grimacing.

I filled my mouth with slippery organs and chewed viciously on them, focusing on just getting it all down. I didn't know how much I would eat or how much I *could*, and so I just continued with my meal, slipping into an almost mechanical state.

Tolin fell into silence, his face grave as I consumed his friend. I began to feel sick at some point but managed to eat the better half of Ansom's torso. When I simply couldn't down anymore, I sat down across from Tolin, sighing. I looked at the mangled mess between us and felt my stomach roll.

I suddenly put my hands over my face, a chuckle escaping my bloodstained lips. "Jesus Christ…what the hell, right?" I laughed harder, clutching my sides and doubling over in my chair, "Oh my GOD, what the FUCK!?" Tolin looked uneasily at me as I howled, tears streaming down my face.

I recovered slightly, wiping my eyes. "Oh, I'm sorry, did you want some? I totally forgot to ask."

"You've lost your goddamn mind," Tolin hissed, his face pale.

"Yeah, maybe I have," I said, the humor leaving me, "but it doesn't matter now. It's done. And now that I'm finished, I don't really have a use for you anymore."

I reached for my gun and saw understanding fill Tolin's eyes, my intentions clear. As I brought the gun up to the table, Tolin burst into ribbons of red, translucent tendrils exploding from his body.

It only lasted a split second before I put two barrels of buckshot through his chest. Blood spewed from Tolin's mouth, his body jolting from the blast. He looked at me for a second, fear and hatred filling his face…and then he slumped over dead.

I exhaled. What a fucking mess…

I don't know how long I sat there, the air reeking of death and gun smoke. Blood pooled around my feet and I watching the veins of red drip down the table. My stomach begged to reject the contents that now filled it. I burped and then coughed, spitting out a chunk of Ansom.

The wind howled outside and the windows filled with curious snowflakes. The fire began to die and I realized it was time to go.

I wearily stood, wiping my hands on my pants. I had a long

way to go still, back down the mountain. But as I began to gather things from around the cabin, I felt a strength fill me, replacing the fatigue. It was a burning determination that jetted from my chest, across my arms, and out the tips of my fingers.

I donned Tolin's bloody jacket and wrapped Ansom's around my neck like a scarf. I tore their shirts into long swathes and wrapped them around my hands and up my arms. When I was satisfied, I picked up the hatchet and looked down at its razor sharp blade.

"You're a little smaller, but you seem to kill just the same."

I walked behind Tolin's lifeless corpse and pulled him back into a sitting position. I cocked his neck to the side and began to hack his head off. It only took a couple whacks before I tore it from his shoulders. I found a crude-looking satchel in the corner of the cabin and stuffed it inside. Mind numb, I walked over to Ansom's head and picked it up from the corner of the room where it had rolled. I shoved it into the satchel as well, looping the bag around my shoulders.

"I still have use for you," I muttered to the empty room. So far my plan had worked, but I wasn't counting on its continued success. Not here, not in this place where everything was mercilessly taken from you.

When I was finished, I gave the room one last look. Content, I went to the door and pulled it open, stepping out into the cold snow.

It was time to find Jess and feed The Pig.

And I knew just who to go to.

The trek down the mountain was a long, gray blur. My mind receded into itself and all I focused on was putting one foot in front of the other. The snow froze me, the rocks bled me, and my body trembled beneath the weight of what I was about to do. I honed myself around a singular vision and let the rest blow away into the wind.

At some point the snow turned to rain and the slush beneath my boots melted into mud. The cliffs and protruding rock descended back into forest and I pushed on. Down…down…*down*. I forever descended the steep slopes, shotgun in one hand, hatchet in the other.

The congested interior of the woods began to thin, and I soon found myself at the foot of the great mountain. I could barely recall a single memory of my march other than the pain in my feet and the ache in my back. Everything was a gray haze and a panting discomfort. I didn't slow, didn't stop, didn't even look back. There was only what lies ahead; there was only what I had to do. I refused to think about alternatives or other paths that might be available.

The only thing left was The Pig and me.

And it would *not* be my end.

The gloom overhead thickened, and as I walked across the empty expanse of rolling grassland, I began to hear thunder at my back. It started as a distant rumble, but as I put miles between myself and the mountain, I heard it grow in intensity. The timid growls grew into vicious blasts that shook the sky and rattled my ears.

I caught flashes of lightning, long snaking veins of red and neon blue. They cracked the clouds, sparking across the gray from the corners of my vision.

I had set something in motion.

And I felt the Farm beginning to unravel.

The forest that divided the island grew in the distance, a line of color on the horizon. I walked toward it, my mind a cage holding back the insanity I had unlocked in myself. I could hear it, feel it, almost taste it.

The madness.

The air rippled around me. The hair on my arms rose as the sky was molded by violent energy. Lighting twisted the clouds like strands of DNA, followed closely by a cannon blast thunder that shook the earth. But I did not look back.

The woods drifted closer and I noticed that the Farm was eerily...empty. There were no signs of Suicidals or Pig Born anywhere on the vast plains. The great red gashes in the sky were devoid of new arrivals and reborn souls. It was like everything had frozen and the very nature of the world stood paralyzed.

I entered the woods and began the final plunge toward my destination. A wind ruffled the foliage overhead and it sounded like screaming. The canopy of green sparked with flashes of red and blue as more thunder crashed down upon me. I shifted the satchel on my shoulder and felt the severed heads knock into one another. I felt blood leaking from the fabric and drip down my leg.

And still I walked...and walked...and walked...and knew this was my last journey. Whatever fate awaited me, whatever end I would meet...I knew it would be my last. I simply could not continue beyond this, for if I did, I knew I would lose myself entirely.

Beyond whatever pieces I had already lost.

Dried blood coated my face, clung to my skin, and lined my lips. I tasted dirt and copper and violence as I licked sweat from them. My hair hung in clumps across my eyes and I smelled the taint of death on my clothes.

Suddenly, as I neared the end of the forest, I heard a voice call out to me. It was like an echo down a long hallway, a muffled cry from beneath a pool of numb pain.

"N-nick?" A female voice.

I slowed, chest heaving. I felt nothing as I turned and stared between the trees, seeking out the source. A dozen yards away stood a small group of Suicidals, watching me with cautious eyes. I started into their faces, my eyes dark and empty, until I spotted one I recognized.

She stepped out from the group. She looked terrified.

"Jesus *Christ*...Nick, is that you? It's me...Megan."

I just looked at her, bloody knuckles tightening around my hatchet. Megan...yes...I remembered someone named Megan.

She took a hesitant step forward, fear pooling in her eyes. "D-do you remember me?"

I said nothing for a moment and then slowly nodded.

"What the hell...what happened to you?" she asked, her voice quiet. She took a quick look over her shoulder at her companions and then back at me. "What's going on?"

I opened my mouth, my voice sounding like the hinges of a rusty gate. "I'm getting the fuck out of here."

Megan swallowed and pointed behind me. "Did something happen? Did...did you do something?"

I hefted the satchel and averted my eyes.

She took a step closer. "Nick...have you seen the sky above the mountain?"

"I have to go," I said quietly, starting to walk again.

"Nick!"

I stopped and looked over my shoulder at Megan and her companions. The way they were looking at me...the *fear*...

"I'm glad you're ok," I said. "Find some place safe if you can."

"Nick, WHY?" Megan pleaded.

I turned away. "Cause Hell's coming.

I didn't wait for another question and let the trees swallow me up again. I couldn't help them. I couldn't worry about them. They were on their own, just like me. Just like we all were.

After a little bit, I saw light begin to filter in from between the trees and I knew that I was reaching the end of my road. I expected to feel something...maybe fear or hesitation. Maybe relief. Anything. Instead, as I stepped across the woodland threshold and onto the other side of the island, I felt absolutely nothing but the darkness in my heart.

Rain began to pelt me as I left the woods. My boots sank into soggy earth. My clothes fluttered in the wind, now nothing more than filthy, bloody rags. My fingers tightened around my weapons and I readied myself for what I needed to do.

I looked toward The Barn and suddenly stopped, my eyes going wide. I gazed out at the scene before me and felt something stir in my stomach, like a nauseous bubble of sickness. I heard my jaw pop as I grit my teeth and my hair blew across my face.

"Goddamn it," I whispered.

Standing between me and The Barn were hundreds of Pig Born, silent and still, their unmoving eyes trained on me. Their contorted, mutated faces were twisted into snarls of rage and hungry hatred. Drool and pus leaked from their angry mouths and we watched one another like gunslingers before the draw.

Even the two snake creatures that were coiled around The Barn's smokestacks were still, their long faces trained in my direction, their lidless eyes unblinking as they observed my entrance into their territory.

I let out a long breath and summoned my voice.

This was it.

"I need to talk to Danny!"

My demand rolled across the distance between us and the Pig Born didn't move. They didn't even react, they just stood there, glaring at me.

"To hell with this," I growled.

I raised the shotgun over my head and blasted two rounds into the sky, "GET THE *FUCK* OUT HERE DANNY!"

After a moment, I saw the Pig Born part. Danny emerged from the ranks and I saw hatred in his eyes. He began to walk toward me, fists clenched, and I stood my ground and reloaded my last two rounds.

"I knew it would be you," Danny snarled, drawing closer.

"Who the *fuck* else would it be?" I asked, snapping the barrels closed.

Danny stopped a couple feet from me, the wind whipping between us. It was as if the Farm itself was gasping for life.

"What have you done?" Danny asked, his eyes furious slits.

I just watched him, unmoving.

Danny pointed toward the sky at my back. "Have you seen this? Look!"

For the first time since leaving the mountain, I allowed myself a glance back. And what I saw took my breath away.

The clouds in the distance had been ripped apart to reveal hundreds of thousands of blazing red and blue comets that painted the heavens like neon streaks across a canvas. Lightning webbed around them, igniting the sky with brilliant color. It was as if the hands of the universe had dipped their fingers in paint and dragged them across the expanse of the sky.

Danny saw my surprise and awe and his voice cracked with anger. "So let me ask you again: what did you *do*?"

I slowly faced him. "Before I answer that, I need two things from you."

"Oh this should be good," Danny snorted. "Listen here, you pathetic—"

I suddenly snapped, a furious rage erupting in my chest. "SHUT THE FUCK UP!" I advanced on him and raised my gun. My sudden aggression rooted him in place as I slammed the barrel of the gun under his chin.

I leaned into him, my face inches from his, my eyes blazing. "You don't get to talk right now, do you understand me? Not a goddamn word or so help me I'll blow your motherfucking brains out the back of your skull."

Danny's eyes went wide, his sudden disadvantage paralyzing him. I heard the Pig Born stir but ignored them. They wouldn't dare make a move with Danny in such danger.

"Do you have any idea what I've gone through to get here?" I spat, quivering, the madness begging to be released. "Do you have any clue what it's like to be one of us? Do you!?"

Danny didn't move, the shotgun digging into his skin.

"Now I want you to listen to me because I need something from you," I continued, my voice dropping to a guttural growl. "I need you to find Jess for me and bring her here. And then, and ONLY then, will you take us both to feed The Pig. Have I made myself *crystal* clear?"

Danny mumbled something, but the gun pressed his jaw closed. I lowered it slightly and Danny swallowed before repeating himself.

"She's already here, Nick."

I felt my mind blank for a split second. "What did you say?"

Nick cocked his head behind him. "She's here. She came

looking for you not too long ago. She refused to leave and so I—"

I pressed the gun hard beneath his chin. "You did what?"

Danny raised his hands. "I locked her up in one of the new arrival rooms. She's ok. I didn't know what to do with her; she absolutely would not go away. I threatened her with Pig Born, The Pig, everything I could think of. But she would not leave me alone."

My eyes narrowed. "Why the hell wouldn't you just kill her? You have no patience for us, so why lock her up?"

Danny blinked. "Jesus, Nick, I'm not a monster.

After a moment, I waved my hand at him."Then get her! Now!"

I lowered the gun and allowed Danny to turn. He motioned to the Pig Born. "Bring her here."

He turned back to me as the Pig Born left and disappeared inside the long building connected to The Barn. Thunder cracked overhead and Danny and I stood staring at one another, hatred sparking between us like the lightning in the sky.

"How did you do it?" Danny asked quietly, his voice hostile.

"Shut up," I said, grinding my teeth, "before I waste these shells on you."

After a couple tense minutes, I saw the mass of Pig Born stir as someone walked through them. My heart began to race and I felt a lump form in my throat. I shot a look at Danny and then back at the menacing crowd of mutations.

And there she was.

I felt a surge of emotion rise in me like the dawning sun at the sight of her. Her clothes were in rags, her hair a tangled mess, but her eyes…her eyes shined at the sight of me.

"NICK!" she screamed, elation lacing her voice. She broke away from the Pig Born and sprinted for me. Danny stepped back as she bolted past him and into my arms, hugging me fiercely, burying her face in my chest.

I wrapped her up into me, my breath draining in a relieved gasp. I kissed the top of her head and felt the knot in my heart unravel as I pressed her against me.

"You're here," I sputtered, stone turning to water. "You're here...you're here...oh, Jess I'm sorry...I'm so sorry."

She looked up into my face, her eyes brimming with tears. "I didn't know where to go, where to look. Nick, I was so scared, I thought the Keepers...I thought they..."

"It's ok," I said, my eyes welling with sadness and relief, "I'm here. I'm ok."

Danny cleared his throat, interrupting our brief reunion. "Look, this is very heartbreaking, but I won't be able to hold back this horde of angry Pig Born forever."

I smiled at Jess, tears rolling down my face, and then looked up at Danny. "You'll take us to The Pig?"

"You said you had something for me," he said, unmoving. "Let's see that first. I've been more than fair."

"Did he harm you?" I asked Jess, ignoring Danny for a moment. "Did he touch you?"

Jess shook her head, pulling away. "He...no I'm ok. I'm ok, Nick."

Danny spread his arms. "See? Now can we please get on with this?"

I slung the satchel down from my shoulder and tossed it at Danny. "That should cover any inconveniences."

Danny caught the bag and looked at me cautiously. He opened the flap and his eyes went wide.

"What...what is this?"

Jess clung to my shoulder as I gripped the shotgun in one hand, the hatchet in the other. "It's the gods you're so afraid of. The monsters on the mountain."

Danny's head jerked up, disbelief plastered across his face. "You don't mean—"

I nodded. "Those belong to the Eyes of the World."

Danny just stared at me, and then looked back down at the severed heads. "They're gone...it can't be..."

I jerked a thumb over my shoulder. "I imagine those comets in the sky are a bunch of very concerned and pissed off entities, rocketing toward us to find out just what the hell happened."

Danny looked past me at the distant horizon. "Angels...demons...my god..."

"I can't image it'll be good when they get here," I said, "but Danny...they're not here yet. You have a very limited window to do whatever the hell you want. The Pig's leash has been severed. It's all or nothing now. You want to make a move? Do it. Because they're coming," I pointed at the neon comets, slowly blazing toward the earth, "and when they get here, it'll be too late."

Danny continued to stare at the descending forces of Heaven and Hell. I saw his mind working urgently, quickly, gears turning, options stripped and then assembled. He looked at Jess and me before turning toward the Pig Born.

"Inform The Pig what's happening! NOW!"

I saw a stir among the crowd of monsters as one of them broke away, sprinting for The Barn. I surveyed the sea of mutated faces and twisted features. The army of The Pig. They were all staring at the sky, the impending conflict surfacing in their dull minds.

"I did you a huge favor, killing the Eyes," I said to Danny, "now I expect you to hold up your end and take us to The Pig."

Danny looked at me cautiously, the wind blowing across the grasslands. "Give The Pig a second to digest all this. I'll uphold my end, don't you worry…but before I do, I have to ask you something."

Jess shifted at my side and I nodded. "Ok, what?"

Danny took a step closer, lowering his voice. "Why do this? Why kill the Eyes for us? Why help The Pig?"

"Because," I said wearily, "I just want to get the hell out of this goddamn place."

Danny looked down at the satchel again. "You certainly went to great lengths just for the opportunity. You know there's no guarantee The Pig will send you back. The way things are…I think you might have a better chance here."

I looked at Jess. "We're not staying." Jess smiled sadly and then slowly nodded in agreement.

Suddenly, the air splintered as a furious shriek deafened us all.

We covered our ears as the piercing cry thundered into our skulls, the echoing scream cracking the sky.

It was the roar of The Pig.

As the blast faded, Danny's face paled. "Oh, fuck…"

Jess was squeezing my arm urgently, pointing towards the opposite side of the Farm, "Oh my god, Nick…"

I turned and looked.

The color immediately drained from my face and I grabbed Jess.

The dead sun exploded across the horizon like a black hole, a blinding blaze of scorching violence that consumed the expanse of the heavens. Tendrils of inky darkness shot from the detonation like cracks in a pavement, shooting out and then up toward the neon comets, obliterating them from existence.

The shockwave came next, blasting across the forest like a hurricane. It knocked us to our knees, the ripple of heat burning my eyes as I squeezed them shut in pain. My ears rang and I felt the earth shake beneath my feet.

I shielded my face and looked up to see a second blast erupt from the dead sun, a cosmic detonation that plumed out like rolling thunder. A wall of midnight darkness swept the distant sky as it plowed across the Black Farm toward the mountain.

The wall of titanic, ebony energy slammed into the distant summit and I gasped, watching the immense power plow across the world.

And then the mountain was no more.

Slowly, we all got to our feet as the aftershock rumbled in the distance. The sky where the comets had been was now stained with streaks of darkness that hung in the air like wet tar. There were no signs of the descending intruders or the mountain. The world groaned and then righted itself, a long gasp escaping on the wind as it tended to its new, horrific scar. The wall of still moving energy bloomed ahead of itself and then settled over the earth like falling mist.

After a moment, I found my voice. "I think you just lost half the Farm."

Sweat stood out on Danny's face and he licked his lips nervously. "Wh-what the hell? What was that?!"

Still recovering, Jess swallowed hard. "I think The Pig just blew up the competition along with half the world."

Danny blinked and turned in place, looking back at The Barn. The army of Pig Born was still getting to their feet, exchanging grunts and snorts of concern. Even they were scared. The two snake-like creatures coiled above the Barn and bared their teeth at the sky, thick strands of drool leaking from their snarling mouths.

"This isn't the end," I said to Danny. "You may have wiped out the initial wave, but they'll be back. The Pig just pointed a huge spotlight over all of us."

Danny was recovering now, the shock fading. "I know. But Jesus Christ, if The Pig can do that..."

I stepped forward. "Hey, don't forget about our trade. This changes nothing. We still need to see The Pig. Sooner rather than later. I have a feeling shit is about to hit the fan here and I want no part of it." I gripped Danny's arm, my eyes bloodshot. "I just want to get out of this god-forsaken place. NOW."

Still staring at the sky and the after effects of the explosion, Danny nodded distractedly. "Ok, ok...yeah, come on. Let's get this over with."

Without lingering any longer, we followed him toward The Barn.

17

I stood with Jess in an empty room, waiting for Danny to return. I knew this place. I had been here with the Hooves, awaiting our chance to pledge our allegiance to The Pig. How times had changed. My boots scraped over the barren concrete as I hugged Jess to me. She was trembling and I realized I was, too. The weight of what we were about to do was pressing in around us.

"How long is he going to be?" Jess asked quietly.

"I don't know," I said, stroking her hair. "I'm sure The Pig isn't in the mood to see visitors. Might take some convincing."

I pulled away from her and took a long breath. "Before he comes back though, there's something we need to do."

Jess looked into my eyes and I saw fear in them. I stroked her cheek lovingly. "You trust me, right? You know what we're about to do?"

I saw the fear grow and felt it reflected in myself. Jess nodded. "I know...and of course, I trust you. You've done nothing but try and protect me since we arrived here."

I cupped her face in my hands, "There's just one more thing we have to do before we escape this nightmare."

Jess's eyes begged for clarity, "What is it, Nick?"

I suddenly stuck my fingers down my throat and pulled her into me. I felt myself gag and then my stomach lurched.

I pulled my fingers from my throat right as my gag reflex gave in. I pressed my lips to Jess's and projectile vomited down her throat. I felt her buckle in horror, desperately trying to shove me back, but I held her tight, my mouth sealed over hers.

Jess sputtered as another wave filled her. She gagged, then swallowed, frantically trying to escape my clutches. I felt puke splash from her nostrils and run down my chin as she tried to eject the vile remains of Ansom.

After she drank down the third splash of vomit, I pulled away, gasping. Jess fell to her knees, dry heaving, panting, confusion and disgust rattling her. I quickly knelt down and put my hand on her back, urging her to hold it in.

"I'm sorry," I hissed, "this had to be done. Trust me, please, this is the only way we're getting out of here."

She looked up at me, coughing violently, her eyes bloodshot. "What the hell, Nick!?"

I stroked her head as her seizures passed. "Just trust me, please, I'm begging you. I'm sorry I had to do that, but it was necessary."

Jess wiped her mouth and shuddered. "How...why...?"

I turned my head and spat, my own stomach rolling. "It's better if you don't know the details."

Still shaking from the shock, Jess stood. I helped her, apologetically stroking her arm. I desperately hoped she had ingested enough of Ansom, the bits of gore now spreading their purity through both our bodies.

Well, that was if there was any truth to my insane hypothesis. One way or another, this would be the end of us. And I found some comfort in that.

Suddenly, Jess and I jumped as Danny walked through the doors in front of us. Heat rolled from the chamber at his back and I could hear the scrape of enormous hooves on the concrete. My stomach lurched and I felt fear spread through me like cancer.

"The Pig will see you," Danny said quietly.

Jess clutched my arm and I nodded, my voice not quite steady, "Ok...let's get this over with."

Danny pointed at the shotgun and hatchet shoved into my pants. "Leave those. You know you can't bring them with you."

I pulled the weapons out and tossed them aside. Didn't have any use for them anyway, no matter where we were sent.

Danny turned and motioned for us to follow him. I slid an arm around Jess and tried to calm my racing heart. The looming violence ahead of us was terrifying and insane. I tried not to think about how it would feel, about how much pain we'd suffer. I heard Jess whimper at my side as we entered the chamber.

The Pig towered before us like a statue.

The furnaces behind the titanic creature cast its shadow across our faces as we approached, and I felt darkness a I've never experienced. The Pig snorted a blast of foul breath across the room as we walked towards it, and I fought to control my already upset stomach.

The Pig was just as large as I remembered, a quivering mass of flesh and hooves and teeth, its eyes dark and intelligent. The two fleshy tubes jutting from its sides quivered, the unseen heads roaring down at us through the roof of The Barn. For a horrifying split second, I wondered if we'd be eaten and spat out as newly created Pig Born.

Danny held up a hand and we stopped, just feet away from

the God of the Farm. The Pig ground its teeth together and a strand of thick drool slithered between its lips and dripped to the floor.

"These are the two," Danny said reverently, his head bowed slightly.

The Pig breathed heavily through its flaring nostrils, cocking its head at Jess and I. I felt like it was staring into the deepest wells of my soul. I looked at my feet, heart pounding. Jess was trying not to hyperventilate, her breath stuttered and desperate. Together we stood, absolutely terrified. I felt like The Pig could see every thought and action I had taken since arriving on the Farm. I shuffled my feet, throat dry, and desperately tried to mask my thoughts. If this monster somehow knew what I had been up to, what I had done...

Finally, The Pig opened its mouth and let out a long, squealing roar. I dared not move, the noise paralyzing me in place as spittle flew across my face. I clenched my hands into fists to stop them from shaking, my bladder releasing.

Piss running down my leg, I slowly looked up as The Pig shook itself and then lowered its mouth. Its jaws opened like a ramp leading to hell's darkest pits, its tongue rolling out like a long, wet worm.

"You first, Nick," Danny said from behind me.

I jumped, having momentarily forgotten he was still here. I looked back at him, shaking my head. "No...we go together."

Danny stared at me for a moment and then raised his voice to his master. "They wish to go together. Do you accept that?"

The Pig didn't move, its mouth split open to reveal a cavern of teeth the size of kitchen knives. I stared into the gaping maw and felt a wave of terror rock me. I squeezed my eyes shut and then forced them open, a gale of dizziness sweeping through me.

"You may continue," Danny said behind us. "Approach The Pig and climb into its mouth."

Jess was crying and I felt like I would start at any second. I felt Danny's hand on my shoulder, guiding me forward. Our footsteps echoed in the empty chamber, the roar of the twin furnaces sending ripples of heat across my already sweaty face.

"I love you, Jess," I whispered, voice shaking.

"I love you, Nick," Jess said, tears flowing down her face.

I squeezed her hand. "When we get out of here, let's try for another baby. I want to start a family with you."

Jess exhaled grief. "I would really, really like that."

Chest heaving with terror, I halted directly in front of The Pig's waiting mouth.

"Please..." I hissed, my voice barely a whisper.

As I climbed into the expansive jaws, my muscles turned to liquid. The Pig's tongue squished beneath my hands and knees as I crawled along it. My shoulders scraped the rows of teeth above me as I reached back and took Jess's hand, pulling her up behind me. Foul heat poured over our faces and saliva soaked us, the stinking, filthy mouth a long tunnel of death.

The Pig raised its head and closed its mouth around us. Jess immediately began to scream as horrific darkness encased us. I held her hand like a vice, my other guiding us slowly through the squelching black.

I had barely started to crawl when The Pig bit down on us. I screamed so hard I felt blood rupture from my throat, a line of massive teeth crunching into my leg. Bone and flesh were torn as I rolled in its mouth, its tongue tossing me across to the other side for another bite. I heard Jess howling as well, a primal sound that blasted from her lips.

As I bled into its mouth, my body rolling into another bite, something happened.

The Pig retched.

I heard its displeasure immediately, a squealing roar that amplified from its throat.

"JUST KEEP GOING! PLEASE!" I screamed, tears of agony rolling down my face. I could feel my knee bone scraping along the bottom of the mouth, an exposed nub of bloody white. Below that was gone, bitten off.

The hand clutching Jess's was slick with blood and slime, but she held onto it with fierce determination, her screams echoing in my ears. The walls of the colossal mouth closed in around us, pressing in tight and I felt blades of pain shoot across my body.

The Pig retched again as our blood spewed from our ruined flesh. I felt it gag and the mouth creaked open, its tongue flopping around us, trying to push US back out. I grit my teeth, screaming, and reached ahead of me with my free hand, clutching a long tooth. Muscles trembling, I howled, pulling us forward, deeper into the mouth.

"COME ON, YOU FUCKING BASTARD!" I bellowed at The Pig. "FINISH THE JOB!"

I jerked Jess along behind me and The Pig bit down again, angry at my refusal to eject from its jaws. My vision exploded with stars of blinding pain as its monstrous teeth plunged into my stomach, tearing my guts apart.

I vomited blood, the agony beyond anything I had ever felt before...

...but I kept crawling, defiance shattering the walls of my

throat as I screamed. I was almost to the back of its throat, a pulsing pit of darkness.

Suddenly, Jess was shoulder to shoulder with me. I felt her squirm at my side, a ruined mess of flesh and blood. The Pig snapped its jaws again, and in that brief second, I saw her legs cleaved from her body at the thigh. Her eyes bulged and her face streaked with saliva and trails of thick blood.

"Keep...*moving*," she croaked, her voice a harsh, guttural escape, almost dream-like through the agony.

I ground my teeth through the searing horror and gripped another tooth, pulling my body into the deepest part of its mouth. Jess held onto me as I suddenly slipped, the massive tongue frantically trying to push me out of its throat.

I clung onto her arm as I felt my insides roll out of my stomach, squirming through the gaping hole in my gut. As they made contact with The Pig, I heard it scream, and a sickly smoke sprang from where they slithered.

I grabbed wet gums and hauled myself forward, now staring down the long black of its throat. Jess wrapped her free arm around me and helped me along, breath blasting from her fractured chest in wet heaves.

I heard sizzling and saw that my intestines were searing into the bottom of The Pig's mouth. Great wafts of charred smoke filled the tight interior of our fleshy coffin and I gagged at the smell, blood squirting between my teeth.

"One...more...push," Jess gasped, fighting to stay conscious through the pulsing pain.

And that's when The Pig vomited. It was a tidal wave of soaking filth that splashed across us like a burning ocean. I screamed as it gushed into my eyes, new pain rattling my skull with relentless fury.

I felt Jess slip as the vomit poured over us, sliding back towards the front of the mouth. I desperately grabbed her arm and screamed, using every ounce of strength I had to pull her back toward me. My arm quivered with effort as I shoved her ahead of me and down into the throat.

Howling, I shimmied behind her and pushed. I saw her head slide forward and then she disappeared down into the squirming black. The Pig tossed its head in horror, our bodies living poison fighting to be digested.

"*LET-ME-GO!*" I roared, surging forward in a last ditch effort.

For a moment, I thought I hadn't made it, its tongue rolling around me, but I squirmed past it, pressing myself against the walls of its mouth.

And then I was sliding down its throat.

Down into the waiting expanse of its reeking maw.

Down into the end.

As the clutches of darkness took me in its arms, I heard The Pig scream with unbridled terror.

18

I screamed, gasping and clawing at my face. The walls of my vision rocked with trembling agony and images flashed before my eyes like blurry photos. Pain shot through my body like my bones were being deconstructed, one molecule at a time. My hands groped at my ruined limbs, desperately trying to stem the flow of crippling agony. My throat felt like it would rupture as my howls rattled from my chest.

"Nick!"

The world shook and gentle hands caressed my face with tender reassurance. The streaking red that filled my vision shook, stirring the horrific images. But then, slowly, they bled back into the corners of my trembling mind, replaced by the reality I now found myself in. I scrubbed the confusion from my eyes and blinked, tears running down my face.

Jess stared down at me, perfect and unblemished. Her eyes glowed with warmth, her face twisted with concern. I felt her hands cupping my face, her soft skin like the smoothest silk. Tears flowed from her eyes, welling in those endless depths of purest blue.

"Jess?" I croaked, my voice a shaking mess.

She let out a relieved gasp, a smile splitting her face. She leaned down and hugged me fiercely, squeezing me tight, her head buried in my shoulder.

Amazed, I took her in my arms and looked around.

We were back in our house, sprawled out on the couch.

"Please tell me this isn't a dream," I cried, chest hitching with unbearable relief.

Jess sat up on me, wiping trails of tears from her face. "We did it, Nick; we're back. We made it out of that awful place. Oh, Nick..." She collapsed back into me and together we wept. I felt an immense weight lift from my shoulders, uprooting and drifting away into the nothing.

Jess and I held on to one another, lost in the bliss of the moment. We had done it. Done the impossible. Against all odds, we had escaped the Black Farm.

"We beat them," I sobbed, kissing Jess like it was the first time. She kissed me back, crying, laughing, filled with elation and gratitude and life.

"I love you, Nick," she wept, our lips meeting again.

We stayed like that on the couch for a long time. Eventually, we fell into silence and just lay there. Jess rested her head on my chest and I stroked her hair, breathed her in, filled myself with the promise of a fresh start. We had overcome tremendous obstacles, suffered through the darkest hell, and made it out onto the other side.

At one point, I looked at the coffee table and saw the array of empty pill bottles we had left behind. I shuddered at the sight of them, and again relief swept through me like a tempest. How foolish I had been, how utterly selfish and horrible. I squeezed Jess tighter and kissed her forehead, swearing in that moment that I would be everything she deserved.

The path we had chosen, the choices we had made...I would

forever close the doors to those dark passages. Not because I knew about the Black Farm, not because I feared its horrors...but because I wanted to be a better person for Jess. Because I needed to appreciate what a wonderful treasure life was. In that moment, I saw the happiness I had been blind to before. I felt the joy of being alive—to burn with affection, to cradle and share the overwhelming love I felt in my heart.

Jess breathed against me and I knew she was lost in her own thoughts, swept away by the incredible weight of what we had just suffered. I stroked her tear-streaked cheek and whispered in her ear just how much she meant to me. We kissed again, still shaken by our passage.

Eventually, Jess pointed towards the window, her voice the softest whisper. "The sun's coming up."

I turned my head and saw she was right. Faint traces of purple tickled the sky, soon joined by gentle pools of pink and orange. We lay there, unmoving, and watched the day begin anew.

Five Months Later

I sat in the darkness of my living room, staring into the shadows. The house was still, swathed in black as deep night swelled around me. The snow had finally stopped, a blanket of undisturbed white coating the cold earth. Faint embers glowed from our fireplace and I turned my bloodshot eyes to watch them die.

I raised my hands and realized they were shaking. I ran them through my hair, exhaling heavily. My chest hitched and I swallowed down a gasp crawling up my throat. I closed my eyes and concentrated, desperately trying to empty my mind. I placed my head in my hands, leaning over in my chair, sweat coating the back of my neck.

Suddenly, a light went on in the hallway and I heard the gentle patter of footsteps against the wood floors. I dragged a hurried hand over my eyes and turned to see Jess staring at me. Her silhouette was a painting of dark beauty, her stomach protruding with our unborn son. She unconsciously ran her hands over the swell of her belly, as if to comfort our child.

"Nick," she asked quietly, "are you ok?"

I struggled to respond, terrified for a second that my voice would betray me. "I'm ok, sweetie. Just…can't sleep."

"Will you come back to bed with me? Please?" she asked, her voice laced with concern.

I tried to smile in the darkness. "Of course…just…give me a second?"

Jess hesitated for a moment and then turned off the hall light. But instead of retreating to the bedroom, she glided over to my side and crouched down before me. She took my hands in hers and stared up into my face.

Shadows couldn't hide the tears in my eyes or the tremble of my lip. I felt naked and exposed, emotion gurgling in my chest like a ghost.

Jess's eyes melted when she saw me. "Oh Nick…"

I sniffled and let out a sob, hiding my face from her. "I'm sorry…I'll be ok…please…"

Jess pulled my hands away from my face. "Hey, hey, it's ok…honey, it's ok. We're not there anymore. You're here with me and your wonderful son."

Tears flowed freely down my face, my vision blurring, my voice a desperate whisper, "I'm sorry…"

Jess cupped my face in her hands, her eyes sad. "Baby, you have nothing to apologize for. You're not going back there, neither of us is. It's all right…it's over."

My hands shook violently as another cry escaped my lips. I scrubbed my eyes, heart fluttering. "Jesus, Jess…I can't get it out of my head…everything I did…" I craned my head back, hyperventilating. "Every time I close my eyes I think I'm going to wake up there, and I'll be standing before The Pig."

Jess stood up and stroked my hair, pressing my cheek to her stomach. "I won't let that happen, Nick. You're safe here with me and with our baby. That nightmare is over and it's never coming back."

I squeezed my eyes shut and sighed shakily, trying to calm myself. My heart began to slow as Jess continued to rhythmically run her fingers through my hair. It was over…

Suddenly, I felt the baby kick beneath my cheek and I jumped in surprise. I looked up at Jess, and as our eyes met, we both began to laugh. It was the most wonderful sound I had ever heard, burning away the mood like a wildfire.

"Feels like someone is concerned about Daddy," Jess said quietly, smiling.

I wiped the tears from my cheek and kissed Jess's stomach, whispering, "Don't you worry, little guy; I'm going to be ok. And I'm going to show you just how wonderful life truly is. I promise."

I hugged Jess and she hugged me back, the knot in my chest unraveling further.

"Come to bed?" Jess asked after a moment.

I stood, wrapping an arm around her. "That sounds wonderful."

As we went to the bedroom, I couldn't help but speculate one last time on our journey through the Black Farm. In truth, I didn't know what kind of state we had left it in or what fate The Pig had met. Even now, the forces of the afterlife could be locked in brutal conflict, moments away from destroying existence itself.

But for now, I could only guess the repercussions of my actions. I knew that one day I would probably find out when I walked back through death's door. But until then...

I climbed into bed with Jess, pushing my troubled thoughts away. I mentally locked them in a vault never be opened again. I knew that my family would be my strength against the darkness that awaited me behind that door. That murderous voice calling out to me...

Jess pulled the covers over us and snuggled into me, sighing comfortably. I wrapped her in my arms, exhaling into the dark room.

Soon Jess was asleep and I knew I wasn't far behind. I

breathed in the silence and emptied my head of worries. As I was about to close my eyes, I looked out the bedroom window at the night sky. A vast canopy of twinkling crystals glowed down at us, perfect and pure.

In the distance, I spotted a shooting star, a flash of light plummeting from the majestic heavens.

And for a second, I thought it glowed red.

About the Author

Elias started writing at age fifteen and hasn't stopped since. As he experimented with different genres, he felt pulled to the darker side of fiction. He lives in New England and can usually be found muttering over his keyboard and nervously looking over his shoulder. He thinks horror deserves some fresh concepts and is doing his best to breathe new life into the genre.